SKYHEIST

ROBERT M. BRANTNER

Skyheist

Copyright ©2021 Robert M. Branter

Robert M. Brantner
Maryland
SkyheistBook.com

In association with:
Elite Online Publishing
63 East 11400 South #230
Sandy, UT 84070
EliteOnlinePublishing.com

ISBN - 978-1-956642-21-6 (Paperback)
ISBN - 978-1-956642-99-5 (Hardback)
ISBN - 978-1-956642-98-8 (eBook)

Printed in the United States of America

SKYHEIST

ROBERT M. BRANTNER

For my mother, Deni. My **entire** life happened because she started as a stewardess.

Table of Contents

Part I

Big Planes
(and a boat)

Prologue

The Boat

The boat was perfect. That was Eric Mansfield's assessment… perfect. And that was saying something. Eric had spent twenty-three years in the Navy, where he retired as a Petty Officer First Class. And the majority of the time he spent there was on boats or working on boats.

It took twenty-three years for Eric to end that long-term relationship, and now he was looking for another long-term commitment in his new life as a civilian. And this boat might very well be that relationship which he sought.

As a California native, Eric had always been drawn to warmer weather. However, rather than return to the west coast, post retirement, Eric decided that Florida would be the ideal place for him to start his new life—for a little while at any rate. During his time in the Navy, Eric had had some exposure to Florida, but never had the pleasure of having been stationed there. When Eric left the Navy, he decided that the gulf coast would be the ideal spot to start his search for the perfect boat. He spent several months traveling up and down the coast, going as far south as Naples, and as far north as Pensacola. The balance he found was, just outside of Tampa, across the bay in St. Petersburg. It also proved to be an area where his ethnicity wasn't an absolute deal-breaker. Not that St. Pete was so progressive that they would give him a job too which he was qualified. He would still be relegated to a job that was definitely beneath him, but here he would at least be allowed to work around the boats, if not on them. And this made the decision to come to St. Pete, the correct one.

In the mid-1960's there were many who didn't want black people to even come anywhere near their boats; too many in America were quick to judge someone based on the color of their skin. Here, Eric was given enough of a chance to afford him proximity to the profession to which he had dedicated his life.

Eric was dressed casually this evening. He wore short Khaki pants, an opened button down "aloha" shirt, and tennis shoes. Even at forty years of age, he was in good shape and wore his hair short and neat. On his well-defined left bicep, he had a single Navy tattoo, the only souvenir of twenty-three years of service. But in the dusk of the Florida evening, the souvenir melted away, just as his time in the Navy had. The blue ink merged with his flesh, becoming invisible. But for the color of his skin, he fit in perfectly as he walked down the dock, taking in all the boats surrounding him. However, no matter how beautiful the other boats were, it was the beauty at the end of the dock that was compelling him forward, producing an almost gravitational force, beckoning him onward.

Although Eric hadn't immediately spotted the boat when he arrived in Florida, once he did, he knew in his heart it was his destiny. It was this boat that induced Eric to seek employment at this particular marina. For Eric it had been love at first sight. The kind of love that makes a man settle down and set down roots... even if the roots don't run deep.

The boat was a 1961 Chris Craft Conquest. It had two 350 horsepower engines, three cabins and even two heads (or bathrooms in non-Navy speak). It was a brilliant white with blue trim and teak wood throughout the magnificent vessel. It was the latest in marine technology Chris Craft had to offer. And best of all—it had an owner whom was almost never there. As Eric strolled down the dock, looking at this sliver of nautical perfection, he couldn't help but to think of the vessel's owner. He was some stockbroker living in New York. Eric knew this little nugget of information thanks to research he had done, delving into the files on the owners in the marina's office. However, anyone could have summarized this information from just looking at the stern of the boat. Emblazoned on the backside, in royal blue lettering, were the words "*Bull Market, Wall Street, NY.*"

The information that the average passerby would not be privy to was the fact that the stockbroker who purchased this boat had only taken it out for a total of ten days since he bought it. One was a two-day outing, followed later by two four-day outings, the most recent of which was earlier in the year, while it was still summer. In fact, not only was this wonderful piece of marine engineering going to waste, all signs pointed to the fact that it would continue to do so for the foreseeable future. The owner had contracted with the marina to take care of the boat and keep it in good working order. It was unlikely that he would be able to make it down to St. Pete again until the following summer. As Eric thought about this last little piece of information, he looked out at the setting sun. The October sky was bathed in a brilliant orange, casting a beautiful hue across the water, illuminating everything around it in subtle colors. The outside temperature was still in the mid-70s. In New York it was probably below freezing, with a blanket of snow on the ground. He couldn't help but to wonder why someone would invest so much money in such a vessel, just to tie it up at the dock and let others care for it.

Eric checked the lines on the yacht and then stepped aboard to inspect the interior. He wondered what the owner would think if he saw him boarding the boat. He wondered if the Wall Street broker saw a black man entering the *Bull Market*, unescorted, would he look at him and think he was a thief, there to make off with his yacht? Eric shook his head. God, he hated racists. He would have been right, of course. Eric would absolutely steal the boat, but it was a shame that he would be judged solely by the color of his skin. Eric shook his head again as he climbed back onto the dock and slipped the lines.

While this act would be Eric's first as a thief, he knew it would not be his last. He also realized that this theft would not be as random as some teenagers taking off with a ski-boat, going for a joyride. This was to be far more long term and more meticulously planned.

Eric had been born and raised in East Los Angeles until he was sixteen. It was at that age that Eric made his break. He enlisted in the United States Navy, claiming he was eighteen. Although war clouds were on the horizon, Eric told this lie prior to the United States entering the Second World War. After basic training, Eric started training in one of the few roles he could hold as a black man in the Navy at that time: a cook.

Eric was intelligent and personable. He did well in the Navy. After the events of Pearl Harbor, despite the systemic racism, Eric eventually worked his way out of the galley and into what he felt was a more meaningful role. Through hard work and determination, Eric was presented the opportunity to train as a marine welder. He was then transferred to the destroyer escort, *USS Mason*.

As the war raged on, Eric distinguished himself and developed an excellent reputation amongst his colleagues and superiors alike. After the war he was able to transfer to other Naval vessels, as he steadily moved up through the ranks. He finally finished his career as a Petty Officer First Class aboard the aircraft carrier, *USS Midway*.

After the *Midway*, Eric felt he had finally topped a long and distinguished career. He realized it was time to leave military life and find a boat of his own.

He could then travel the world at his own leisure. The only problem with his plan was an enlisted man's retirement would not provide him with the money he would need to get a boat worthy of his skill and experience. He realized that if he were to live his dream, he would need to use his mind. It was up to him to figure a way to make his dream a reality.

If Eric had merely wanted a 'boat,' something as mundane as a 16-foot fishing boat, that would have taken no effort whatsoever. These boats were common in the waters off the coast of Florida. But a 41-foot Chris Craft was something else entirely. This would take planning and forethought.

When Eric first saw the yacht, he was struck by how flawless it seemed, though *Bull Market* hadn't been the first. In fact, it was the third boat that Eric had set his sights on. However, the first two were, sadly, in committed relationships. They both had owners that loved and doted on them. After two weeks of watching each boat, Eric realized they were in long-term relationships that would be nearly impossible to break up.

When Eric chanced upon *Bull Market*, he felt that this was a boat that had real potential. His heart soared when he noticed that the owner hadn't even bothered to put 'St. Petersburg' as the homeport on the stern of the yacht.

Eric watched the *Bull Market* for a month. The only activity the boat saw during that time was that of the marina staff. At the end of the month, Eric put his plan into motion, walking into the main office, and requested an application for employment.

The only job Eric was offered was one not worthy of his experience. He had seen combat, worked on an aircraft carrier, and risen to the rank of Petty Officer First Class. Yet the manager of the marina couldn't see past the color of Eric's skin and would only give him a job emptying the trash cans. Well, that was fine with Eric. A job as low profile as janitor would mean that he wouldn't raise any suspicion when he disappeared at the same time as the *Bull Market*. More so, if their opinion of him was so low that this was all the management of the marina thought him capable of, they wouldn't think him capable of masterminding the theft of the yacht.

As Eric looked around at the deserted dock, he pulled the last line from the berth. *Bull Market* was now free floating. Eric headed topside to the bridge and started the two motors that would slowly liberate the craft from its prison in St. Petersburg.

Eric had worked out the general framework of the plan when he first retired from the Navy. Once he found the boat, and later employment at the marina, he fine-tuned his strategy. He just needed to wait for the right time to execute the plan… a plan he was now committed to, be it successful or not. However, he knew in his heart it would succeed. It had to. The alternative was unthinkable.

During the month Eric had spent watching the *Bull Market*, he laid the foundation for what was to come. He manufactured new registration numbers and a new name for the boat, which he would use to cover *Bull Market's* true identity. Although it might not stand up to intense scrutiny, it should be enough to alleviate any suspicion from the Coast Guard at a passing glance.

However, it was the research and planning he had done in his recent job as the marina's janitor that would truly keep him safe as he liberated the *Bull Market*.

It is funny how no one ever seems to take notice of the custodial staff. Even as they are emptying the trash can you are using, they seem invisible. Occasionally they may warrant a "thank you" (but more often than not, they would not even receive that), but mostly they were never seen. Even if Eric had been discovered late at night entering the marina office (where he could go through the files on *Bull Market)*, he would have simply been ignored. It was this ability to become invisible, while gathering intelligence, that had allowed the last piece of his plan to come together.

The day before Eric liberated the *Bull Market*, the marina's manager received a call from the ship's owner, asking him to contact him at his earliest convince.

Per marina policy, the manager, Kevin Summers, pulled the file of the *Bull Market*. Looking through it, he thoroughly familiarized himself with the yacht's owner. He also verified that the phone number matched the one on file. The number Mr. Summer's secretary had written down was not the owner's home number, but his office number. Mr. Summers returned the call to New York at once. After all, Mr. Frost was paying him a sizeable sum to keep his boat in good repair.

After only one ring, a woman's voice answered the phone, "Morgan Stanley, Bradley Frost's office."

"Yes, this is Kevin Summers. I'm the manager of the marina in St. Petersburg where Mr. Frost keeps his boat. I have a message to call him."

"Yes, Mr. Summers. Mr. Frost is expecting your call. Please hold."

Less than a minute later, a man's voice came on the line. "Mr. Summers? This is Brad Frost. I wanted to let you know that I'm going to be making a little more use of my Chris Craft. My wife is getting tired of the cold here in New York, and I told her I would take her on an extended vacation to Bermuda. I just wanted to alert you so you wouldn't be concerned when the *Bull Market* turned up missing."

"Yes, sir. That won't be a problem at all."

"Good. Not sure exactly how long it will be. Frankly, I think I will end up leaving my wife in Bermuda for a good deal of the winter. I'll be back and forth between there and New York while I take care of business back home. But I wanted to make sure you knew what was going on."

"Absolutely, sir.   I will also make sure we discontinue charging you for the servicing and upkeep of your boat."

There was a brief silence on the other end of the line.   When Mr. Frost spoke again, the tenor of his voice had changed slightly.   "I appreciate that Mr. Summers.   However, I would like to keep the payments the way they are now.   I will continue to send the checks every month just as I have been doing and I would like the same itemized bill.   Tax considerations. I'm sure you understand."

Nodding, Kevin Summers said, "Yes, sir.   I absolutely understand."

"And Kevin, may I call you Kevin?"

"Absolutely Mr. Frost."

Mr. Frost's voice lowered a little more.   He now was speaking in an almost conspiratorial tone, "I would like to keep this conversation between you and me."

Kevin started to smile.   His wife? Sure. He had seen this so many times before.   It seemed the more money you got, the looser your morals became.   This would also explain why the payments would continue and the billing should remain unchanged.   Well, if that was the way this New Yorker wanted to play it, that was fine with him.   The marina would continue to receive the payments and there would be less work for Kevin and his staff.   This was nothing new.   He was happy to play along.

"I assure you, Mr. Frost, that won't be a problem at all. And I can guarantee you perfect discretion."

"I knew I could count on you, Kevin." The line went dead.

As Kevin hung up the phone, he imagined the stockbroker in his window office, looking down upon the island of Manhattan. He had no way of knowing that in reality he had been connected to a phone number in the Bronx that would be disconnected by the end of the week. He also did not realize that he had not been talking to Brad Frost, but a friend of Eric Mansfield's. Further, he was ignorant of the fact that the phone number he had retrieved from Brad Frost's file was a number that his janitor had changed weeks ago to match the one in the Bronx. All Kevin Summers saw was what he expected to.

As Eric watched the marina disappear into the distance, he smiled, enjoying the moment. In a few hours he would be well out of sight of land. There he would shut the yacht down and start changing the boat's identity. Hours later, he would turn south and head towards the Caribbean. By the time the New York stockbroker realized his boat was gone, the identity of the Chris Craft would have been forever changed. As the coast of Florida faded in the distance, along with the day's sun, the boat was no longer Brad Frost's, but now truly belonged to Eric Mansfield.

Chapter One
Maintenance

"Ladies and Gentlemen, this is your captain speaking: I'm sorry to inform you I have a bit of bad news. During our walk around preflight check, we found a slight problem with one of our systems. I'm not sure how long the delay will take, but we will certainly let you know just as soon as we get some more information."

The feel inside the small cockpit was that of a mid-evil dungeon. Darkness had almost completely consumed the dying sapphire of the evening sky, providing little help in lighting the compact room. Most of the light present was the dull orange glow produced by scores of lights illuminating dials and indicators throughout the small compartment. Most of these came from behind the first officer, at the workstation of the plane's flight engineer. The captain of the jet aircraft turned around and looked across at the man sitting behind him on the opposing side of the cockpit.

"Stu, you up for a walk? I'd like to see the damage for myself."

The second officer turned from the wall of dials, his face bathed in the half-light emanating from the instrument panel. "Sure Arnie. Give me just a minute." He manipulated a few controls before standing up and taking his hat. The captain followed behind him.

As Arnie and Stu left the cockpit, the captain turned to the first officer. "Gary, give maintenance a call and see how fast they can get out here. I'm hoping it's nothing, but somehow I feel this will take a while."

"Sure thing, boss. You and Stu going to wait down there for him?"

"Probably."

When they left the cockpit and entered the plane's cabin, they felt a hint of the chilly November evening. However, when they stepped off the Boeing 727 and onto the stairs leading up to the plane, the full force of the dark St. Louis night hit them. The captain followed the flight engineer down the stairs until they reached the tarmac below. Most of the passengers were on board, so there was not much passenger traffic to make their way around.

At the base of the stairs, Stu led his captain around the nose of the jet and to the main landing gear on the right side of the plane. As they walked, Stu noticed a few early season snowflakes flurrying around the ground equipment. The sight alone sent a chill through the young flight engineer and he pulled his coat tighter around him. As he did so, he glanced over at the captain. Arnie, like most captains, didn't wear a heavy overcoat like the junior officers often did, as the duty of the walk around preflight fell primarily to the plane's second officer. However, Arnie took the temperature in stride and put on airs of being perfectly comfortable. Stu marveled (and was slightly irritated) about how he could do this.

Much to the disappointment of the captain, Arnie found just what he expected: a massive puddle of fluid reflecting the lights that illuminated the ramp. Even though the darkness of the evening masked the color of the puddle, both men knew it would have the dark red tinge of Skydrol; the sweetly sick odor gave it away at once.

"Take a look over here, boss," Stu said to the captain as he maneuvered his way around the enormous puddle, and over to the lines leading to the brakes. He pointed the beam of his flashlight at the long ropy cables leading from the wheel well down to the gear trucks supporting the two tires and the massive airplane.

The light fell on a large gash on one cable, nearly severing the line.

"What do you think could have caused that?" Arnie asked Stu as the two stood watching the slow dripping, as the lifeblood of the hydraulic system ebbed.

"No idea. It looks like it was cut intentionally."

"Yeah, I've seen a number of gripes that looked like they were intentional. But for the life of me, I can't think of any reason why anyone would want to hurt the bird."

Stu gave a laugh. "I guess I'm still getting used to being in the civilian world. In the Navy there were lots of people who wanted to hurt us."

Arnie nodded. "And you had it easy. I was in Korea. They were shooting at us there."

"I was lucky. I missed that one. Still, I'd rather be here than in the military."

"Amen to that."

A moment later a gruff voice came from behind them, breaking the spell.

"What the hell did you do to my plane?"

Both turned to see a man behind them in greasy overalls. Arnie took a step forward, extending his hand.

"Hi, Arnie Whitmore. My second officer here found this when he did his walk around." Arnie swept his arms, motioning to the puddle.

Stu positioned the beam of his flashlight at the nearly severed hydraulic line. "Pretty sure this is the problem."

The mechanic turned to the captain. "He's pretty sure this is the problem, eh?" He then turned back to Stu. "Just how old are you boy?"

"Twenty-eight. How old are you?"

"All right guys, enough." Arnie said with authority. "I need to tell the passengers something. Even if the problem's bigger than just the severed line, this is going to have to be replaced. How long do you think it's going to be?"

The mechanic took the flashlight from Stu with a glare and moved closer to the wheel well. He then shone the light over the length of the landing gear and into the well.

"Good news is, from just a cursory glance, it looks like the cut here is the only problem with the system. I think we might even have another brake line in stock. Bad news is, I'd guess we're looking at... at least, a two hour's wait while we replace the line."

"Two hours? It's the 1960s. We're putting men in space. You'd think we could change a hydraulic line in less than two hours." Stu exhaled.

"At *least* two hours," the mechanic corrected him. "Even if everything goes right, we're doing the job at night and it's dark out. That'll add a bit of time. I'll also want to go over the entire system and make sure nothing else is wrong. I'd hate to see you guys lose your hydraulic system again, but this time at 35,000 feet." Both pilots unconsciously nodded their agreement.

"I'll have to head over to stores and find a line to replace it with," the old mechanic continued. "But I doubt that should take too long. Tell you guys what, I'll get a few of my guys over here and get to work. While I'm doing that, you're free to see if operations can find you another bird. But I wouldn't hold my breath. As far as I know, everything's accounted for tonight."

"Thanks. We'll head back up to the cockpit and see what we can do from our end. Keep me apprised of your progress. And if there's anything I can do, just let me know."

"You've got it," the mechanic said, returning the flashlight to Stu. In the dim light, it was hard to tell, but Stu was sure he saw the older man give him a friendly wink before he turned and headed back to the door marked "maintenance" under the main terminal.

"Ladies and gentlemen, the captain just informed me that while the repairs to the plane are going smoothly, it will still be a little more than an hour before we're ready to depart. While you wait, we'll be coming through the cabin to provide a drink and snack service. We apologize for the inconvenience, and if there is any further assistance we can provide, please don't hesitate to ask."

Sara hung up the airplane's interphone and headed into the forward galley.

"How are you doing Liz?" she asked the other stewardess working in the front of the plane as she pulled the curtains closed behind her.

"I'm fine. Just a little tired, that's all."

Sara shook her head. "I can't tell you how much this pisses me off." Liz raised an eyebrow at the other stewardess' use of language. "Oh, come on. No one can hear us. I mean really, this is the third mechanical delay I've had this month. Don't you think the airline could keep the planes in better repair?"

Liz shrugged. "I haven't had any problems."

Sara looked Liz up and down. She was only 21 and had the perfect look for a stewardess. She was very thin and exceptionally beautiful. She also was, as all stewardess were, very single. "How long have you worked here?"

"About six months."

"Well, when you've been here as long as me, you'll start to look at things differently."

Sara was considered very senior at only 25 years old. She too had been hired at 21 and was now finding it harder to keep the weight off. She was growing increasing nervous every time she went to weigh-in. She hadn't busted yet, but she knew it was only a matter of time. This was not an old woman's game, and she was becoming an old woman.

Liz looked at the scowl on her superior's face as she finished setting up the beverage cart.

"You ready Sara?"

"Just a minute," Sara growled. She then opened her small makeup bag and fished a lipstick out. After a quick touch up, she put the makeup away and opened the curtain, flashing a warm radiant smile as she left the galley ahead of Liz, who was pushing the beverage cart. She then stopped at the first passenger in first class, and purred, "Sir, I am so sorry for this inconvenience. Now what can I get you to drink?"

"Good evening Captain," a tall man said, ducking as he entered the cockpit.

All three flight officers turned to see a man dressed just as they were entering the cramped room.

"I'm Alec Edwards. I just got in from London. Didn't think I'd be able to make it home tonight."

"I'm glad to hear our little mishap benefited someone at least. What equipment are you on, Alec?" the captain asked.

"I've been on the 707 for a little over a year now. What's up with the delay?"

"My fault," Stu said with a grin, raising his hand. "I found a severed hydraulic line on the walk around. Maintenance said they need to replace it before we can go."

"Ouch. How long will that take?"

"Good news is, they said only a couple of hours. Bad news is that was almost three hours ago." As he spoke, Stu looked at his watch and fidgeted.

"Any clue to how much longer?"

All three shook their heads. It was Arnie who spoke. "Not sure, but I don't think too much longer. They haven't canceled the flight, so that's a good sign. You have a seat yet?"

"Oh yeah. The flight's wide open back there. They were able to get me a nice one in first class. I just wanted to come up and say 'hi' and see what's going on. I'll get out of your hair."

"Make sure to change out of the uniform and get a drink. Sleep will make the trip go a lot faster," Arnie continued. "I doubt it'll be too much longer."

"Heading back to change now. And thanks, guys." As Alec left the cockpit, a short woman with dark hair, looking very tired and frazzled, replaced him. All three turned as she entered, hoping it would be someone from the maintenance department. When they saw it was only the gate agent, Stu and Gary returned to their work.

"Hi, Captain. How are you guys doing?"

Arnie exhaled. "Getting tired but hanging in there. Any new word?"

"Not from maintenance. However, I did want you to know that we had a passenger just show up wanting to get a last-minute ticket on the flight."

Arnie shrugged. "And?"

"Well sir, he has a lot of equipment with him. Part of his job, I guess. Anyway, he said he's willing to pay the extra charge for the additional luggage, but it has to make *this* flight. I just wanted to check with you first, to make sure. It might take a few minutes to get everything out here, and he was insistent that everything must go."

Stu backed up his seat and turned to the woman behind him. "How much is a last-minute ticket? Pretty expensive, right?"

The woman smiled for the first time. "Quite."

"Boss," Stu continued, "If it's OK with you, I can head downstairs and make sure everything makes it on. It'll also give me an excuse to check in again with the maintenance guys."

The captain only shrugged. "Knock yourself out." He then looked at the gate agent. "Gloria, I'm fine with the additional passenger if you are."

"Thank you, sir. I'll let him know we can get him on. And I'll be sure to let him know that you guys are personally ensuring his equipment will make the flight as well."

Stu got up from his station and moved his seat full forward to the flight engineer panel. Stu and Gloria headed down the stairs parked against the side of the plane. As Gloria continued towards the terminal, Stu split off to the other side of the aircraft, to the forward cargo compartment. There he found a ramp agent lying on a belt loader, awaiting further instructions.

"Hey," Stu called, getting the man's attention. "I've got a favor."

"What's up?" the ramp worker asked, getting up from the inclined position.

"We just got a last-minute passenger with some equipment that has to make the flight. It should be here soon. Can you load it up here in the forward cargo compartment for me?"

"We've already got the front loaded. Is the back OK?"

"I'd prefer the front. I told him I'd take care of it personally and the front will be the first to be unloaded. He's a last-minute passenger, so he paid a lot more for his ticket. I want him to think of TWA next time he flies."

The man on the belt loader shrugged. "I guess. Whatever you say."

"Thanks a lot. I'm going to go check-in with the maintenance guys. I'll be back in a few minutes. If you need anything, I'll be back by the wheel well."

Stu casually made his way over to the two men working under the wing, focused on the landing gear.

"Hey guys. How's it going?"

"Slow," one of them said without looking up.

"Yeah, I know it's getting late. If you guys don't mind, could I get an update to pass along to the passengers? We're starting to get a lot of questions."

The mechanic closest to Stu now turned. His face and clothing were covered in slick black grease, and the unmistakable red stain of hydraulic fluid.

With a sigh, he said, "We're just about done. There's still a few more lines to connect and then a system's check, but it shouldn't be too much longer."

"Thanks. I appreciate it."

"One question: how the hell did you guys sever the line in the first place? I've never seen anything like this before."

Stu shook his head. "Damned if I know. We're just starting off. We saw the crew as we swapped out, but they didn't say anything. They told us it was a good bird."

"Yeah? Well, they lied."

Stu looked at his watch. 10:45 PM. "That's an understatement."

Stu then glanced over at the forward cargo bay. "Thanks guys. I'm going to check on a few things over here. If you need anything, let us know."

Now fully returned to his work, the mechanic grunted, "Will do."

Stu made his way back to the forward cargo hold. It was now open and he could see the belt loader being positioned next to it. Inside of the bay there were a series of thick blankets and nets providing a barrier to the cargo already loaded, ensuring it would not shift. Behind the forward barrier he could see a large load placed on a pallet, cloaked in shadow.

"Front part of the compartment's full. Is the aft end of the forward cargo compartment OK?"

"Oh yeah, that's fine. I just want to make sure his stuff's off-loaded first."

"You know, you could just call ahead and have Denver unload the aft first."

Stu flashed a grin. "You know those Denver guys aren't nearly as good as the St. Louis crew."

This brought some laughter as another ramp agent started struggling with several large canvas bags.

"What the hell does he have in here?"

"I don't know what they are to him, but they're money to us."

The new ramp worker grunted. "More like money to our owner."

The ramp worker next to him rolled his eyes and added, "Like that asshole needs more money."

Stu shook his head and started back to the stairs on the other side of the plane. "Just get the stuff loaded. If you need me, I'll be in the cockpit."

"Whatever." Was the last thing Stu heard as he made his way back into the plane.

As Stu exited the stairs, heading out to check on the baggage, the late arriving passenger replaced him. Stu and the new passenger shared a glance as they passed, and the new arrival made his slow assent up to the Boeing 727. A minute later, he emerged from the darkness into the dim lights of the cabin.

Many of the passengers were asleep at this point. The stewardesses had finished their service and were currently sitting on their jumpseats awaiting further instructions.

As the late-arriving passenger slowly walked into the plane, both forward stewardesses turned to look at him. At once it was apparent he did not belong.

The first thing that stood out to Sara was the man's rumpled appearance. Whereas everyone on the plane that evening was wearing either a suit or a dress, this man was clad in old baggy blue jeans, a loose fitting, black sweatshirt, and an old baseball cap pulled low, obscuring much of his face. Over the sweatshirt, he had on an extremely worn, olive-green army jacket. Further, while most of the passengers had either a briefcase, or a small elegant carry-on suitcase, this man carried an equally worn green duffel bag, matching his coat.

The man had a quiet demeanor as he made his way onto the plane. Beneath the cap, shaggy black hair poked out. His skin was well tanned, indicating a heritage from somewhere warmer than where they were. Probably Mexico, Sara thought.

Yet, however out of place this passenger might have appeared, he had purchased a ticket (and an expensive one at that) and he was entitled to the full service that came with that purchase.

Sara at once rose from her seat and met the passenger at the door. She smiled warmly and purred with a slight southern accent, "Welcome aboard, sir."

The late arriving passenger looked over at her, keeping his head low, and gave a curt nod.

"What seat do they have you in this evening?"

The man fished inside of the deep pocket of the old army jacket, adjusting the strap of the duffel bag. He pulled out a slip of paper.

"Looks like 17C," he said in almost inaudible tones.

"Very good, sir. That's just down the aisle here. If you'll just follow me." Sara led the man to the center of the plane to the unoccupied isle seat. Although there was already a passenger in 17A, the middle seat between them was empty.

"May I give you a hand with your bag?" Sara asked with a false smile.

"No, I've got it."

As the new passenger reached up to put his bag in the overhead compartment, the napping man by the window in seat 17A half opened his eyes, appraising the newcomer. Unnoticed by all, he rolled his eyes at the new arrival.

As the passenger in seat 17C sat down, Sara said unconsciously, "If you need anything sir, just push that call bell above you and we'll come right away."

17C started to look up to comment, but Sara had already turned around and was heading back to the front of the plane.

Chapter Two

Demands

"Ladies and Gentlemen, good news from the cockpit. We're happy to report that our maintenance team has fixed the mechanical problem and we're good to go. We have just a few more paperwork and housekeeping items to go over, and then we'll be underway."

Arnie hung up the PA and looked at his crew. Gary was going over the logbook while Stu was pouring over the performance paperwork.

Arnie then looked out the forward window. The ramp crew swarmed around the ground equipment as the ballet to get a plane into the air started once again. Once the Auxiliary Power Unit, or APU, was on-line, the external power was pulled as the driver of the pushback tug plugged in his interphone for communications with the cockpit. As this was happening, out of the corner of his eye, Arnie could see the stair truck pulling away. Several other ramp workers removed the chocks from the tires of the 727.

"Cockpit, this is ground." The voice was staticky and heavy with sleep. This irritated Arnie. This guy would be in bed soon whereas this crew's night was just beginning. Where the hell did he get off being tired?

"How are you guys doing tonight?" Arnie asked.

"Tired." The captain rolled his eyes.

"I hear you," he conceded. "We'll be ready in just a couple more minutes. Just finishing up with the numbers now."

As he spoke, Stu reached forward, dropping the performance worksheet on the pedestal between the two pilots.

"Good here, boss," Stu said, returning to his own instruments.

"Logbook checks. Everything's in order on this side, boss," Gary said, handing the log to the captain.

"Very good. Pressurize hydraulics," he winced, "and call for pushback clearance."

"Pressure's good boss. System's working perfectly," Stu announced.

"Ramp, TWA 798 gate two-seven, ready to push."

As Sara finished the safety announcement, she hung up the cabin PA mic. After putting away her briefing script, she joined Liz in taking drink orders. The stewardesses in the back returned to their jumpseats.

Sara was halfway through taking drink orders when the call chime went off. As they taxied out, the lights had been dimmed. The passengers not already asleep, were now starting to drift off. When the chime sounded, it shattered the serenity that lay thick in the cabin. Sara glanced back and saw it came from somewhere in the middle of the plane. She instinctively knew it was row 17.

Before Sara could make any moves towards the beckoning light, Kathy, one of the stewardesses in the back, had already unstrapped her seatbelt and was heading forward to answer the call. Sara watched hypnotically until the passenger she was currently taking a drink order from said, "Scotch with a little water."

The spell broken, Sara returned to the passenger, her plastic smile firmly in place.

"Yes, sir. I'll have that to you just after takeoff." Again, a slight southern accent highlighted the corners of her voice. She then moved on to the next row and continued to take drink orders; the disturbance in the middle of the plane forgotten.

"Sara." It was Kathy. Behind her was the passenger from row 17. However, it wasn't the tan-skinned man whom had arrived at the last minute. Instead, it was the dozing passenger by the window.

"This gentleman here said he needs to use the lavatory and that it's an emergency."

"All right but just…"

"I'm sorry," the passenger cut her off in a low, hushed voice. "I don't need to go to the bathroom, but I needed to talk to you without the man beside me hearing."

"Sir, I'm sure there's no need to…"

"Listen to me," he interrupted her again. "I think he has a gun."

Unconsciously Sara rolled her eyes. She caught herself at once and put her "stewardess face" back on. Kathy looked more concerned.

Before responding, Sara took a moment to look around to see if they were gathering attention. So far, it seemed not. Sara leaned in slightly and matched his low voice. "Thank you for bringing your concerns to our attention. Do you have any proof that he has a gun?"

"When he reached up to put away his bag, I saw a suspicious budge. I didn't think much of it then, but a minute ago he took off his jacket and I'm sure I saw a gun flash in his waistband."

"Sara!" Came a voice from the cockpit, the door still opened. It was Stu calling her.

"Sir," again, a hushed tone, "let me go tell the pilots what you saw."

"Ma'am, I'm not leaving the ground while that... man... has a gun."

She scanned first class. There was a seat open. 4B. "Sir, take a seat here. I'll be right back."

She glanced at row 17. The man in 17C appeared to be growing agitated. Kathy leaned over and whispered, "He looks upset."

"I'm sure it's nothing. Let me go talk to the guys up front."

It was a short walk as Sara passed through the open door of the cockpit. Stu was smiling but looked tired.

"We're ready to go. Why don't you finish the drink orders after we're airborne?"

"Captain," Sara said, ignoring Stu, "We have a gentleman up here who said he saw a gun on the passenger that joined us last minute."

Even in the darkened cockpit, Sara could see everyone looked crestfallen.

"How sure is he?" Arnie asked.

Sara turned and looked at the man now occupying 4B. He fidgeted nervously. She then looked past him into coach. Seat 17C looked even more agitated.

"The last thing I want to do is head back to the gate." She glanced back again. "But I think it might not be a bad idea."

Everyone nodded reluctantly.

"You want me to make the PA boss? I can say it's a problem with the hydraulics again."

Arnie pondered this for a long second before replying. "That sounds good, Stu, but don't give a reason yet. Gary, you call company and inform them of the situation. Have them notify the police. It might be nothing, but I don't want to take any chances. I'll call ground and let them know we need to return to the gate."

Everyone started nodding their agreement when panic broke out in the passenger cabin.

The sound of the bullet erupting from the gun was deafening. Even outside, the large caliber projectile would have made a loud noise. In the stillness of the barely lit cabin, it sounded more like an explosion than a gunshot. Everyone in the cockpit flinched. There was a palpable stillness for perhaps half a second before the entire cabin erupted in screams of panic.

Without thought, Sara rushed out of the cockpit, pulling the door closed behind her, ensuring the pilots were locked safely inside. She then started down the aisle as passengers began to get up, supposedly trying to rush to an exit.

"Quiet!" Sara screamed as she struggled to make her way down to the passenger in seat 17C.

Over the PA, one of the other stewardesses, Sara thought it was Kathy, began, "Ladies and gentlemen, please remain in your seats ..."

"Sir," Sara said to the man in 17C, "Just calm down. I'm sure we can all be reasonable here."

Sara was still five rows away and had to raise her voice to be heard. As she called out to the man in 17C, the rest of the cabin fell into an uncomfortable silence. All struggled to hear what she had to say.

Everything was still for several heartbeats as Sara looked into the eyes of the gunman. He was now standing, but still slumped. He was no longer wearing the worn, olive-green jacket, but he still was wearing a baseball cap with the brim pulled low. She could see most of his face, but definition was obscured as the lights in the cabin were still dimmed for takeoff.

Sara started walking slowly to the gunman, keeping her eyes locked with his. As she advanced, the sulfur smell of gun smoke filled her nostrils.

"Whatever you want, I'm sure we can be reasonable."

"What do you know about reasonable?"

"I know that everyone here wants to get out unharmed. I'm sure we can make that happen."

The gunman now scrunched his face as he considered her words.

"OK. I'll work with you, but there are a few things I want first."

Sara nodded slowly. "I'm sure there is. And I'm also sure we can make that happen."

"First, I want to talk to the man in charge."

Sara kept nodding. She even forced a slight smile. "OK, we can do that. Now, what man do you want to talk to, the police?"

"Are you stupid? I don't need the police. I need the guy up front. The captain."

"I'm sorry sir, but we can't allow you in the cockpit."

"Did I ask to get in the damned cockpit? You have a phone, don't you?"

Sara wore a calm façade she did not feel. Despite her best efforts, she struggled in vain to keep her entire body from trembling. "There's a cabin service interphone at the rear of the plane."

"Don't you play me," 17C said as he waved the gun. "I want to use the phone at the front of the plane."

Sara nodded again. "That's fine. There's an interphone up there too. If you want to follow me, I'm sure the captain would be anxious to speak with you."

17C looked around at the other passengers, transfixed in their conversation. "First, you tell everyone to back up against the windows. If anyone tries to jump me, I'll put a bullet in him. I swear to God I will."

"Ladies and gentlemen," Sara said in a voice slightly louder, "I need everyone to please move as close to the windows as possible, providing us a wide berth. Please cooperate and I promise all of this will be over soon."

As soon as Sara slammed the cockpit door, Arnie said, "Oh hell." Immediately he rushed to the transponder and input the code denoting a hijacking. He then took command of the radio and called the tower.

"St. Louis tower, this is TWA flight 798."

"Confirm, TWA *flight* 798?"

"Confirm *flight*. We are *flight* 798." He said, giving code to the personnel in the tower that a hijacking was taking place. "I'm not sure of our current situation, but I know a shot has been fired, and the cockpit has been locked down." He then unkeyed the mic and turned to the others. "Start up the APU and shutdown the engines."

Gary responded, "It'll take a minute to spin up the APU. You want me to wait until the APU is on-line or just shut the engines down now?"

The captain took a moment to consider the options. If he shut the motors down before the APU was on-line, the plane would go dark for want of electrical power. This could acerbate the problem in the back. He knew that most hijackers didn't know the first thing about an airplane—certainly not enough to start the engines—and without the motors running; they weren't going anywhere.

"It sounds quiet back there. Stu, what do you see?"

The flight engineer slid his seat back and got up. At the cockpit door, he glanced through a peephole and assessed the situation behind them.

"It looks like Sara's talking to the gunman. At least, I think that's what's going on. She's standing mid-cabin and everyone seems quiet. But kind of hard to tell from here."

"Why the hell doesn't one of the other stews call?" Arnie said under his breath. He then added at full volume. "Wait for the APU until shutdown. A few seconds isn't going to make a difference."

"TWA flight 798, what is your current situation?"

Arnie keyed the mic. "Tower, we don't know yet. Please stand by."

"Hey, boss." Both Arnie and Gary turned to Stu, who was still at the door. "It looks like Sara's coming forward. And it looks like the gunman's behind her."

"You sure?"

"No, but I think so."

"I guess we'll know in a few seconds," Gary added.

Stu glanced at his panel and quickly returned to his seat. "APU's up boss."

"Change over the power and kill the engines."

Obediently, Stu removed the flow of power from the aircraft's three engines to the lone APU. Almost immediately afterward, he reached forward and pulled the three fuel levers, starving the three JT8D engines of Jet-A. It was only a second later that the engine's roar quieted to a whine as the jets lost momentum.

Arnie had the interphone in his hand almost the moment the chime came from the cabin.

"Sara, is that you?"

"Yes, sir," she replied robotically.

"Is he beside you?"

"Yes, sir." She answered in the same tone.

"Are you the only one who can hear me?"

"For the moment, sir."

"Listen, if you can talk freely, call me Arnie, or use any of our first names. If you can't, call me, or anyone else up here, 'Captain.' Do you understand?"

"Yes, Captain. Captain, there is a gentleman back here who would like to talk to you."

"Go ahead, put him on."

There was a moment of silence until a man's voice replaced Sara's. "Is this the captain?"

"Yes, it is. To whom am I speaking?"

"Now you listen to me: if you do what I say, there's no reason anyone has to die. But if you don't, not one of you'll be getting off this plane alive." The hijacker's voice was excited and his words rushed.

"Now, just calm down," Arnie said in a much slower cadence. "I'm sure we can all…"

"Don't tell me what to do! I'm the one with the gun! Do you understand?"

"Yes, I understand"

"No, *do you understand*?"

"Yes, sir. I understand you. What do you want?"

"That's better. Now look, I don't want to hurt nobody, but I'm not afraid to either."

"As I said, I understand. What do you need?"

"OK. First, I want a full tank of gas."

"A full tank?"

"The plane! I want you to fill the plane!" the hijacker shouted.

Speaking slowly, Arnie said, "We're ready for takeoff. We already have a full load of fuel."

"Don't bullshit me. I know you don't go from St. Louis to Denver with full tanks of gas. I want a *full* load."

Arnie looked at the other pilots in the cockpit. All seemed to be thinking the same thing: He knows more than he's letting on.

"I think we can make that happen. What else?"

"I want a perimeter set up around the plane. No vehicles within half a mile, except for the fuel truck."

"All right, sir. I think we can do all of this, but what will we get in return? Can you give us a show of good faith?"

There was a lengthy pause as the hijacker seemed to ponder his response.

"I can let the women off. How's that?"

"That would be great. Besides the fuel truck, can we bring a stair truck up the plane? To get the ladies off?"

"No," the hijacker snapped decisively. "You can use the stairs in the back of the plane."

"Sir, you sound reasonable. Why don't you just put the gun down and let all the people go? I'm sure all of this can be worked out so that no one gets hurt."

"Sure it can. But that ain't gonna happen with me putting the gun down. You think I'm stupid? A Cuban takes a plane and then gives up? You guys don't like us too much right now. I won't last a day. Now, here's what I want: A full tank of gas and I'll let all the ladies go. Then I want one hundred thousand dollars in cash. You understand?"

"What else?" the captain asked, anger touching his voice.

"I think we're starting to understand each other now. Then we're going for a ride. You're going to take me home."

Arnie closed his eyes in frustration and opened them again, feeling trapped. "And where might that be?"

"Are you even listening to me? Cuba. I'll be home, and I'll be safe. Kennedy made it so that no one can go there now. You can't touch me there, and with the money, I'll be set for the rest of my life."

"I'm not sure we can make it all the way to Cuba from here."

Any traces of amusement left the hijacker's voice. "Don't bullshit me, man. I know the range of a 727. You can make it there easy. I want a damn fuel truck, and I want it here in half an hour. If it's not, someone dies. If it gets here, all the ladies go. I want my cash within two hours. If I don't get my cash, then someone dies. I get my money, everyone else goes. You understand?"

"I understand," Arnie said through gritted teeth.

"Oh, and captain, tell the boys in the tower, only one driver. He can also do the fueling. If I see more than one body, someone dies."

There was the click of the interphone being hung up before Arnie could respond.

Chapter Three
Fulfillment

"TWA flight 798, you there?"

The voice on the radio was a new one. It was different, deeper than the tower controller they had been talking to before.

"We're here. Go ahead."

"This is John Reynolds. I'm with the St. Louis Police Department. Have you made contact with the hijacker yet?"

"We have. He has a list of demands."

"They always do." Arnie could almost hear the smile in the man's voice. "What does he want?"

"He wants the plane fueled within the next half an hour. Then he wants a hundred thousand in cash. He says he wants that within two hours. He then wants us to fly him to Cuba."

"That's good. We can work with that. Captain, I want you and your crew to hang in there. We're setting up an assault team as we speak."

"Yes, sir. John, was it?"

"Yes."

"John, you should know, I don't think this is just some deranged nut."

"Why do you say that?"

Arnie shook his head. "Little things. He knows too much. You know what I mean."

"No, sir. I don't."

"He knew that even though we're just starting off the flight, that we could carry more fuel. He knew that our plane had a set of aft airstairs. Things like that."

"Boss?"

Arnie turned to Stu, giving him a nod.

"Boss, I think he's military."

Arnie raised an eyebrow and Stu continued. "He sounds somewhat uneducated, but he's very precise. The money, the time. His resolution of letting passengers off when one gate is hit, then letting the others off when another demand is met. Also, who uses the word 'perimeter?' I'm telling you boss, he's military."

"How sure are you?" Arnie sounded doubtful as asked the question.

Stu shook his head. "Just a feeling."

Arnie stared at the flight engineer for a long second and then reached for the mic. Before he could key it, Stu added, "And that was a service .45 shot. I'm sure you know that sound as well as I do."

Arnie closed his eyes and exhaled before keying the mic. "We think he might be military."

"Roger that, captain. If he is, it will make a difference."

"I understand."

Gary turned around and gave Stu a questioning look. Although as copilot, Gary outranked the flight engineer, he was actually a year younger than Stu. Whereas Stu had gained his flight experience in the Navy flying fighter aircraft, Gary was a civilian pilot. He had put himself through college working as a flight instructor, amassing experience and flight time as he continued his education. This experience put Gary in a position to be hired with TWA earlier than Stu. It would be another year after they had hired Gary until Stu had fulfilled his obligation to the military and was free to apply to the airlines as a pilot.

While this lack of military experience didn't affect Gary's ability to fly an airplane, it made him a little more uninitiated with military operations.

Stu leaned forward and whispered to Gary, "If he's military, he has a plan. He's not just some nut making all of this up as he goes."

"But Cuba?"

"He said it's his home. But I think he's also trying to make a political statement. The embargo still really pisses a lot of people off. I think he's trying to make a point, and a hundred thousand will set you for life in a place like Cuba."

"How's that different from just some nut? Why does the military angle make a difference?"

"Like I said: he has a plan. It also means that he might be more willing to die. If he's just doing it for the money, I think he'd fold. But if it's a cause he really believes in..."

"Are you two going to let me talk to the guy in the tower?" Arnie snapped.

"Sorry Boss."

"Sorry."

"John, you were cut out, say again."

"Yes captain, I was saying I can get you a fuel truck in the next ten minutes. How much do you want? I can give you as much or little as you think's prudent."

"I'm thinking, meet this demand. Top off the tanks. If he does know the capability of the plane, he might have an idea of the range. The last thing I want is some asshole with a gun up here telling me I can't land while I'm running out of gas."

"How much gas will it take you to get to Havana?"

"A good deal, but we'll have the range to make it there easily. But I don't know what this guy's ultimate goal is. If he changes the plan midstream, I want to have the gas."

"Understood."

Arnie then turned to his crew. "Gary, I agree with Stu... if this guy's military, he has a plan."

"Is it wise to play into his plan?"

"Why wouldn't it be," Stu said. "First priority is to get the passengers off, right?"

"Agreed," Arnie affirmed. "We take on the gas and get the first group of passengers off. We then hope they can come up with the money so we can get the rest off."

"Then what?" Gary asked.

Arnie shrugged. "I'm making this up as we go. After we get everyone off, we can worry about the next step."

"He wouldn't kill anyone, would he?" Gary pressed.

Arnie looked at Stu. "You said you weren't in Korea, right?"

"Just missed it."

Arnie nodded. "I flew Corsairs there. Most of the officers were reasonable, but some of the enlisted..." his voice trailed off.

Stu nodded his agreement. "I know what you mean, sir."

"So, what do we do?" Gary looked a little paler than he did a few minutes before.

"Like the book says," Arnie answered. "We wait."

It was quiet as the grave in the back of the cabin. Although it was now past eleven PM, no one was sleeping. The gunman sat in the stewardess's jumpseat, his eyes wide as he surveyed the passengers. Sara was alone, across from him in the plane's galley. The remaining three stewardesses were holed up in the back of the plane.

Everyone onboard flinched when the chime sounded throughout the cabin and the light illuminated above the cockpit door.

Sara had made the tactical decision to keep the cabin lights low to try and lull the hijacker to sleep. She thought it might have the added benefit of putting some passengers to sleep as well, easing their anxiety. However, the tactic proved fruitless. The fear was palpable.

Sara looked at the gunman and the cabin interphone next to him. He didn't move. He only stared back at her.

"Do you mind if I get that?" She finally said. Her voice was icy and there wasn't the faintest trace of a southern accent now.

"What? Is it the cockpit?"

"Who else would it be?"

"Don't mess with me," he said in a low growl. He then waved his gun at the phone. She crossed the galley and reached for the handset next to his head. He shot her a look, and she hesitated a moment, her hand motionless next to his head, before she completed the action and picked up the phone.

"This is Sara."

"Sara, its Arnie."

"Yes, captain."

"All right, he's with you. That's good. Let him know the fueling is complete. When can he let the first of the hostages go?"

Sara looked over at the gunman and asked, "The captain said the fueling is complete. Are you going to keep your word and let the women go?"

The gunman narrowed his gaze. "Isn't that what I said I'd do?"

"When?"

"Tell one of your girls in the back to open the door. The women can leave, but I see one man head out, I start shooting."

"Captain," she said. "He said one of the stewardesses in the back can open the aft airstairs and the women can exit. Would you like me to make an announcement?

"Hold on," came the reply. After a brief pause, the captain's voice returned, "Stu said we should move the women to the back and the men up front. That should keep anyone from making a break for it."

"Good idea, sir. Let me see if that's acceptable." She cupped her hand over the handset and repeated the idea to the gunman.

"Don't try anything funny."

She rolled her eyes. "Don't worry." She then pressed the button signaling the back of the plane and explained the plan to the other stewardesses.

A few minutes later, the men were in the front and the women started exiting out of the aft stairs. Once the last of the women left, Liz raised the door again. Once more, everyone was trapped in the plane.

"John, can you give me anything?"

"Well captain, we're still debriefing the passengers, but they're consistent that he has tan skin, black hair and is wearing ratty clothing. Not too much help on identifying the gun, but a few of the women said that he was wearing a green jacket when he first boarded. From the description, it sounds military."

"At least we're getting somewhere. The women are off."

"We'll get everyone off before this is done. You guys hang in there."

Arnie could hear exhaustion in the police officer's voice. He was tired as well. As he looked around the cockpit, he could tell his entire crew was exhausted. The adrenalin rush of the initial hijacking had long since worn off.

"Gary, why don't you try to grab a bit of shuteye?"

"Don't need any. I'm fine, Arnie."

Arnie gave a thin smile. His crew had been excellent. "Gary, I don't know when this will be over and we still might need to fly. If we do, I'd like to have at least someone in the cockpit who can keep their eyes open. Maybe we can wear this bastard down through attrition."

"All right." Gary said in a defeated tone. He slid his seat back and stretched out, closing his eyes.

"Did the guy in the tower say anything about the money?" Stu asked in a whisper.

Arnie looked at the pilot next to him. Gary was already asleep.

"Only that they're working on it."

"Do you think they really are?"

"Don't know. Hundred thousand's a lot of money. Might take them some time to scrape it together. Especially at this time of night."

Stu nodded.

A few minutes later, "Captain," came over the radio. Both Arnie and Stu sat up straight and looked over at Gary. He was still out.

"Go ahead," Arnie said in a low voice.

"Captain, this is Richard Stack. I'm with the FBI and I'll be replacing Officer Reynolds here."

"Well, Officer Reynolds has been doing a good job so far. We've got half of the passengers off the plane."

"But he can't get you the cash. I can."

Arnie glanced over at Stu. Both shared a look. "In that case, good to be working with you, Richard."

"You can call me Dick."

Arnie hadn't expected this informality from a fed. His tone softened a bit, and he said, "In that case, call me Arnie."

"OK. Arnie it is."

"All right, Dick, what's the situation?"

"We're having a hell of a time getting the money together, but we're making progress. I'll keep you in the loop."

"What's the problem?"

"How secure is this line? Is the hijacker listening in?"

"No. We've locked down the cockpit and all communication with him is through our lead stewardess."

"Any chance he can listen in?"

"No."

"All right then; given the release of the woman, the FBI is willing to deal. But we would like to keep him on the ground if at all possible."

"I think we're all in agreement there, Dick."

"However, if we can't keep him on the ground, we'd like to do our level best to get this son of a bitch."

"Going to be hard to do from Cuba. Didn't you hear Kennedy severed all ties with them?"

"You're right ... If he stays in Cuba, it will be hard to get him. But we believe that there's a chance that he's not going to stay in Cuba. If that happens—if he comes back here—we want plans in place to get this guy."

Arnie looked at Stu, who was listening in. Stu gave a shrug.

"He said he was from there ... that he wanted to go home. Why would he come back to the US?"

"Once you've lived an American life, it's hard to step back to a place like Cuba. Trust me, there's a good chance he'll return."

"OK, I can understand that. But what does that have to do with the money?"

"He didn't specify how he wanted the money. We need to get to a bank so we can get new, uncirculated hundred-dollar bills. All sequential."

"So you can track him." Arnie looked at his watch. "His deadline is fast approaching. Will you make it?"

"It'll be close."

"Where the hell's my money?"

"We're trying to get it."

The gunman gripped the handset and growled, "You think I'm messing around here? I told you that if I didn't get my money, I was going to start shooting people."

"I realize that," the captain said on the other end of the line, his voice calm and even. "But you have to realize that it's the middle of the night. The authorities are trying to get the money as fast as they can."

"They ain't working fast enough. Now I'm going to have to start killing people."

"Listen to me. Think about it for a minute. You've already bought a great deal of goodwill by releasing the women. I'm talking to the authorities and they want a peaceful resolution to this. That's why they're bending over backwards to get you your money. They're telling me they need a little more time, and I believe them. However, if you start killing people, you'll be forcing their hand. They'll send an assault group into the plane, and then the only thing you'll get will be a cheap funeral. Now, if you're serious, let them do their job."

The gunman surveyed the cabin. It was still dark, and despite the fear in the group, some hostages had drifted off into an uneasy sleep. He weighed his options for several long seconds before answering.

"I'll give you one more hour. But if the money doesn't come by then, I'll start shooting people. Maybe I get killed, but maybe I won't. But you'll all know I ain't screwing around, and you might start taking me seriously!"

Arnie flinched as he heard the hijacker slam the handset back into its cradle. He hoped the unit wasn't broken. Communication would still be possible, but from the back of the plane, it might be more difficult.

"Dick?"

"I'm here, Arnie."

"He says that if he doesn't get the money in an hour, he'll start killing hostages."

"How credible do you think he is?"

Arnie rubbed the bridge of his nose. "He hasn't killed anyone yet, but we've also met his demands up to this point. Also, even if he really isn't willing to kill anyone, he's got to be getting tired. So, if we're dealing with a tired, trapped, desperate—and possibly stupid— animal… Well, I wouldn't want to take any chances."

There was a lengthy silence. "Dick, you still there?"

"Yeah Arnie, I'm here. Listen, here's the deal: I think you're right; this guy might not be a killer, but he seems to know his way around weapons. He's armed, and he's probably tired. I've been talking to Washington and they've authorized the money. It's on its way now from the bank. We've managed to get more or less what we want: new sequential hundred-dollar bills."

"What's the plan after we get him the money? Do you think we can end this here?"

"Very much so, yes. Once we get the passengers off, we can send in an assault team. They know you're in the cockpit, so they'll be sure not to catch you in the crossfire. We believe he'll be so focused on the attack, that his bullets shouldn't be a threat to you, or any of your men in the cockpit. I think we could resolve this whole thing within the next hour or so."

"I hope you're right."

"And Arnie, make sure you get your stewardesses off the plane with the rest of the passengers. One less group to be caught in the crossfire."

"Sara?"

"It's me, Arnie."

"Good. Listen, tell this guy his money's on its way. When it arrives, I want all the passengers off the plane. And I want you to get him to let you and your crew off too."

"I don't know if he'll go for that."

"Do your best. The money will be here soon."

Sara slowly hung up the handset and rubbed her eyes. She then got up and approached the hijacker.

He looked to be sleeping, but as she got within a foot of him, he raised his head, and his gun with it, pointing it at her.

"I just wanted to let you know that the captain said your money will be here soon."

"Good." He lowered his head and gun again, but Sara didn't move. After several long seconds he said, without looking up, "There was something else you wanted?"

"Yes. Me and my cabin crew. I would like you to let us go."

"And why should I do that?"

"We aren't any good to you anymore. We aren't any more valuable than any of the other hostages you'll be letting go. And you still have the pilots."

"So, you just want to run?"

Sara glowered. "Yes, I just want to run."

He looked up again, but the gun stayed down. "The others can get off. You stay."

Sara allowed herself a slight smile and returned to the front of the plane.

Chapter Four

Airborne

"This is the plan," Arnie said into the interphone. "You listening?"

"Yeah, I'm listening," the hijacker responded.

"Sara will lower the aft airstairs. A single man will come onto the plane and give you a bag with the money. He will then lead everyone out of the plane. We will then take-off and take you to Havana. Is that acceptable?"

"That'll work. But the blonde is staying."

Arnie gripped the handset as he growled, "That is *not* acceptable. Everyone goes."

Another voice replaced that of the hijacker. "Arnie, it's me."

"Sara, you're getting off this plane. That's final."

"Arnie," she said in a much lower voice, "he's gone back. Listen, I know the police are planning something. I'm not stupid. But the way I see it, I've gotten everyone else off the plane. I can dive into the forward galley and lie on the floor when the attack comes. It's our best chance."

"No, the risk is too high."

"*Arnie*," she pleaded. "I'm a big girl. I can take care of myself. I have a responsibility to these people too. I'm not here just to serve drinks and meals. I'm a member of this crew and I will be saving lives; I will be *doing my job*."

"I don't feel good about this."

"And you think I do? But this is what I'm paid for and we'll get through this together."

"Arnie, you ready for my guys?" The voice of Dick Stack came over the radio.

Arnie leaned over and touched the arm of his first officer, who came wide awake with a start. He then keyed the mic.

"Listen Dick, we've been able to negotiate everyone's egress except for our chief stewardess. Couldn't swing her too. She's going to hide out in the galley. Make sure your guys know where she is before they come in, guns blazing."

"Shit! I wanted everyone off."

"Sorry, I tried. Couldn't make it happen."

"Not your fault. But still, you did good. Don't worry, my guys are professionals. They'll make sure she's OK."

"What's the plan?" All three pilots leaned in towards the center of the cockpit as they listened.

"My guy with the money will drop off the bag and then lead the hostages out with one of your stewardesses.

They will lead everyone out of the back and down the stairs. Have your remaining stewardesses follow the last of the passengers out. Once they're safely out of range, my boys will rush the back of the plane, boarding before he can get the stairs back up. I expect the entire op to take less than three minutes."

"Good."

There were only twelve passengers left on the plane, and two stewardesses behind them. They continued to tick off one by one. Sara stood next to the hijacker, a slight smile on her face as the passengers continued to file off.

As they stood there, the hijacker looked over at Sara and smiled as well.

"You look happy," he told her.

"So do you."

"I should. I have everything I want. I got a bag full of money. I got a jet. And I've got my insurance policy right here." As he said this, he held up a long metallic cylinder. At the top of it was a red button which was being held down by his thumb.

"What's that?" Sara asked, her grin fading.

"This? This is called a Deadman's switch. You see, if my thumb comes off of this little red button, my bag over there, filled with C-4 plastic explosives, will blow this whole plane straight to hell."

As the last of the passengers were leaving, Sara leapt up violently and ran to the interphone and started urgently pushing the call button.

"Goodbye, asshole." Stu grinned, looking out of the cockpit door's peephole as the last of the passengers left the plane.

Suddenly, a blur sped across the tiny window and the cockpit chime started ringing repeatedly. All three men jumped as Arnie picked up the handset.

"Don't let them storm the plane! Don't let them storm the plane!" She screamed. "He's got a bomb!"

"Shit!" Arnie said, looking outside the cockpit window.

Before the captain could key the mic to the outside world, Gary was already talking into his microphone. "The hijacker's got a bomb! Stay back! Stay back!"

"Say again?" Came Stack's voice.

"He has some kind of bomb," Arnie answered this time. "Don't approach the plane or he'll blow up this aircraft!"

The hijacker was laughing as he watched Sara rush forward. She made no effort to keep her voice down or hide what they were planning. He continued to laugh as he casually strolled to the back of the plane. As the two remaining stewardesses disappeared down the airstairs, he activated the switch to close the door. As the door started to slowly lift closed, in the darkness he could just make out several figures, all clad in black, frozen in place. This made the hijacker laugh even harder.

The assault team was 20 feet from the plane when the call to stand down came. The members of the team were frozen momentarily. Was this some kind of trick? Was the assault called off? The men dressed head to foot in black gear stood exposed when they first heard the soft whirr of the hydraulic motor. Moments later, the aft stairway door crept slowly closed. The leader of the team made the judgement call: if they weren't going to carry out the op, they would withdraw.

"Fall back! Fall back!" he commanded his team. As silently and stealthily as they had appeared as black wraiths in the night, they withdrew. Moments later, they were gone, enveloped into the inky darkness.

"Dick, what's going on? Did you copy about the bomb?"

"The withdraw orders been given. They're pulling back. What's going on?"

"I don't know. Give me a minute. All I know is my stewardess said he had a bomb, and this plane is gorged with gas. I'll get back to you in a minute."

Arnie punched the cabin call button.

"He's in the back. He closed the door, Arnie. Did they stop? Are they coming?" The panic was clear in her voice.

"Yeah Sara, they called off the assault. What can you tell me?"

The voice that replied wasn't the voice of his stewardess, but that of the hijacker.

"I've got 20 pounds of military grade C4 attached to a remote Deadman's switch. If my thumb comes off the button, we all get blown straight to hell."

"What? You don't trust us?"

"Shiiiiit. How dumb do you think I am? Do you really think I can't see an assault team coming just because they're dressed in black?"

"Sorry about that," Arnie said through gritted teeth.

"I'm sure you are. Now listen up, because I'm not going to repeat myself: I've got my money and I've got my gas. Now I want you to get this damn plane in the air and get my ass to Cuba before the police can try to kill me again. Understood?"

"Look, it will take a little while. We need to get a flight plan together and we need clearance from air traffic control before we can…"

"Hold it! Just hold it! I've been patient with you so far, but I'm starting to get tired of your bullshit! I know you have maps up there and I know you have more than enough gas. All you need to do is takeoff and turn south. You can figure out the rest on the way. The alternative is, if we're not in the air in ten minutes, I'm detonating the bomb. There is no way any court is going to spare my ass. I'm dead either way. The only chance I have of surviving the night is getting in the air. That goes for all of you as well... including the pretty blonde back here. You have ten minutes... either we go, or we're all gonna die!" The line went dead.

Arnie looked at the other two men in the cockpit.

"He said he's going to blow up the plane if we don't take off. And Stu, I think you're right: he's military."

"Why's that, boss?"

"He said he has 20 pounds of military grade C4."

Stu shook his head. "That's way more than he needs."

"What are the chances we can wait him out?" Gary asked.

"No dice. He said he's going to die in an assault and his only chance is getting airborne." Arnie looked at the other two pilots and added, "He's right on that score. I believe him when he says if we're not in the sky, he's going to detonate the explosives."

"Arnie," Stu said, "What's the point here? Let's just take him to Cuba. It's only money. And it's marked at that. I don't want to sound like I'm giving up, but you have us, Sara, and not to mention a fairly expensive plane here to think about. Besides," he added with a grin containing no humor, "it's a lot warmer in Cuba than it is here."

Arnie turned to Gary. "Your thoughts?"

"You're the boss, boss. But I'm with Stu. I say we just go."

Arnie nodded as he keyed the mic to the tower.

"Dick, it's Arnie. Look, this guy has us in a box here. We're all in agreement. We're going to takeoff and start towards Havana. If you can, please coordinate with your people to get us a route? ATC can just radio it up to us."

"Arnie, I don't think that's a good idea. I want you to hang on a little longer."

"Sorry Dick, that's a negative. We're all in agreement. We're going."

Dick's voice had a bit of a quaver in it as he said, "Arnie, I've got a psychologist and he's saying this asshole's full of shit. He won't do anything. Just stay there a little longer."

The sleep deprivation and stress of the whole situation finally got to Arnie as he transmitted, "Look *Dick*, I understand that waiting sounds like a great idea when you're up there in the Air Traffic Control Tower. You'd get a really nice view of the fireball and everything if you're wrong, but I'm not willing to take that chance. I have a crew—one of which is a young girl in her twenties—to think about. I also have a very expensive plane that I promised TWA I would bring back in one piece. So, with all due respect, *sir*, we *will* be taking off."

"You know Arnie, I can shoot your tires out."

Arnie looked at the two other men in the cockpit. They all nodded. "Stu, reduce the loads for engine start."

The minutes between the first indications of an engine whining until the plane finally lifted off were the most stressful of the crew's lives. All were well aware that there were numerous ways that the FBI could stop their departure. They also knew that the FBI thought the hijacker was bluffing. They, however, weren't so sure. It's one thing to have someone on the ground analyzing a hijacker from miles away, but quite another to have a man sitting mere feet from you with a bomb.

The most stressful moments happened once the throttles were advanced to take-off power. As they started rolling down the runway, this was where they would be the most vulnerable. Vulnerable from an attack from the FBI (no matter how well intentioned), vulnerable from the hijacker (If he did have a bomb, no one in the crew wanted to deal with that while the 727 was rolling down the runway at 150mph). And they were also vulnerable from themselves. All three men were exhausted and strung out from the evening's events.

It wasn't until they were climbing through 3000 feet and the flaps were retracted, that the three pilots began to relax, however slight it might have been.

"Hey boss?" Stu asked.

Arnie turned, looking over his shoulder. "What's up?"

"It occurred to me, if he has a bomb, perhaps we can mitigate any damage it might do if we keep the plane depressurized."

Gary chimed in. "That's a good idea. We could just cruise at 10,000 feet."

"Maybe we could go higher. Climb to 41,000 feet and knock this bastard out." The captain added. "We have oxygen, he doesn't. Time of useful consciousness at that altitude is less than thirty seconds."

"I'm not so sure that's such a good idea." Both sets of eyes turned to Stu. "Well, two things. First: I don't want to put Sara in any danger. And second: he said he has a Deadman's switch. If he lets go of that, we're all dead."

Arnie swore silently beneath his breath. "Dammit Stu. You're right. I'm not thinking straight. Of course, 10,000 feet would be best. I also need you to work up a flight plan towards Cuba."

"No problem, boss. I'm on it."

Nodding, Arnie turned to the co-pilot. "Gary, you take the plane. I want to see what's going on back there."

Stu looked up from his paperwork on the desk of his workstation and said, "I don't think that's a good idea, either."

Arnie shook his head, his irritation apparent. "Why's that?"

"This asshole told us he wanted us to stay up here. We should call Sara first and make sure it's OK." He then added quickly, "I don't want to see anything happen to you or Sara, boss."

Arnie nodded, "You might be right." He then picked up the handset and chimed back to the cabin.

It was several seconds before Sara's familiar voice answered.

"What's up, Arnie?"

"I take it you can talk."

"Yes, sir. He's pacing up and down the aisle."

"I want to come back there and talk to him."

"I'll ask. Just a minute."

Arnie heard her hang up the handset. He fumed as he waited. "This is my goddamn plane." He muttered.

"Boss, it's all good. We'll be on the ground before you know it," Gary offered.

The chime from the cabin split the air just as Gary announced that they were leveling off at 10,000 feet.

"Cabin's at 5000 feet and climbing boss. I should have it completely depressurized in a few minutes."

"Would you all shut up!" Arnie snapped. "I can't hear myself think. And Stu, where the hell's my flight plan?"

"Just a few more minutes, sir," Stu offered weakly.

He then picked up the handset, "Sara?"

"Sorry captain, he said no one comes back here."

Arnie unbuckled his seatbelt and started to rise. "This is my goddamn plane. I'm coming back!"

"Arnie, we don't need you shot. If anyone should go back, it should be me."

"I'm in command here, Stu."

"Yes, sir. You are. And with all due respect, that's why you need to stay up here."

The captain seemed to consider this for several long seconds before he spoke into the handset again. "I'm sending the flight engineer back. Does he have a problem with that?"

He heard a hand cover the handset and Sara's muffled voice. He never heard the hijacker's response, but she quickly came back on, "He said only the flight engineer. If anyone else comes back, he'll blow up the plane."

Arnie nodded as he settled back into his seat. "Fine. Stu, go back there and let me know what's going on."

"Yes, sir," Stu said, undoing his seatbelt and rising. As he did so, he passed forward a chart to the men. "Here's the flight plan. We'll cross the Gulf of Mexico, skirt the West Coast of Florida, pass over the Keys and then into Cuban airspace."

Arnie nodded. "Thanks Stu. This is good work. Sorry I snapped."

Stu offered a tired grin. "We're all tired. But first rounds on you."

Now both Arnie and Gary were smiling as Arnie conceded, "You've got it."

Stu was gone for almost fifteen minutes before he returned to the cockpit.

"I think I made some progress boss," he said as he closed the cockpit door behind him.

"What up?" Gary asked.

"The guy's a nut. But a well-armed nut. He has a semi-automatic handgun and a duffel full of C-4. I'm sure he has an assault rifle in there as well. No question this asshole's military. Probably an E-1 prick. But he's got his hands on some good hardware. More than enough to blow the plane. He seems calm enough, though. Says he just wants to go to Cuba. He's convinced he can live the easy life with a hundred grand."

"How's Sara?" the captain asked.

"She's a trooper. Rattled, but hanging in there. Unfortunately, this asshole knows we don't want anything to happen to her. She's his best leverage, and he knows it. He stressed he wants us to stay in the cockpit until we land."

"Looks like that should be another three hours from now," Arnie said. "How are you guys doing?"

"A bit strung out, but I'm fine." Gary said.

"Same here. I'll just be glad when this is all over."

Outside there was a high overcast of clouds, blocking the moon and stars. Arnie nodded and looked out of the window into the darkness enveloping them.

Chapter Five
The Fed

The phone rang at 11:30 PM. In Washington, D.C., Paul Owens was sound asleep. Paul was usually an early to bed person, much to the chagrin of his wife. Leslie Owens liked to go to sleep closer to midnight. However, after five years of marriage, and Paul's work with the federal government, his circadian rhythms won out.

Leslie had just drifted off when the bell of the phone shattered the calm of the night. Her irritation was exacerbated by the fact that it wasn't until after the fourth ring that her husband picked up the receiver.

"Owens." His voice was almost unrecognizable, thick with the slur of sleep. Even in the dark of the night, Leslie could hear Paul come to full wakefulness.

"How long ago?" His voice was now clear and alert. Leslie leaned over and snapped on the lamp on the nightstand. Paul involuntarily blinked back the light but showed no irritation.

"National Airport? Around an hour, unless I skip the shower." Silence. "Probably twenty minutes." Silence. "I'll do my best. When is the flight scheduled to leave? Yes, sir. I see. I'll be there as soon as I can."

Paul hung up the phone and jumped out of bed, heading across the room to the dresser where he began to change out of his pajamas. As he did so, he started to answer his wife's unasked questions.

"That was the Chief of Staff. It looks like there's a hijacking in St. Louis. The hijacker hasn't made any demands yet, but local police are on the scene. Local FBI's on their way."

He was pulling on his pants as his wife asked, "What does this have to do with you?"

"The Chief of Staff's making me lead."

"Why would he be making *you* lead?"

"Long story. No time to explain. There's a jet at National waiting to take me to St. Louis."

"A jet?"

"A private plane. They want me there yesterday. They're waiting for me right now."

"You said a hijacking. Are they still on the ground?"

Paul looped a tie around his neck as he answered. "They are for now. With any kind of luck, it's going to stay that way."

"I still don't understand why they're sending you. You said the FBI is on the scene, right?"

Paul smiled and put on his jacket as he crossed the room to kiss his wife. "Like I said: it's a long story. Go-bag's in the downstairs closet, right?"

His wife nodded, frustrated. She knew she wouldn't get any answers tonight. "You need the go-bag? How long will you be gone?"

A go-bag was a suitcase or duffle bag most in federal law enforcement kept packed so they could depart at a moment's notice. Inside, the essentials were already packed, and at least a few days' worth of clothing to get them through. Paul had kept a go-bag packed and ready since he first went to work for the Treasury Department, but this was his first time utilizing it.

"If I knew that, I wouldn't need the go-bag." His grin was unconvincing, but Leslie accepted it. Paul was already a Federal agent when she married him. This was what she signed up for… even if this was the first time he was being called into action.

Paul kissed his wife one last time and gently closed the door behind him, heading downstairs. As she clicked off the light, Leslie heard a car approaching as headlights washed across the window. She heard the front door close. A minute later, a car door closed with a heavy thud. The lights then washed over the window again as the car disappeared into the night.

They sent a car? Leslie thought. *What are they getting Paul into?*

When Paul arrived at Washington National Airport, he was met by another federal agent. This man's clothing, like Paul's, was somewhat askew, as if he too, dressed in a hurry. However, this man was younger, and looked far more awake.

As Paul got out of the car, the driver rushed around to the trunk to retrieve his go-bag. As Paul slung the duffel over his shoulder, the other man approached him, extending a hand.

"Special Agent Owens, I'm Jon Rooney."

He shook the younger man's hand. They then headed towards the waiting plane. "Paul Owens. Nice to meet you. What have you got for me?"

"Not much, sir. I have a dossier, but it's pretty thin."

Paul glanced over to the younger man and noticed he was carrying only a briefcase. If he had a travel-bag, it must already be on the plane.

"I wouldn't expect much. Do you know the current status?"

As they talked, the door to the Lear Jet opened and the two men nodded to the captain as they ascended the stairs.

"I've been told it just you two. Is that correct?" the captain asked.

Nodding, Paul said, "Yes. Are we're fueled for St. Louis?"

"Yes, sir. And then some. We have a full load of gas just in case things change."

Paul snorted, stifling a laugh. "It's a hijacking," he said sarcastically, "How much can things change?"

"Yes sir," the captain said with a laugh of his own.

As they entered the small cabin of the corporate jet, a stewardess pulled the door closed behind them. As the captain took his place in the cockpit, both federal agents were offered beverages as they took their seats and fastened their seatbelts. As they did so, the engines started spinning up. Both declined, resuming their conversation.

"Latest I have is, they're still on the ground in St. Louis. The hijacker demanded a hundred thousand dollars. The FBI told him they're working on it. He also said he wants the plane fueled—full tanks."

"Did he say where he wants to go?"

"Cuba."

Paul grinned. "Of course." He then added, "Did he specify how he wants the money? And how long until the FBI can get it?"

"He didn't specify, and the Bureau already has the money. All hundreds. All sequential."

Paul looked out of the window as the plane moved. They were the only activity on the airport at that hour. Other than the blue lights denoting the taxiways, all was dark outside. Nodding, he said, "That's something. Does anyone besides us know what's on the plane?"

"I don't think so. FBI's on the scene, but I don't think they've been told."

Paul said with a snort, "I'm sure they'll be thrilled to see me."

Nodding without humor, Jon said, "I only have you until St. Louis. You're on your own after that." He then reached into his briefcase and pulled out a plain folder and handed it to Paul. "This is everything we have on the crew and the plane. It's a Boeing 727-100. It was doing a late-night flight from St. Louis to Denver. They experienced some kind of mechanical delay."

The Lear Jet slowly turned onto the runway and then accelerated. Moments later, it lifted off into the night sky. As they climbed, Paul looked outside at the US Capitol as the plane banked, following the Potomac River on the departure.

"There was a last-minute addition to the passenger list," Jon added. "The ground crew said he looked like a shady character. He wouldn't have made it except for the mechanical delay."

Still looking out of the window, Paul said, "How's that?"

"He arrived looking for a ticket after the plane's scheduled departure. The only reason he made that flight was the mechanics were still fixing the plane."

As they continued to climb, Paul returned his attention back inside and opened the folder. After looking through it for a minute, he said, "It says here the plane's brand new. What was the problem?"

"Some issue with the hydraulic system. Not sure exactly what yet. Some kind of leak, I believe."

Paul nodded and looked back at the folder. After another minute, he asked, "Why do they think he's shady?"

"He wasn't dressed right. His clothing was old and worn. Casual. The stuff you'd wear doing yardwork. Not the clothes you'd fly in. You travel sir, have you ever seen anyone dressed like that on a plane?"

Paul shook his head. "No, everyone's always dressed up. Do we think the two are related?"

Jon shrugged. "I don't see how they could be, but we're looking into it."

"Did he say anything about the cargo? *Our* cargo?"

"Nothing. It's probably just a crazy coincidence."

Shaking his head, Paul said, "We'll know soon."

Paul returned his attention to the world outside. As they climbed above a cloud layer, everything beneath them dissolved. All was black, save the red flashing of the plane's anti-collision light, illuminating the clouds around them in rhythmic, red pulses.

A few moments later, Paul opened the folder and started looking through the thin file again. As he did so, he said, "Jon, what about the hostages?"

"He said he'd let the women go once he was fueled."

"And?"

"They should be fueled by now, so I'm hoping they're safely out."

Paul nodded. "And the rest?"

"He says the rest will be released once he has the money."

"I would assume the FBI has an assault team in place." Paul turned over a page in the folder without really looking at it.

"Yes. Once they get the passengers out, they're going to storm the plane. It should all be over by the time we land."

Paul nodded and was silent. Jon looked at him, trying to figure out what was going on in his mind when Paul raised a hand, summoning the stewardess.

The woman at the front of the plane rushed up to him.

"Yes, sir? What can I do for you?"

"The pilot said the plane is fully fueled?"

She turned and looked towards the front, and then back at Paul. "I'm sorry sir, I'm not sure. But if he said it is, I'm sure that's the case."

Paul pursed his lips. "Would you do me a favor and tell the guys up front to work up an alternate flight plan? There's a chance we might need to change our destination."

"Of course, sir. Where to?"

"Guantanamo Bay, Cuba."

"At once, sir."

As she headed back towards the front, Jon asked, "Do you really think that will be necessary?"

"Paul shrugged. "Don't know. But I want to have all bases covered." Paul looked at his watch. "The women should be off of the plane by now. If the FBI delivers the money, the rest will be off soon."

"I've been told that the FBI has orders not to let them take off."

Paul exhaled and blinked the sleep out of his eyes. "This whole situation looks fishy. It's a hell of a coincidence that this guy hit *this* flight, don't you think?"

"I don't know. There are so many planes out there…" His voice trailed off. Jon then said, "Sure, this one has cargo… but does that really mean anything other than our bad luck?"

Paul considered this. "And the maintenance delay?"

Jon shrugged.

"If you don't mind, would you have the stewardess bring us some coffee? I have a feeling it's going to be a long night."

As the Lear Jet was approaching the top of descent, the first officer came back into the cabin.

"Special Agent Owens?"

Paul looked up from the folder. "Yes?"

"I just got news from St. Louis. The 727's airborne."

Paul nodded. The bags under his eyes were pronounced and his unshaven face added to the weariness of his appearance.

Jon stood up and roared, "What the hell?"

"Sorry sir," the copilot continued, "I just got a message to pass the information to you guys. They said they got the passengers off and were going to storm the plane when the guy produced a bomb or something. He then told the crew to take-off or he would blow them all up."

Jon's mouth hung open. Paul had been expecting this.

"I take it they're on their way to Cuba?"

"They're heading southeast."

Paul gave the man a weary smile. "So, I take that as a yes."

The copilot returned the smile. "It's a solid probably."

"Tell the captain…"

"He's already working on it, sir. I've got to get back to the cockpit. I'll let you know if anything changes."

"Thank you. Please do."

The color seemed to have drained from Jon's face, but Paul just looked tired.

"How did you know?"

Paul shrugged. "Unlucky guess."

Jon looked around the plane then back at Paul. "You know what this means, don't you?"

Another tired smile. "It means we're going to need more coffee."

Chapter Six
The Emergency

Arnie, like the other members of his crew, was struggling to keep his eyes open. They were now skimming the West Coast of Florida, more than halfway to their destination, when an explosion shook the plane. Instantaneously, all three members of the crew were wide awake, the remnants of fatigue driven from their minds.

"What the hell was that?" Arnie roared.

Stu was shaking his head. "It looks like the A system hydraulic pressure's dropping, but not fast. Electrical is fine. Nothing to report on pressurization. We're still depressurized."

"Re-pressurize the cabin. See if it holds pressure."

"Yes, sir." Stu had earlier switched from automatic to manual pressurization, giving him direct control of the cabin. He now switched it back to the automatic system and waited.

"What are you seeing back there, Stu?" Gary asked.

"Nothing. Not holding pressure. Switching back to manual." Several long seconds later, Stu said, "Outflow valve's closed... still nothing. You want me to go back and take a look Arnie?"

Arnie considered the question for a few seconds before answering, "Yes."

"Should we call back first?" Gary asked.

It was a few more seconds before Arnie answered, "No. Something's going on back there. I want to know what it is."

Stu got up and opened the cockpit door. At the first crack, Sara flew in, crying. A moment after she entered, the acrid smell of smoke filled the cockpit.

"What the hell's going on back there?" Stu said.

"I don't know. He had me locked in the lavatory ever since you went back to the cockpit," Sara answered, fighting back tears.

Stu looked at Arnie, who shook his head. "Go. Let me know. I'm standing by."

Stu left the cockpit and entered the back of the plane.

The chime from the cabin came almost at once.

Arnie picked up the interphone. "Stu, is that you?"

"Yeah, it's me. The entire cabin's filled with smoke. Something back here burned."

"Do you think it was the C-4?"

"I doubt it. If it were, it probably would have taken out the entire plane."

"Well, something happened back there. That sure as hell wasn't turbulence."

"Yes, sir. Let me look around. I'll get back with you in a few minutes."

"Wait. Where's the hijacker?"

Exasperated, Stu said, "I don't know. Give me a few minutes and I'll get you some answers."

Arnie nodded, unseen by the flight engineer. "Just let me know."

The three in the cockpit waited for almost fifteen minutes before the knock came. At Arnie's nod, Sara opened the door.

"He's gone."

"What do you mean, gone?" Gary asked.

Stu shook his head. "I mean, I can't find him anywhere." He then produced a plain black bag. "And he left this."

Arnie and Gary looked at the bag with a questioning look. Sara recognized it at once. She said, "You mean, he left…?"

Stu nodded. "Yes, he did. And it would seem the money's all there."

"What money?"

Sara said, "That's the bag with the ransom money."

Arnie's face was a mixture between rage and bewilderment. "None of this makes any sense. We're ten-thousand feet above the water. He just can't be gone. And if he is, why would he leave the money?"

Stu shook his head, his own irritation and confusion showing through. "Fine, then you're welcome to go find him. I'll wait here for you."

Arnie closed his eyes and nodded. "OK guys, we're all tired. Let's just take a deep breath and talk this out. Now Stu, tell me what you saw."

Stu exhaled and took his seat. Sara was now sitting on the jumpseat in the cockpit, located beside the flight engineer's station. After another few moments, Stu began to talk.

"When I went back there, the cabin was filled with smoke. You all knew that. It's almost clear now. I walked the length of the cabin looking for him. I searched the lavs and then the overhead bins. That's why it took me so long. I didn't want him jumping out with a gun and surprising me. But nothing was there. I couldn't find hide nor hair of him. As I was checking the cabin, I noticed that the smoke seemed to dissipate through the cabin floor. After I finished my search and didn't turn up anything, I followed the smoke. Several rows back I could see it going through the floor, and I also heard the rush of air. I then lifted back the carpet. It looks like he cut a hole in the floor leading down to the cargo hold. I looked down but couldn't see much. I don't know if he was hiding down there or not, so I didn't go down to look, but it was making a hell of a racket. One thing I did see was there is a big hole in the side of the plane. It's hard to see much; it's really dark outside, but I'm pretty sure that the cargo door's gone. I looked around as best as I could in the low light but couldn't see much else. If he is down there, I think he'll have a hell of a time getting back into the cabin, so I'm not worried about that. But if I had to take a guess, I don't think that's where he is. With a big hole in the plane, it would be hard to stay down there."

"Was that the explosion we felt?" Gary asked.

Stu nodded. "I'd guess so. It's why the plane won't pressurize. Also, why the A-system hydraulics are losing pressure. I think the explosion nicked the hydraulic line. On my way back, I saw the bag sitting on the seat next to the hole. It was open and I could see it was full of money, so I grabbed it."

"We're losing hydraulic pressure?" Sara said, unconcerned with the talk of the missing hijacker, or the bag of money left behind. "Can we fly like that?"

Arnie gave a forced smile. "We'll be fine. We have back-up systems. Worse case, we have manual reversion. That means we can fly the plane with cables."

Sara didn't notice the look Stu and Gary gave each other. Both knew if it came to that, they *were* in serious trouble. Stu looked to his hydraulics panel. Only the hydraulic fluid level in the A-system was falling—and that was at a very slow rate.

"What about the landing gear?"

Now Arnie's smile was genuine. "Don't worry. We've got it covered." He turned to Gary. "However, if our guest has left us, I think it might be best if we land."

Gary nodded. "I couldn't agree more, sir."

Paul Owens was dozing off when a hand touched his shoulder. He had been over the folder so many times; he felt he was on a first name basis with the crew. Paul tried to use his time on the small jet productively, but he finally surrendered to the fact that a little sleep would be more beneficial than going over the thin file for the umpteenth time.

Startled to full wakefulness, Paul opened his eyes to see the copilot next to him.

"Are we starting down?" Paul asked groggily.

"Not yet, but we will be soon. But not Cuba."

"What happened?"

"The flight had some kind of problem. It looks like they're making an emergency divert to Tampa."

As Paul was assimilating the information. The copilot added, "The captain's up-front making arrangements for us to follow. We should be on the ground somewhere around half an hour to forty-five minutes from now."

"We're not landing first, are we?"

"No, sir."

Paul nodded. "Good. The way this night's been going, who knows where the hell they'll end up."

Chapter Seven
Two Feds

The sun was low in the sky, illuminating the morning in a brilliant orange glow. As the door of the Lear Jet opened, it was a vast contrast from the temperature they left the night before in Washington. Rather than cold, brittle air, hot, sticky humidity rushed to fill the small cabin of the jet.

As Paul stood, Jon asked, "What do you want me to do, sir?"

"Head inside and call Washington. See what you can find out. I'm going to see if I can find the guy from the Bureau who's in charge out here."

"Do you think the FBI's on scene already?"

As the two men talked, they stepped out of the plane and descended the short flight of stairs onto the tarmac. Across from them, maybe 300 yards away, was a dormant 727 with a deep red "TWA" emblazoned inside twin golden globes on its tail. Surrounding the plane were numerous police cars and men in uniform.

"Oh yeah. They're there."

Paul crossed the ramp and was met at once by a police officer who began to challenge him. Preempting the confrontation, Paul held up his badge.

"I need to see the agent in charge." As he did so, he flipped his badge over to reveal his identification.

"Seriously?"

Paul was tired, and in no mood to be questioned. "Now!"

The officer, unused to being address thus, took a step back. "Sorry, sir. Right this way."

The FBI agent in charge was a local. Of that, Paul had no doubt. Rather than a suit, the man was wearing a blue tee shirt with an FBI badge stenciled on the breast. He also was wearing short pants and tennis shoes.

Paul gave a weary smile as he said, "The FBI has a lax dress code in Florida."

The man spun to face Paul. "This is a closed scene. Who let you over here?"

The police officer started to say something, but Paul cut him off. "I'm Paul Owens, Treasury." He pulled out his badge and identification. The FBI agent looked at the credentials before Paul added, "And I'm taking over this investigation."

The FBI agent's mouth dropped open for a long moment before he said, "Uh, no."

Paul smiled. "Sorry, my boss' orders trump your boss."

"How's that?"

"My orders come directly from the Secretary of the Treasury."

"I don't care if your orders come directly from…"

"Whose orders come directly from the President of the United States. Sorry. Johnson's President now. Bobby may still be the top lawyer in the land, but his word's no longer law."

Deflated, the FBI agent stuck out his hand. Greg Stephens."

"Paul Owens."

"Sorry about the attire. I was called out half an hour ago. My wife caught me on my morning run. She took the car out to find me and told me she got a call from Washington. She said they wanted me out here immediately. It's the first time they've ever had her track me down, so I thought it might be better to skip the suit and shower."

"Good call."

"But they said nothing about you. Why's treasury out here? And why put you in charge?"

Ignoring the question, Paul asked, "Have you gone through the plane yet?"

Greg looked up at the jet and then back to Paul. "My guys started a few minutes ago. We just got the crew off. They're now sweeping the plane to find the hijacker."

"What do you mean, 'find the hijacker?'"

Greg shook his head. "This is one of the weirded things I've ever heard of. The guy disappeared in flight. Even stranger, he left the money behind."

"You know about the money?"

Greg gave Paul a confused look. "Of course I know about the money. The FBI provided it."

Paul nodded. "Oh, that money."

"When they were in flight," Greg continued, "they had some kind of explosion. One of the pilots went back to assess the situation. Once he got back in the cabin, he couldn't find the hijacker... but he did find the ransom. Or at least most of it."

"Most of it?"

"The ransom was a hundred grand. We recovered all but three one hundred-dollar bills."

Paul nodded again, but it was apparent his mind was elsewhere. He then asked, "How could the hijacker disappear?"

"Didn't they tell you?"

"I've been on a plane all night on my way here. Well, I was originally going to St. Louis and then Cuba, but I ended up here. Has anyone been in the cargo holds yet?"

Greg gave Paul a questioning look and said, "You really haven't heard anything, have you? I think you should come over here and have a look."

The two feds walked around the plane to the right side of the aircraft. As they crossed the nose, the other side of the plane came into view. It became immediately apparent what Greg meant. Where the forward cargo hold door should have been, there was a mass of scorched and melted aluminum aircraft skin.

"This was the explosion the pilots felt." Greg then motioned over to the wing. The leading edge had an enormous dent in it. "The cargo door almost took out the wing. They had to make an emergency landing. Out experts are saying they couldn't deploy the slats."

"Slats?"

"Something they say they need to slow the plane down for landing." Paul nodded his understanding as they approached the plane. However, as Greg watched Paul, he seemed unconcerned with the wing. He was focused on the enormous breach on the side of the aircraft. As he approached, Paul looked inside the gaping hole. Under his breath, he said, "Shit!"

"What?"

"You haven't removed anything from the plane?"

"No. Why."

"Do you have any money on you?"

Greg shrugged. "A few bucks, I guess, why?"

"Would you mind showing me?"

Greg narrowed his gaze.

"Please."

Greg shrugged and pulled out his wallet. Inside he produced three old one-dollar bills, a new five-dollar bill, and a worn twenty.

"How old do you think those bills are?" Paul asked.

Greg looked at the money. "Date's on them. Two years, two years, three years, one year and this one's four years old."

Paul nodded. "Sounds about right. Now, how much longer do you think those bills will stay in circulation?"

"I've never thought much about it."

Paul smiled again, the weariness heavy on his face. "Most people haven't. I'd be surprised if any of those bills, except for the five, will be around for more than another year. What do you suppose will happen to the bills?"

A shrug. "They'll be destroyed, I guess."

"Right again. How?"

Greg shook his head. "Look agent Owens…"

"Paul."

"OK, look Paul, I don't really have time for this."

"You're right. I'm sorry. I'll cut to the chase. The bills are collected by the local banks and then sent to a central bank where they are all gathered together to be delivered to Denver to be destroyed."

"So?"

"This plane was carrying just such a shipment."

Greg looked to the hole in the plane's side and then back at Paul. "I take it the shipment was more than the hundred grand the perp left behind."

"Your department *almost* lost a hundred-thousand dollars in new, uncirculated, sequential hundred-dollar bills. My department *actually* lost somewhere around ten to twelve million dollars in old money. All denominations and random serial numbers."

"Are you sure you want to do this now? You look beat," Greg said with some compassion.

The two men had spent the better part of an hour going through the plane, but as expected, producing no results.

Once they returned to the FBI field office, Greg got a quick shower and changed, looking more like a typical FBI agent.

They now stood behind the glass of the interview room where Arnie Whitmore, Captain of TWA 798, sat patiently.

"You know better than I how important the first 48 hours are. The clock's running."

Greg nodded. "Do you want to conduct the interview with me?"

"Not this one. I just want to observe."

"OK. You're the boss," Greg said as he stood and exited. A minute later, watching through the one-way mirror, Paul saw Greg enter the interview room.

"Captain Whitmore."

"What's going on? Is this how you treat everyone who's suffered a hijacking?"

"I'm very sorry captain. First, I would like to stress you are *not* a suspect."

"Well, I feel like one."

"I understand. It's just we need to get as much information as quickly as we can. The first few hours after an incident like this are critical to getting vital information on what happened. Even the most insignificant detail could crack the case. I know you're tired, but I promise you, all of us are. We just want to get to the bottom of this. You and your crew are our best chance at doing that."

Arnie nodded. "Fine. What can I do to help?"

After an hour with Arnie, Greg then moved onto Gary, Stu and finally Sara. Each interview lasted roughly an hour where all told their story with little variation in the narrative.

Once Sara was dismissed, the four members of TWA 798's crew were taken to a hotel in downtown Tampa. All were told to get some sleep and order anything they wanted from room service. They were instructed not to leave their rooms until either Greg or one of his subordinates allowed them.

Paul was pouring over the transcripts, sitting at Greg's desk when Greg entered his office.

"You look like hell."

Paul looked up and smiled. "It's been a long day."

"Why don't you get some sleep? I can handle things from here."

Paul nodded. "I will, but first I want to spend a little more time with this. If I don't, I won't be able to sleep anyway."

"It's your call," Greg said. He took the chair across from his desk. "What are your thoughts?"

Paul put down the transcripts and sighed. "Consistent story. But not too much so."

Greg nodded. "I agree. If they're in on it, they didn't coordinate their stories."

"Is that what you think? The crew's in on it?"

Greg pondered the question and then shook his head. "No, I think it's unlikely. When questioned about the cargo, none gave any indication that they knew what they were carrying. They all seemed genuinely surprised when we told them what was on board."

Paul picked up the transcript and flipped a few pages and then read. "Stephens: Did you go outside of the plane?

"Whitmore: The captain normally doesn't do the walk around. The flight engineer takes care of that. But after Stu reported there was a break in the landing gear's hydraulic line, I went out with him to take a look.

"Stephens: Break? I heard it was a cut in the hydraulic line.

"Whitmore: Break, cut, whatever. The plane was broken, and we had to get it fixed before we could go.

"Stephens: Did you look inside the forward cargo hold?

"Whitmore: No. Why should I? The problem was with the hydraulic line in the landing gear.

"Stephens: I'd think as the captain of the plane, you'd be interested in all aspects of the ship.

"Whitmore: The cargo holds are only of interest to me if there's a live animal or hazmat inside.

"Stephens: Hazmat?

"Whitmore: Hazardous materials. Short of that, all I care about is the weight and that it's loaded within balance.

"Stephens: So, it would be a surprise to learn that there was special cargo on board?

"Whitmore: What kind of cargo?"

Paul put down the transcript and looked at Greg. "He seemed surprised when we told him what was in the cargo hold."

Greg nodded. "They all did." He then picked up another transcript. "Stephens: Did you look in the cargo hold during your pre-flight inspection?

"Powell: No. I just look at the parts of the plane we have control over. The cargo holds aren't a part of the inspection.

"Stephens: Aren't you curious what's in the cargo hold?

"Powell: No. Why would I be? It's just bags and mail and junk like that. Besides, the ramp guys are usually blocking the entrance. I just duck under the belt loader and continue my inspection.

"Stephens: So, you have no idea what was in the cargo hold?

"Powell: No, but I'm starting to think it was something important."

Greg put down the second transcript. "The copilot says he never left the plane and the flight attendant says she doesn't even have authority to go outside, short of boarding with the rest of the crew on the stairs."

"You know, if they were in on it or knew something, they certainly wouldn't be admitting to it. They could be feigning ignorance."

Paul leaned back and pinched the bridge of his nose. "Could be." He then leaned in, "Greg, you're FBI. You have to have seen this kind of thing before. What do you think?"

Greg laughed. "I've never even *heard* of anything like this."

"Maybe not the value of the loss, or the method in which the crime was committed, but a thief's a thief."

Greg shook his head. "Well… if you want my opinion…"

"That's exactly what I want."

"Look, here's the thing: as you said, a thief is a thief. But you're talking about over ten million dollars here. And every one of them reacted with the same level of surprise I'd expect from anyone who didn't have any foreknowledge. If you want my opinion, the crew wasn't involved.

All three pilots and Sara were gathered together in the hotel bar. They had been interrogated at least three times. Arnie and Stu, six apiece. It was now three days after the hijacking, and this was the first time all four were allowed together.

They were all sitting in a dark corner of the restaurant bar, and all had a large tumbler of scotch in front of them, except for Sara; she was drinking white wine. Aside from the four crew members, the bar was empty. It was like most every other bar one would find in a hotel. The lights were dim and the smell of old cigarette smoke hung thick in the air. Even at ten in the morning, with no one smoking, the smell permeated everything.

They talked in low whispers, and they all couldn't help but to keep their heads on a swivel. Despite the empty room, all were vigilant for prying ears.

Gary took another drink and rattled the ice around in his glass before looking at Stu for what seemed to be the hundredth time.

"Stu, it was a pallet of money in the cargo hold. You must have seen something."

Stu shook his head. "Why does everyone keep saying that? Gary, it wasn't all that long ago that you were a flight engineer. When did you ever look in the damn cargo hold?"

Gary looked at Arnie and then back at Stu. "But a whole pallet of money?"

"Look Gary," Arnie said, coming to Stu's defense, "from what that fed said, it's not uncommon to be carrying money to the mint to be destroyed. We just wouldn't know about it."

"You know what," Stu said. "I think it was one of the ramp guys that did it. They probably called one of their friends when they saw the plane was loaded with all of that money."

"Why not just take a stack of bills?" Sara asked. "It seems like a lot of trouble to take it all."

"Wouldn't work. Apparently, the money's wrapped up tight from what the fed was saying. Wrapped in plastic wrap or something. He said to the casual observer it wouldn't even look like money."

"Then why'd they keep asking us over and over again what we saw?" Sara said as she lifted a trembling glass to her lips.

"They said it was over ten million dollars in untraceable bills. They've got to do something."

Stu took another drink of scotch and growled, "Then find the asshole who hijacked our plane. With all the information we've given them, they must have some kind of idea."

Arnie shook his head. "Look, we need to just stick to what we know. They can't do anything to us if we haven't done anything wrong. And we didn't do anything. All of this will blow over soon and we'll be home before we know it."

Stu drained the last of the scotch in his glass. "I sure as hell hope so. Because if they're going to hang anyone out to dry, it's probably going to be me."

"Why?" Gary asked.

"Because I'm the one that was outside on the walk around. I was the one that found the cut hydraulic line. I was the one who had more interaction with the guy than anyone else. I'm the perfect scapegoat."

Gary grinned. "Sara was with him more than anyone. Maybe they'll go after her."

Sara lifted her trembling glass and took another drink. Both Arnie and Stu scowled.

"Not funny, Gary," Arnie said as he finished his own drink.

Chapter Eight
The Investigation

"What do you think?" Paul asked, leaning back in his chair.

"It's your investigation," Greg replied. "I just work here."

"Yeah, but you have a lot of experience investigating. I have next to none. What would you do if you were in my place?"

Greg shrugged. "You've had these guys for a week now. We've kept them separated *and* we've let them congregate. The entire time we've kept them under surveillance and turned up nothing suspicious. It seems to me if they had anything to do with it, we'd know by now. They've all agreed to keep this matter to themselves. And let's not lose sight of the fact that, if they *are* innocent, they're all victims. They were threatened, had parts of their plane blown up from under them *while in the air*, and managed somehow to land the plane without anyone dying. They've been cooperative and done everything we've asked of them. You want my opinion; these guys are heroes. I'd cut them loose."

Paul nodded. "I'll make the call. What else do you think?"

"Well, the flight engineer said he thought the hijacker was military. I think we should start there. Call every military base in the area and see if they have anyone matching our guy's description working there."

"I agree. Also, the pilots said that they thought the guy was enlisted. That's probably a good place to start. It sounds like someone who would have access to the kind of explosives our guy used to blow the door."

Paul nodded again. "What else?"

"You've been trained, what do you think?"

Paul scratched his chin. "Walk the crime scene?"

Greg grinned. "You're catching on fast. Keep it up and we'll steal you away from treasury."

"Steal?" Paul said with a wry grin. "That would be ironic, wouldn't it?"

"How long are you guys going to keep the plane here?" Tampa's Chief of Police asked.

"Why?" Paul replied as he walked across the ramp towards the dormant aircraft.

"Because I've got two guys guarding this piece of crap 24/7. Also, it's taking up ramp space and the airport people are bitching to me about it and I'm getting tired of their shit."

"We'll let TWA have the plane back as soon as the investigation is over," Greg said, answering for Paul.

"Chief," Paul said, "You were a detective, weren't you?"

"Yeah, I was. So, I don't see why a hijacking is taking so long to investigate. And I don't see why I need two men on this hulk at all times."

"Chief, I promise, we'll end this as soon as we can. Please, just have a little patience." Paul said, trying to keep his demeanor friendly.

The Chief shook his head and walked away, muttering under his breath about the 'damn feds.'

Greg followed Paul up into the plane for what seemed like the thousandth time.

Inside, the plane was stifling. Even with all the doors opened and the over wing exits removed, it felt like a sauna inside.

As the two men walked the plane again, they held flashlights even though there was more than adequate light this time of day.

As the two looked at each individual seat, Paul called Greg over.

"What have you got?"

"This brown stuff. I found it on the inside of the seat pocket here." As he spoke, Paul pointed to the edge of the seat pocket. On it was a line of discoloration, like something had scrapped against the top of the opening.

"So?"

"Look up."

Greg did so. Seat '17C' was denoted above him. "The hijacker's seat."

"If it weren't for the seat, I wouldn't have even bothered. Do you think it could be important?"

"Looks like dirt."

With a shrug Paul said, "Doesn't feel like dirt. It's a little tacky and sticky."

Greg now touched the substance and rubbed it together. "Could be char from the explosion. A lot of stuff got burned back here."

"Inside the seat pocket?"

"Maybe an ember flew up and started to smolder but never caught. The hole's just right over there. It's possible."

Sniffing it, Paul said, "Doesn't smell like char. It's also lighter. More brown than black."

Greg nodded. "It's probably nothing, but let's get a sample for the lab, anyway."

The two continued to examine the cabin and stopped at the hole in the floor.

"What do you make of this?"

Greg shrugged. "What of it?"

"It looks like he drilled a pilot hole and then sawed out an opening." Paul leaned down closer, studying some discoloration around the hole. "What's that over there?"

"We saw that earlier. It's dried blood. The edges are jagged. He might have cut himself as he lowered himself through the floor."

Paul nodded. "Yeah, that makes sense."

"We have a sample in the lab already."

Paul nodded. "Of course." After he spoke, he seemed to contemplate the opening in front of them. Then he finally said, "Here's the big question: How is it the stewardess didn't hear the sawing?"

Paul looked to the front of the plane and back at the hole. His shirt was already soaked through. "She was locked in the lav."

"Yeah, but it had to have made a hell of a racket."

"Loud plane? Maybe she didn't hear it over the jet engines? I know it was noisy on the plane ride down here from DC."

"Probably."

"We let everyone go yesterday. Do you think we should bring her back?" Paul gave Greg a wry look and added, "You were the one who convinced me to cut everyone loose."

Greg shook his head. "No, you're right. I think that horse is dead. I'm just grasping at straws here. Let's take a look in the cargo compartment again."

Rather than risk injury, the two agents left the plane and entered through a ramp leading into the cargo hold. Crawling inside, they found it just as hot as the cabin of the plane had been. There was less light and everything inside was catalogued with tags. The two carefully maneuvered on their hands and knees, preserving as much of the scene as possible.

There were still several bags up against the walls, untouched since the hijacking. On the floor there were three steel pipes. Each one had a tag on it.

Paul picked up a pipe and handed it to Greg, saying, "This must have been how he got the pallet out of the plane."

Greg nodded his agreement. "Probably got the pallet on these pipes and rolled it out of the opening once the door was blown off."

"There's not enough of them here to roll a pallet as large as the one that was back here."

Greg nodded. "Not with just these three. But I would assume that a bunch of others left the plane with the money."

Paul looked around. "That makes sense."

Greg replaced the pipe to the area that Paul had picked it up from. As he released it, it clanged loudly as it hit the floor, punctuating the silence of the cargo hold. "But how the hell did he get the pallet on the pipes in the first place? The money must have weighted a ton."

Paul was studying the floor, not looking at his partner as he answered, "Not a ton, but close to it. That's a good question: how *did* he get the pipes under the pallet?"

Both men continued to look over the floor of the cargo hold until the heat got the better of them, and they exited the plane.

"Greg, you're the expert here, but I think we're done. Unless you can think of anything we missed."

Shaking his head, Greg answered, "I can't think of anything. We've gone over every inch of this beast and recorded everything."

"You realize once we return the plane to the airline, Hughes will fix it and put it back in service as quickly as he can. And if he can't fix it, he's going to scrap it for parts. Either way, once we let it go, it's gone."

Greg's expression was grim. "I think we're done here."

"OK." Paul reached out his hand. The FBI man accepted it in a firm grasp. "Greg, it's been a pleasure. I've learned a lot from you."

Greg smiled, accepting the compliment. "And for a money guy, you're a lot more competent than I expected."

This brought a chuckle from Paul. "Any chance you might want to see this thing through?"

"How so?"

"You've been a big help. I could put in a request and see if I could get you TDY in Washington."

Greg scratched his chin. "The family's here."

Paul nodded. "I understand."

"And they'd probably expect me to wear a suit."

"They probably would."

"And of course, there's no chance we'd be able to close this case."

"Even less so without your help."

Greg looked over to the plane and then back at Paul again. "How soon before you'd need an answer?"

Chapter Nine
A Warm Trail

Paul and Greg's desks were facing each other. However, it seemed like they spent more time talking to other people on the phone than to one another.

The office was small and felt smaller still because of the clutter inside. Aside from the two metal desks, covered in papers with a telephone each, there were also a series of filing cabinets against the far wall. On the near wall, there were four chairs for visitors, but they were useless; piled on all four were numerous stacked files. The one redeeming quality of the room was the large window facing outside. The edges of the window were frosted over on the exterior, with beads of condensation on the inside. Outside there was a gently falling snow. The wall separating the room from the hall outside was frosted glass. On the door (also frosted glass), the name "Paul Owens" was stenciled in bold, black letters.

Greg had been in Washington for three weeks, returning home on the weekends to spend as much time as possible with his family whenever he could. On the weekday evenings, more often than not, he was a guest at the Owens household, having dinner with Paul and Leslie.

Despite the cold temperatures outside, the interior of the treasury building was stifling. Both Paul and Greg had their coats removed, ties loosened and sleeves rolled up.

"Yes, I understand. Thank you for getting back with us. If you hear of anyone with missing ordinance, please let us know. Yes, sir. Thank you again." Greg hung up the phone with a dejected look. Glancing over at Paul, he saw that he was still on a call of his own. Greg waited an additional three minutes before Paul hung up his receiver.

"Sorry, boss," Greg said now that he had Paul's attention. "Just got off the line with MacDill. They don't have anyone matching our John Doe's description. They also have all of their ordinance accounted for."

Paul exhaled. "MacDill was a long-shot, anyway."

"You were on the phone for a while. Anything on your end?"

Paul shook his head sadly. "Not much there. Just a report from the lab. More results are being sent up."

"Really? That took a while."

Paul grinned. "The results are coming from your end of the house."

Chuckling, Greg said, "I'm TDY Treasury. Can't hold FBI against me now."

"Maybe we should send you back there and you could get Hoover to work faster."

Holding up his hands in mock defense, Greg said, "I never want Director Hoover to have even a hint of my existence. That guy gives me nightmares. Why do you think I jumped at the opportunity to work with you? Even if it meant I was spending my weekdays away from my family."

The last comment broke the levity and Paul said, with a more solemn tone, "Look Greg, I really appreciate your coming over to give me a hand. Investigation isn't something we really do a lot of here. But Secretary Fowler really wants to keep this one in-house."

"Paul, seriously, don't worry about it. All kidding aside, I'm glad to have the opportunity to work here for a little while. Besides, once we crack this case, I'm sure it will be a big feather in my cap."

"*If* we crack this case."

"Relax. These things take time. A break will come."

The break came three hours later with a knock on the door.

Paul got up, while Greg was on another call. However, the call was unimportant and Greg focused more attention on the knock than he did on the person on the other end of the line.

Paul moved slowly, but deliberately, across the room. When he opened the frosted glass door, on the other side was a man whom appeared to be a courier of some kind. This impression was driven home as Paul signed a sheet of paper before taking possession of a package. He then closed the door and returned to his desk.

"I'm sorry, I missed that last part. Could you repeat it, please?" Greg said into the receiver and then ignored the caller again.

Paul removed a few contents from the folder and started reading the report. The minutes passed by slowly and Paul's expression didn't change much. Thinking this was yet another fruitless delivery, Greg's attention drifted back to the caller. It was a minute later that the former FBI man noticed his partner's eyes widen.

"Jeff, I'm sorry, would you mind if I called you back in a few minutes? I think there's something here that needs my attention. Thanks."

Greg hung up the phone and looked expectantly at Paul. After several long seconds, Greg broke the silence. "Well?"

Paul looked up, as if noticing Greg for the first time. "What? Oh. Sorry. It's probably nothing."

"Probably. But since there's no such thing as nothing, what have you got?"

"Well, this is the report from the FBI. There were no hits on fingerprints or anything, but the report also had the analysis of that dirt we found in the seatback of 17C."

"You mean the sticky dirt that we decided wasn't dirt?"

"Yeah, that one. The lab says it's some kind of cosmetic."

The statement hung in the air for a few seconds before Greg said, "So?"

"Well, scanning the initial report, it would seem it's not the makeup you might find in any woman's handbag."

Greg leaned in closer. "Continue."

"The report says it's the kind of makeup one would apply to their skin to make them look tan."

Greg's eyes grew wide. "This changes everything!"

Paul shook his head. "Not so fast. It doesn't really change anything."

"Are you kidding? If that lab report is telling us what I think it is, we've been looking in the wrong direction. We've been looking for a Cuban. This means that our hijacker might be white!"

"Greg. I'm not sure how much of a breakthrough this really is. We still have a composite sketch from our eyewitnesses on the plane, and we've distributed it to all the military bases in Missouri, Colorado and Florida. Nothing's comes back as a match."

"But those sketches were of a Cuban. If our guy's a Caucasian we've been looking in the wrong place."

Paul shook his head again. "It might change his skin tone, but not his basic appearance. We've already sent them a sketch of what he looks like."

"We've also been looking for an enlisted man. Our guy could be an officer. The pilots all thought he was enlisted. Probably for the same reason we did: most officers are white. If our guy's a white officer, rather than a Hispanic enlisted man..."

Paul obviously did not share his partner's enthusiasm. "Greg, we've distributed sketches. They haven't turned up anything. I'd think if the sketch matched an officer, rather than an enlisted man, we would've heard."

"Trust me, eyewitnesses are notoriously unreliable. We did an exercise at Quantico where we were sitting through some bullshit lecture and some nut busted into the room. Made a hell of a disturbance. Two uniforms came in and chased after him. After a few crazy moments, they all disappeared out of the back door. The entire thing couldn't have lasted thirty seconds.

"The entire room was buzzing when the uniforms came back in and told us they hadn't caught the mustached man and need our help with a description. They then spent a while interviewing us individually, putting together a composite sketch. When all was said and done, the sketch wasn't too bad. God knows, it's how I remembered him: fair skin, dark hair, mustache, wild, deep-set eyes. There were some variations, but we all mostly agreed.

"Well, they then brought in the man who had barged into the room. We all recognized him. Except he had shaved off his mustache. The one thing we all agreed on about him was now gone."

"So?" Paul asked.

"So, he hadn't changed a thing. He never had a mustache. But that was the first thing we were told when the uniforms came in looking for him. And we were a class of supposedly trained observers. Ideas can be put into anyone's head. That's why eyewitnesses don't deserve near the credit they get."

"So, you saying…"

"I'm saying that by telling everyone who might know our suspect was Cuban, we may have taken the actual perpetrator out of the mix."

"So, what do we do now?"

"You're not going to like it."

Paul closed his eyes and pinched the bridge of his nose. "Why?"

"The best results will mean more travel."

Paul let out a rueful laugh. "We've blown through so much money so far, what's a few more hundred? What's your plan?"

"Let's get another sketch together, just like last time, but this time with a white guy. We'll talk to the sketch artist, soften his features and make him white. We'll then go down to the military bases and see if it rings any bells."

"You think by changing the skin tone it will change the results?"

"It will be more than just the tone. The color of the eyes, hair… all of those features were based on what we expected to see." Greg then pulled open a desk drawer and removed a file. He flipped through it for several seconds, waving a piece of paper in the air. "Here it is!"

"What?"

"A witness report: 'He had blue eyes.' That's what one passenger said. We dismissed it because everyone else described him as having brown eyes and black hair."

Paul got up and walked around to Greg's desk. He looked through a few files before saying, "Where are the crew reports?" Greg reached in and produced another folder. Paul flipped through it for a minute before pulling out a sheet of paper in triumph. "And here, the stewardess says he had brown eyes." He flipped through a few more pages and removed another piece of paper. And so does the flight engineer. And these guys spent more time with the suspect than anyone else."

Greg shrugged. "There were also a dozen other passengers who said his eyes were brown. But they were all looking at the man in whole; seeing what they expected to see. Their brains filled in the gaps when they didn't see something or saw something that didn't quite fit. I'm telling you, we need to redo the sketch and make our perp more Caucasian."

Resigned, Paul said, "And you think that will lead to our guy."

Greg seemed to consider this for a moment and his enthusiasm ebbed, if only slightly. "Yes… and no. Before, we only sent the sketches to the commanding officers. Everything was by courier and nothing was in person. It made sense at the time."

"And there were no hits."

"Right. But this time you and I will take the sketch with us. We'll do one-on-one interviews with personal, showing them the sketches. We might get lucky with fresh eyes and a better description."

"Sounds reasonable. Do we start at Scott Air Force Base?"

Greg was smiling. "Why do you suggest there?"

"The flight originated out of St. Louis. If he was military, he's probably local."

"Greg's smile broadened. "You're becoming more Bureau material every day."

"Do you want to start with some officers?" the general asked.

The room was larger, and more comfortable than either Federal agent had expected. The temperature was very comfortable, and both men had been given fresh cups of coffee upon being brought into the general's office.

The office was much like the lieutenant general they were interviewing: immaculate and pristine. The back walls of the office were covered with framed pictures of various aircraft, most of them jets. There were several models of aircraft on the desk as well. Behind the general, almost as an afterthought, were two framed pictures of him with what one would assume were his wife and kids. While strategically placed, they were by far the smallest pictures in the room.

The desk that the general was sitting behind was of a dark brown wood. Across from him were a pair of very comfortable-looking chairs, in which the two federal agents were currently sitting.

Flanked on either side of the general were two flags: one the American flag and the other the Air Force flag.

The general's uniform was one of perfection. Starched so crisp that it looked like the creases in the uniform would cut anyone who dared to get too close to the man.

On his shoulder the three stars gleamed, perfectly catching the light from the enormous window overlooking the snow-covered Scott Air Force Base flight line.

"No general," Paul answered. "If it's all right with you, we'd rather talk to some enlisted men."

The general shrugged. "Makes no difference to me. The major outside will set you up. Any idea where you want to start?"

"Ordinance." Greg answered.

"Major Walsh!" The general yelled through the closed door.

"Yes, sir?" the major answered, opening the door on queue.

"If you don't mind, these federal boys would like to talk to some of our enlisted men over in ordinance. Would you show them the way?" Although framed as a question, there wasn't a doubt in anyone's mind that it was anything but.

"Right away, sir. If you would follow me."

As Greg and Paul stood, the general added, "Gentlemen, we're always happy to assist you fed boys whenever we can. If you need anything else, Major Walsh will get it for you. If not, you come and see me."

"Thank you, General."

The trio left the office and Major Walsh asked, "Do you have any idea who you'd like to start with?"

Paul looked over at Greg, who then answered. "Preferably an E3, but no one higher than an E5."

"That shouldn't be a problem."

"Collins!"

Roger Collins was lying on his bunk, daydreaming when Major Walsh called his name. The airman had been at Scott AFB for a little over a year and was generally well liked. He kept his head down and tried his best to stay out of trouble. Mostly, he had been successful. His shift had just ended, and this was technically his own time. So, it came as a surprise when the major called his name.

Despite his clean record, a little concern worked its way into the airman's mind when his name was called. It was rare that an officer came looking for him.

"Yes, sir!" Airman Collins answered, jumping to his feet.

"If you would follow me, airman, we have two gentlemen from the FBI who would like to talk to you."

Collin's blood ran cold. "FBI, sir?"

"Did I stutter, Collins?"

"I'm sorry, sir."

The two men walked in silence when Collins was shown into a small interview room. This room was everything the general's office was not: It was small, hot and sparse. The only thing on the far wall was a giant pane of one-way glass.

Paul and Greg were sitting together and starting to lose hope with the first base they were visiting. They had already interviewed three men and while the second was promising– "He's looks familiar, but...

no. Sorry. Can't place him."– there were no definitive leads yet. After their interview with Airman Collins, there would be just one more man to talk with. If neither of these men turned up anything, it would be on to the next base on the list.

Collins was shown to a metal chair at a metal desk. Across from him were two men dressed in dark blue suits.

Once seated, the major gave the feds inside a silent nod and quietly closed the door behind him.

"Airman," The taller of the two men opened a folder and then continued, "Collins?"

"Yes, sir," Collins nodded.

"How old are you, Collins?" the other man asked.

"Nineteen, sir."

"It's great to see you serving your country, son. I'm Special Agent Paul Owens and this is Agent Greg Stephens of the FBI." The first man said.

Collins nodded uncomfortably.

"Airman Collins, first I want to stress, you are in no trouble," Agent Stephens said. Collins looked to the other man, Special Agent Owens. His face was relaxed. Agent Stephens then continued, "We've asked you down here because we need your help."

The last question took the nineteen-year-old by surprise. "My help, sir?"

"Yes." Special Agent Owens looked in his folder again. "Roger. May I call you Roger?"

"Uh, I guess so, sir."

"Look, Roger, we've been told you've been here for a while and you might help us identify someone. Someone who might help us with a case we're working on."

"What case is that sir?"

Special agent Owens chuckled in a friendly manner. "Well, we can't really go into that right now. But if you could look at a sketch and tell us if you recognize the man in the picture, it will really help us out a lot."

"OK," Collins nodded a little more comfortably. "I'll do my best."

Special Agent Owens reached into his folder and removed a pencil sketch of a man and slid it in front of the boy. Collins looked at it and gave it a puzzled look. "Captain Moore, sir?"

Both federal men looked at each other and then back at the boy. "Captain Moore?" Agent Stephens said.

"Well, it looks like him. Captain Doug Moore. The Logistics Officer."

"Logistics Officer?" Agent Stephens continued.

"Yes, sir. He's responsible for everything in ordinance."

The two men looked at each other again.

"Does that help, sir?"

Special Agent Owens smiled. "Yes, son. It helps a lot."

"General, have any of your explosives gone missing in the last couple of months? Specifically, detonation-cord?" Paul Owens asked.

"No, sir. They have not."

"Forgive me, sir, but just, 'no, they have not?' Don't you need to look through records or something?" Greg asked.

"No, I do not," the general replied with an edge to his voice. "If any ordinance goes missing, it would be reported to me. If it were reported to me, I would remember it. So again, I say, no, we have not."

"General," Paul asked, "Please forgive us. We're not insinuating anything. We're just trying to gather information."

The general seemed to relax a bit… but just a bit. "I understand."

"But general, if something did go missing…"

"Like det-cord," the general interrupted.

"Yes, like det-cord. Who would report it to you?"

"That would be the Logistics Officer. Captain Moore."

Paul glanced behind him. The ten men in tow—and Greg—might have been ninjas for as much noise as they made following the Treasury agent. Greg looked relaxed enough. For all Paul knew, he might have done this numerous times before. But the experience was a new one for Paul. Leading an assault force into a potentially hostile environment was not something that a treasury officer did often.

A man in black combat gear crept up next to Paul, looked at him and nodded. Paul instinctively looked back at Greg and back to the man in combat gear next to him and returned the nod.

Another man in combat gear crept up next to the first man. All were holding automatic assault rifles except this man. His weapon was slung across his back, freeing his hands which were holding a large metallic battering ram that would crash in the door to the apartment.

Paul looked behind him again as the men he was 'leading' slowly crept around him and Greg, positioning themselves. The leader of the assault team held up one finger. The man holding the battering ram nodded. Two fingers. The rest of the men lifted their rifles a little higher. Paul felt somewhat naked as he and Greg gripped their service pistols tighter. Three fingers.

Wood sprayed across the room as the assault team stormed into the small apartment amidst shouts of, "FBI! FBI!"

There was a single man sitting on the couch, watching a football game on a small black and white television set.

He threw up his hands as the assault force fanned out into the other rooms. Shouts of "Clear!" and "Clear!" followed as they all coalesced back into the small living room.

Paul and Greg were the last to enter, and the leader of the team confirmed that the man on the couch was the only one present in the apartment.

Holstering their weapons, Paul, followed closely by Greg, approached the man on the couch. He was now face-down, his hands secured behind him. However, his face was clear. A face both men had become far too familiar with. This one might have been of a lighter skin tone and blonde hair, but there was little doubt this was their man.

"Captain Douglas Moore, you are under arrest for the hijacking of TWA flight 867 and the theft of approximately eleven million dollars in federal funds."

Chapter Ten
The Interrogation

When Paul and Greg had had their conversation with Airman Collins, there had been no one on the other side of the one-way mirror. Today it was standing room only. Besides members of the FBI and Treasury Department who had flown in, there were also many members of the Air Force and Defense Department present.

The small interrogation room was crowded as well. Besides Greg, Paul and Captain Moore, there was also Major Marshall Ryan, the Judge Advocate representing Douglas Moore.

"I would like the record to show that Captain Moore has submitted to this interview willingly and intends to cooperate fully," Major Ryan said, more for the benefit of those on the other side of the glass as opposed to the men across the table from him.

Paul nodded. "So noted. And I would like to state that I would hope that Captain Moore will come clean since we have him dead to rights. A confession would save the taxpayers a considerable amount of money. I think we can all agree your client has cost them enough already."

Major Ryan started shaking his head. "I'm sorry to disappoint you Agent Owens, but Captain Moore has done nothing wrong. We can produce logs and eyewitness accounts that show him at his duty station on the night in question."

Paul grinned. "And we also can produce eyewitnesses that put him on that plane. He also had access to a unique explosive that the FBI's lab is now working on to match to stores that went missing from Scott Air Force Base."

"That's bullshit!" Moore said, standing up. "Check the records. Nothing was unaccounted for during my entire time at Scott."

Major Ryan put his hand on his client's arm, calming him. After Moore sat back down, the JAG lawyer whispered something into his client's ear. Moore then whispered back to Ryan's ear while the federal agents sat quietly.

"You guys done?" Paul asked.

"I apologize for my client. However, he's somewhat emotional because of the charges leveled against him. His entire life has been dedicated to his country. Since he attended West Point and then joined the Air Force, Captain Moore's entire life has been one of service."

Paul nodded. "Apparently. Service, not forgery."

Moore started to rise, but Ryan put his hand on the man, calming him once again. "I'm sorry Agent, but I really have no idea what you're talking about. My client affirms that the records will exonerate him."

"You see, that's the problem. Once Doug here... May I call you Doug?"

"Captain Moore, if you please," Ryan answered.

"As you wish," Paul continued. "After Captain Moore was identified as the man accused of hijacking TWA 798, General Bolander, his commanding officer, was extremely cooperative in providing us access to his records. Now, I will confess that at first glance it appears the records are spotless—God knows that from the initial inspection from an agent like me, it looked like there was nothing amiss. But to a team of forensic accountants... well, let's just say there are some inconsistencies." Paul smiled. "Now, I'm not going to claim to be able to identify these inconsistencies myself, but if this thing goes to trial, I have been assured that our men will be able to explain everything to a jury and the facts are fairly self-evident."

The accused conferred quietly with his lawyer as the agents sat patiently. They knew they had him. Finally, Ryan spoke again for his client.

"If your accusations are true, Captain Moore is just as outraged as you, and would like nothing better than to help you find the guilty party."

"Good. So, he will be giving us that confession then?"

"Agent Owens, I object to your condescending tone. Aside from some allegedly doctored records—that by your own admission were done so well that they escaped your capable notice—you have nothing."

"But an eyewitness report." Greg leaned over and whispered into Paul's ear. "I apologize. My colleague just corrected me ... *several* eyewitness reports."

"You know as well as I that eyewitness reports are unreliable. I've even heard rumors that the man in question had dark skin. That he was a Cuban with black hair. As you can plainly see, the captain here has fair skin and is blonde."

Paul sat back and let the statement hang in the air for several seconds. It wasn't until Ryan looked as if his comment had touched home that Paul leaned over to Greg and whispered in his ear. Greg nodded and removed an 8x10 black-and-white photo from a folder. On the picture was a bottle with several test streaks besides it of various shades.

Major Ryan leaned forward, looking at the pictures as they were laid out on the table. He said, "Is this supposed to mean something?"

Ignoring the statement, Paul asked Captain Moore, "Does this look like your brand of makeup, captain?"

Moore looked at Ryan and whispered again. Ryan then said, "Exactly what are you playing at Agent Owens? That my client is a hijacker, or that he's a fag?"

Paul continued, "It's what's called instant tan. The newest thing in tanning. It gives you all kinds of options. You can go light, looking like you had a good day at the beach, or darker. This might allow one to change their complexion from pale to almost Hispanic. And, for the record: I couldn't care less about his sexual preferences. However, this *is* his shade."

Doug smiled and said, "Agent Owens. From what I understand, a fake tan can last well over a week. Surely I would have had some kind of residue left over if I had tried to pull off such a deception."

Paul leaned forward. His expression soured. "Captain Moore, I have tried not to insult your intelligence. I would appreciate it if you would show me, and my colleague, the same courtesy. Removing a fake tan was one of the first things we looked into. It would seem that removing this kind of makeup is far simpler than most of the country realizes."

"There's no way you can prove that I ever even touched any of that stuff." As Moore spoke, he leaned back in his chair. "You can tear my place down from top to bottom and I can guarantee you won't find anything like that."

"Of course we wouldn't. Captain, please understand, as I just said, we are not accusing you of being stupid. Quite the contrary. I think we've shown you're rather clever. The accounting alone was masterfully done. And to leave a tanning makeup bottle behind… Well, that would be beneath you."

Both lawyer and client looked at the accuser, waiting for him to continue. After a lengthy pause, he did.

"Doug… excuse me, Captain Moore, while you cleaned your apartment very well, it's hard to remove every smudge. Our forensic team matched a sample from your bathroom that is the exact color and shade as the tanning makeup found in the plane. It would seem that while you were rather meticulous in your cleaning up afterwards, you missed a little under the sink where the cabinet door closes.

"Now, before you go telling me that this doesn't prove anything, I'm willing to grant you that using an artificial tanner in and of itself, doesn't. But right now, that sample we found under the captain's sink is being shipped off to Quantico. There they will match it against the chemical compounds of the sample taken from the plane."

"There's a problem with your theory, Agent Owens," Major Ryan said. "Fake tan does not simply rub off. If… and I stress *if*… my client had tried to disguise himself in this way, you would not have residue."

Greg picked up the conversation, smiling. "You know, that's exactly what I thought. When Paul and I first received the lab report, telling us it was makeup, I thought it was some kind of women's foundation. Not that I know that much about makeup. All I know is my wife uses it, and it gets all over the phone. So, when I didn't remember any reports of residual makeup on the plane's phone, I thought we had hit another dead end. Then, I read further and saw that it was tanning makeup."

"The kind that doesn't rub off, as you have already admitted," Ryan said.

"Exactly." Greg picked up the photos, looked at them for a moment and then continued, "But if you look here, you can see that if applied too quickly, it can clump. That *can* be smeared off. It would seem that your client tanned himself in quite a hurry. He got the shade right, but it would appear it was heavier in some areas, more than others. Our guess is, when he took his seat in the plane, some of the undried tanning makeup was somewhere around his hand, or lower arm, and it rubbed off in the seat pocket at some point."

Paul then pulled out some more papers and continued, "Also, we have a blood sample we found on the plane. It would seem that when the hole was cut in the floor and Captain Moore descended into the cargo hold, he cut himself. The sample was O-negative. By the way, Captain, what is *your* blood type?" Silence. "No need to answer, we all know the answer to that one."

Major Ryan stood and Captain Moore followed suit.

"Gentlemen, I was under the impression that we were here to find the truth, not just find a convenient scapegoat for your inability to find the actual perpetrator of this crime. When you're ready to have a serious discussion, we'll be happy to provide whatever assistance we can. But until then…"

Ryan looked at the door and gave a nod. The guard at the door opened it and the two were escorted out.

A few minutes after the prisoner and his lawyer left the room, Paul and Greg exited. As they entered the hallway beyond, they were joined by all of the observers from the other side of the glass.

"General, do you have a place we could talk?" Paul asked.

"Of course, If you all would please follow me."

General Bolander led the assembled group to a large conference room and all the men took seats around the large table.

"If there are no objections, I would like to start with you general," Paul said. "What are your thoughts?"

"There's little doubt in my mind that he did it."

"I think we're all in agreement on that count," Greg agreed as everyone in the room nodded. "And given my experience with the FBI, I think a conviction should be relatively easy."

"However,…?" General Bolander said.

"However," a senior official from the Treasury Department replied, "There's the question of the eleven million dollars that's still missing. Getting a conviction isn't enough. A conviction without the money is unacceptable. Wouldn't you agree Agent Owens?"

Paul nodded. "In most cases—sure, all we really want is the guilty party to be brought to justice. But when you're talking about this kind of money... yes, it's a bigger priority to recover the stolen funds."

"And how would you suggest we accomplish that, Mr. Owens?" the general asked.

It was Greg that answered.

"Although I've never seen a theft of this size before, we have some experience extracting information."

General Bolander grunted, "Black ops shit?"

Greg chuckled, "Don't ask questions you don't want the answers too."

"I spent some time in Asia during World War Two. I won't stand for any of that bamboo under the fingernails crap."

"Calm yourself, General," a senior FBI official said from the far side of the room. "We find that psychological... motivation... is far more effective than physical torture."

"Uh, huh." General Bolander nodded. "I'm sure."

"I assure you, sir, when we release your man, he will be none the worse for wear. Admittedly, he may be hungry and tired, but he'll recover."

"Let me make one thing clear, *sir*. The only reason I'm willing to even entertain this is, I agree with you: you have him dead to rights and I'm ashamed that a man under my command would ever show this level of disrespect to our country or the uniform. I also went to West Point, and I firmly believe that Duty, Honor, Country should be something you carry throughout your life." He then shook his head and looked back to Greg. "But I fully expect you to be true to your word. You can screw with his head, but no more."

Greg smiled. "Understood, General. Let's meet again with Captain Moore in, let's say—four days?"

The music had been relentless and the food non-existent. Literally bread and water... and precious little of that.

There had also been a guard posted by Captain Moore's cell who talked incessantly. While the guard wore the uniform of an E-3 Airman, he was, in reality, an FBI agent trained in Psychological Operations. He reported back to Greg that he was relatively sure that they would get full cooperation from the Captain after only three days. However, Greg and Paul agreed to give it an extra day to make sure Captain Moore's cooperation was assured.

The four men—Paul, Greg, Doug Moore and Marshall Ryan—all met in the same interrogation room. However, this time there was not the assembled audience behind the one-way mirror. Now the only one behind the mirror was General Bolander.

Doug Moore looked far different from his previous interrogation. There were dark bags under his eyes and his skin was grey and drawn. It was the Judge Advocate who spoke first.

"Don't think I'm not aware of what's going on here."

"And what's that, counselor?" Paul asked innocently.

"All you need to do is look at my client to know he's been subjected to torture."

Paul affected an innocent look. "Captain, you haven't been ill-treated, have you?"

Moore looked over at Greg and the FBI man shot him a warning glance. "Not at all, sir. I am kind of tired, though."

"All you need to do is look at my client to know that…"

"To know that he's been losing sleep—because of his guilt, no doubt—for the crimes he committed," Greg cut him off.

Greg pulled out the photos of the tanning makeup again and resumed the same line of questioning he had four days prior.

The session lasted several hours, the exhaustion plain on Moore's face, but he still refused to give up any information.

As the interrogation was starting into its third hour, Major Ryan stood up. "I will not allow you to subject my client to any more of this. We're done here. You'll get no more cooperation from us, and I'm planning on opening a formal inquiry."

"On what?" Greg asked with a calm he did not feel.

"The treatment of my client. This kind of abuse is not how the United States operates. And it is certainly not how we do things in the Air Force."

As the JAG lawyer finished, the door to the interrogation room opened. General Bolander emerged.

"It certainly is not major. I'm sorry gentlemen, I have given you latitude here, but you're finished."

"Thank you, General" Ryan said, rising. "Then, if we're done…"

"No, we are not done. This man is under *my* command. I would like a few words with him… *alone*… if you don't mind."

Paul and Greg looked at one another and nodded. "Yes, sir," they both said, rising from their chairs.

Ryan nodded and started to sit down. But before he could, General Bolander said, "I said alone, major."

Ryan started to protest, but with a look, the general shut him down. Nodding, Ryan gathered his papers and followed the two federal agents.

"And gentlemen," Bolander added as they were leaving, "I *mean* alone. I don't want any of you behind that glass. Understood?"

They all nodded and shut the door behind them and left the room.

Doug leaned back in his chair and seemed to relax as the door shut behind the trio. He then exhaled and said, "Thank you, General."

Bolander stared at Doug and took the seat across from him, not saying a word. He then picked up a folder that was left on the table.

"General, I'm glad that you believe me. I swear I had nothing to do with this robbery."

Bolander continued to flip through the pages, remaining mute.

As the silence dragged on, Doug continued to fill the void.

"If there is anything I can do to help, I'll be happy to provide any assistance I can." The general lowered the folder and stared at his subordinate. "I'm sorry, sir. I'm just so tired. They haven't let me sleep in days."

Bolander set the folder down and adjusted it so that the corners were perfectly lined up with the table. Doug started to say something again, but the general held up his hand, silencing him. He then leaned back in his chair and stared at Doug once more.

"Don't think this is over."

"But you said it was over," Doug said, fear washing over his face.

"No, I said that they were finished. If I said it was over, that would be a lie. And I don't lie."

"I know, sir. I've always…"

Bolander slammed his fist on the table, silencing the man across from him. "What the hell is your problem, Captain? The entire time I have sat here, when did I *ever* give you permission to speak?"

"I just thought…"

"The question was rhetorical, *captain*. Goddamit! You were a captain in the *United States Air Force*. You went to *West Point* for God's sake. I went there! Now I feel like I need a shower just being in the same room as you."

Doug started to say something again, but was shut down with a glance. "I don't know what the hell went wrong with you. Maybe it was your class. When I attended… Duty. Honor. Country. It all meant something. You have defiled every single tenant we believe in with one stupid act. You took an oath, but that obviously doesn't mean shit to you, does it? You stole from me! You stole the explosive I was charged to protect! Good God! *I'm* culpable!"

"Sir, in no way are you…"

"Keep your damn mouth shut until I tell you you can open it! Understood?"

Doug shrank back into his seat and nodded.

Bolander shook his head. "And then you stole from every single American when you took all that money. How much was it again? Thirty pieces of silver? Because that's what you did: you betrayed everything you claimed to have believed in. How far would you have gone? Would you have killed those people to get that money? Because you sure as hell tore out the best part of yourself and murdered it dead.

"Everyone out there," Bolander motioned to the door, "knows you're guilty as hell. Even… *especially*… your lawyer." The general shook his head. "And now you're putting him in a shitty position, making him defend a piece of filth like you, when you know you're guilty."

Bolander got up and crossed the room. He looked at his reflection in the one-way glass. He knew that no one was behind it. With his back to Doug, he said, "Here is what you can do: you confess and help those feds out in any way you can. You're going to prison either way, and you know it. The evidence is overwhelming and I promise you I will be there to testify against you at your court martial." He turned and faced Doug again. "If you do all of that, maybe… just maybe… your lawyer can get you some kind of deal. And perhaps you might salvage some shred of what was once your soul."

Without waiting for a reply, Bolander crossed the room and opened up the door. "Gentlemen, he's all yours."

"Gentlemen, is there any room for a deal?"

Doug Moore and his attorney had talked alone for over half an hour before Greg and Paul were brought back into the room. They knew that Moore was done. Now it was just finding the right measure of justice while recovering what he had taken.

Paul and Greg put their heads together and quietly conferred. But it was mostly for show. Outside in the hall, while Moore and Ryan were having their talk, the two feds had decided on their strategy. They had developed the chessboard, and General Bolander provided them the move they needed to enter the endgame. Both were confident that there was nothing that could surprise them at this point.

"There might be. And that's only because we would like to recover the eleven million dollars your client stole. As to any civil suit Howard Hughes—or anyone on the flight, may file—well, that's not up to us."

Moore started shaking his head. "I can't get you the money. It's gone."

Forcing himself to project a calmness he did not feel, Paul looked at Moore and spoke directly to him. "Gone? Would you mind explaining how eleven million dollars can be gone?" Paul then glanced over at Greg and then back at the folder before him. Closing the file, he said, "Look Captain, if you can't give us the money, then there isn't anything that we can do for you. Know at this point we don't even care about your confession. We have no problem with just letting this go to trial. We have you dead to rights. So, it's a few more weeks." He then chuckled, "Hell, with our evidence I doubt the trial will even last that long. It will probably be more like a matter of days. Sir, you will spend the rest of your life in Leavenworth."

But then Doug Moore, with only a few words, muddied the pristine chessboard Paul had so elegantly established.

"I can deliver you my boss. He's the only one who can get you your money back."

Paul and Greg looked at one another, now dumbfounded.

"What do you mean, 'your boss?'" Greg asked.

"I mean the guy that set this whole thing up. The inside man."

Now it was Ryan's turn to look smug. "I think that's enough, Doug." He then turned to the federal agents, "He can get you the man you really want, but we want a deal. If not, you may get your conviction, but that's all you'll get. Now, I ask you: will your bosses be satisfied with that? Oh, and by the way, this offer is good for," he glanced at his watch, "let's say, two more minutes."

Paul and Greg put their head together once more. However, now they were legitimately conferring. Paul wasn't sure how far his authority extended here, but this might be his one and only shot at closing this case.

"If the information you provide is reliable, we should be able to work something out," Paul finally said.

"Three years, dishonorable discharge and loss of retirement," Ryan replied.

Paul laughed. "Whether or not he was alone, he hijacked a plane. He set off explosives in the plane. He stole *eleven million dollars* of government money. The absolute best I can do is twenty years and loss of pension with a dishonorable discharge."

"Eight years."

Paul and Greg conferred again for a quick minute, then Paul said, "Fifteen. I can't do any better than that."

Ryan looked at his client and then at the men across the table from him. He then lowered his voice. "Gentlemen, trust me, my guy's just a cog here. You want the guy who ran the entire operation. Please, give me twelve years. I promise you won't regret it."

Paul leaned over to Greg and whispered in his ear. "What do you think?"

"Nine times out of ten I'd say he was full of crap, but... I just don't know."

"It's going to be difficult justifying twelve years."

"Paul, look, I stand by you, whatever you decide. But it's your decision. It sucks, but it's on you. However, I'd tell you to consider this: I don't think he's bluffing. This might be the only bite you're going to get at this apple."

"How's that?"

"I know these lawyers. You'd be amazed what they can worm themselves out of. And then there's what we went through to get here in the first place. Psy-ops aren't necessarily illegal, but it would work against us at trial. And this guy here, he's JAG; he's a military lawyer."

"So?"

Greg shook his head. "I'm not saying the civilian lawyers are better—some of the best lawyers I know are JAG—but they're different. If this guy has access to the kind of money we think he does... Let's just say I wouldn't want to fight that battle. A team of civilian lawyers could bury us in years of paperwork alone. Twelve years... that's not bad."

Paul nodded, and the two feds leaned in over the table.

"All right councilor, you've got your twelve. Now, Moore, start talking."

Both lawyer and defendant exhaled as Doug Moore started his story.

"An old buddy of mine came up with the idea a while ago. He works for the airline, TWA.

"Anyway, he's over at my house one day, and we're enjoying a couple of beers, and he tells me how he was working a flight to Denver, and onboard they have a pallet of money. He told me that to look at it, you'd never have guessed what was on that pallet. But as the ramp guys were loading it up, he started talking to them and found out what it was. He'd been at the airline for only a brief time at that point, but already he was getting kind of board. So, he tells me, what if we were to steal the money? I laughed it off. We were enjoying a couple of beers so I just figured it was the Budweiser talking. But the next day he tells me how he's been thinking about the plan. How he's working out the details.

Paul leaned in. "He's a pilot for TWA?"

"Of course, he is. You must have met him. Stu Powell. He was the flight engineer when I ripped off the flight."

Chapter Eleven

Skyheist

Doug Moore was dozing off, watching the Dick Van Dyke Show when the phone rang.

Instantly Doug snapped awake, irritated at whoever was calling. He had already had a long day and had an early wake up in the morning. When he growled "Hello" into the receiver, there was no friendliness in his voice.

It was like a bucket of cold water had been thrown over his head when the voice on the other end of the receiver spoke. "We have a maintenance issue here. Flight 798. We could be a couple of hours late." Then there was a click, and the connection was broken.

At first, Doug stood there as he collected himself. The plan had been worked out well in advance. Time would be of the essence. However, Doug still gave himself a full minute before he sprang into action.

The first thing he did was place a long-distance call to Florida. Eric Mansfield picked up the line. The conversation was brief. "Skyheist is a go."

He then called a friend at Scott Air Force Base. He told him he had a hot date and wouldn't be in the next day and asked if he could cover for him. He knew that this friend would do this, as Doug had done the same for him several times in the past.

With the calls made, Doug walked from the living room to the bathroom where he spread out an old bedsheet and started to apply the tan. This seemed to take forever, but he knew he needed to get it right. People would see his face. He needed to make sure they wouldn't be able to recognize him.

Once the tan and wig were applied, he folded the old sheet, being careful not to get any of the tanning fluid on anything in the bathroom. His hands were sticky with the solution, and he opened the door under his sink to retrieve an old towel to wipe off what he could from his hands. It wouldn't be perfect, but it should be good enough. The towel, along with the sheet, would be discarded on his way to the airport, far from his house.

Next, he went to his closet. Off to the side, in the corner, was the wardrobe he would be using. This was just as important as skin tone in disguising who he was. He quickly changed and shoved the soiled sheet and towel into the old duffle bag that would be making the trip.

The last piece of the puzzle he was assembling were the tools. They would be heavy and difficult. A few of the heavier items he would use were already loaded in his car. They included an automotive jack and several small, half inch steel pipes.

In his closet, he removed the remaining items he would be needing. Using a dolly, he started working immediately on getting the parachutes out to the car. Whereas he could explain (if questioned) on why he had pipes in the back of his car ("I'm doing some plumbing work over the weekend") or a jack ("Duh"), two parachutes (one extra-large used for dropping military equipment) would be harder to justify.

Even harder to explain would be the detonation cord. Not only would it be unlikely he could come up with a reasonable explanation for why he had explosives used to take out sections of walls, he would have bigger problems in that possession of military grade explosives is illegal.

He also had a handgun and an assault rifle. Both were in the bag with the det-cord. The rest would be checked baggage.

When Doug finally arrived at the airport, the sun had already set and it was dark outside. It was November, and there were a few random snowflakes swirling on the ground in the bitter wind. He parked in the short-term lot. It was closer to the terminal and time was working against him. He quickly got a cart and loaded everything on it and made his way to the ticket counter.

Inside, the line was short. After a few minutes, he was standing in front of the agent, whom offered to help him. His blood ran cold. He felt like everyone could see through the fake tan he had applied. But confronted with the woman before him, he did his best to stay calm and natural.

"Yeah. I just got a job working for some guys in California on a movie project. They just called and said they need me to get some gear out to a location shoot in Colorado. I was told you've got a plane going there, and I need to get on, like, yesterday."

The woman took in the man's disheveled appearance and ratty clothing and forced a smile. She then tried to explain that this wouldn't be possible. "I'm sorry, sir, but the last flight to Denver has already left. But we have a flight tomorrow morning that I would be happy to put you on." She started working on ticketing for the next day's flight, and Doug felt on the verge of panic. The plan couldn't be falling apart already, could it?

"Look, I hear you. But I really need to get on *this* flight. If it helps, I could add a little extra to the price of the ticket."

This seemed to offend the woman, as she said, "I'm sorry, sir. It isn't the cost of the ticket that's the problem, but the flight's already left."

Doug didn't need to fake the look of desperation on his face. "I was told that the flight was late and that if I wanted to keep my job, me and all the equipment had better be on it. Are you sure there isn't anything you can do?"

Doug did his best to emote pleading while holding up a twenty-dollar bill.

His stomach dropped again as the woman frowned and picked up a phone, talking softly in it for a few excruciating seconds. He knew this was it. She was calling the police. They may never figure out the actual plan, but the weapons and explosives would put him in jail for sure.

He was in a state of near panic when the woman hung up the phone and smiled again.

"Sir, you can relax. You'll be fine. I talked to the gate and you're right. The plane's still on a maintenance delay. If you hurry, I can get you on the flight. Do you have bags to check?"

It was almost impossible for him to answer, so sure was he that it was over. He only motioned to the cart behind him.

"Very good, sir. I'll get someone over here to help me out. Now, I can't promise that your baggage will make this flight, but as I said, there's a flight in the morning and..."

"No," he almost pleaded. "The movie shoots early tomorrow morning."

She looked at him blankly, and started to speak, but he continued, "Please, I need the bags to make it. My boss will have my job if I don't. Please. I've been trying to get a job like this my whole life."

Again, his acting paid off. She picked up a radio and spoke quickly into it. She then turned back to Doug. "I have some help on the way. Your stuff should make it to the plane before you do. However, there will be an extra charge for the larger than normal load."

"No problem," He croaked out. He even forced a smile. "And the Production Assistant—he's my boss—told me to tell you it needs to be in the forward bin. I don't know why, but he wanted me to tell you that. Is that OK?"

Again, a genuine smile. "That won't be a problem."

He then gave her the false name of Juan Diaz and paid for the ticket in cash. He also tried to offer her additional money, but she refused.

A few minutes later two men arrived and took his checked baggage. He again insisted it be put in the forward bin. They reassured him it would be.

He made his way to the plane and felt every eye on him. Once more, he was sure everyone saw right through the façade.

As he walked down the hall, he looked around and noticed he was the only man of color there. He was also woefully underdressed. While everyone else wore suits and dresses, he had dressed down as several of his enlisted men would on their days off.

This had always been part of the plan. From the beginning, when Stu first approached him with the idea, he said that he should disguise himself as a Cuban.

"When everything goes down, their first thought will be you're a criminal. So why not look like one?"

"But Stu," he argued, "being Cuban doesn't make you a criminal. I have several Hispanics who work for me who do a better job than many of my white guys do."

"You know that" Stu agreed, "and I know that. But a good portion of the country sees America as us and them. Bay of Pigs may have been a few years ago, but it's still fresh in everyone's minds. Let's use the country's racism against itself. If they're a bunch of racists who expect to see a Cuban as a hijacker, then by God, we'll give them a Cuban hijacker. They'll all look right at you but never see you. Why? Because they can't get past the color of your skin."

As Doug approached the plane, he realized just how right his friend had been. As he looked around, he saw nothing but disapproving stares. When he boarded the plane, he got more of the same.

Once Doug found his seat, he felt eyes upon him. He was sweating profusely and unconsciously wiped his hand on the seat cushion. To calm himself, he reached into the seatback and pulled out the safety information card and started to look it over.

When the man by the window got up to talk to the stewardess, it didn't matter what he claimed as an excuse, Doug knew it was to rat him out. He knew that if he was going to go through with this; it was now or never. He put the card back into the seatback pocket and pulled his gun out. He then fulfilled everyone's worst expectations.

After the initial shot, there were moments when Doug wondered if he could ever reclaim control of the situation. The plane wasn't full, but there were enough people on board that if they rushed him, he wouldn't stand a chance.

It was only after the panic started, that Doug realized that these people might be scared, but they were also a bunch of untrained civilians. There was panic, but no fight. Fear, but no plan. His confidence returned quickly as the stewardess calmed the situation. He quickly returned to the role of antagonist.

He forced the stewardess to take him to the front of the plane. As he approached, he saw the back of the peephole flash momentarily. Someone was looking through it. He knew this had to be Stu. He took some small comfort in the fact that he wasn't alone. However, he also knew that he would need to deal directly with the captain. Stu might influence the situation, but he couldn't control it.

Doug fought to keep the fear out of his voice as he talked to the captain over the interphone. He could hear a slight tone change when he demanded full tanks of fuel. They hadn't expected him to know that. That 'slip' had always been part of the plan. His use of the word 'perimeter' had also been deliberate. Stu had insisted that his claim of possessing C4 explosives (which he did not) would be met with skepticism if made by a mere street thug. However, if they suspected he had military ties, then the claim would be plausible, and possibly even probable. Doug had argued it led them dangerously close to the truth. Stu countered his argument, saying that it would be the most effective subterfuge. "A good lie is buried deep in truth." Again, Stu was right… for a while, at any rate.

The lights in the cabin were low. The idea was to alleviate tension the passengers might be feeling. Over time, it seemed to produce the desired effect. However, Doug, who had already had a long day, also started to succumb to the lower light and the late hour. He looked over at Sara, who was surveying the cabin. He stared at her for what seemed a long while until she glanced in his direction. He then looked at the coffeepot in the galley and back at her. "Coffee?" He said quietly.

She looked at him and then at the passengers. Although you could sense the tension, all was quiet. She then frowned and went to the galley and poured a cup. As she gave it to him she said under her breath, "You want it with cream? A nice shade of tan?"

In response, he glared at her. "Not funny."

She started to respond when the chime from the cockpit sounded.

Sara glanced at the cabin, then at Doug. "Do you mind if I get that?"

Doug snapped to full wakefulness as the cockpit relayed that fueling was complete. Doug, back in command, barked out orders, letting the women off the plane.

Ironically, Doug was probably more scared than any of the hostages. He had threatened that he would start shooting people if any of the men attempted to leave, but there was no doubt in his mind that if tested, he would fold. Doug made the conscious decision to channel his anxiety into yelling and cursing. The front he put forward was successful, as only the women exited the plane while the men submitted to his commands.

Once the women were off and the aft airstair door was closed, everything settled back down again, and the waiting game resumed. And with it, so did the fatigue.

As the night pressed on, Doug was growing increasingly tired, but he resisted asking for more coffee. Although he wanted it desperately, with hostages he knew a trip to the lavatory was out of the question. If pushed, he would have to wet his pants. Despite the threat of prison and even death (if everything went wrong), this was what scared him most.

The moments continued to tick away at an excruciating pace as the coffee in his system migrated to his bladder. Slowly he was fighting off sleep less and less and now found himself fighting off the urge to urinate.

Finally, he barked at Sara for the handset to the cockpit. Once the captain was on the line, Doug started demanding his money. He knew that once the ransom was in hand, he could let the passengers off and then he could pee.

As he yelled at the captain, the anger and desperation in his voice were now very real.

It had been almost another hour, and Doug was about to concede that he would wet his pants, when the chime from the cockpit came. Sara handed him the handset and relief washed over him as he was told the money would now be delivered. Finally, he could get the passengers off of the plane.

As he hung up, he now focused on the next challenge he would face: The FBI would send in an assault team. They had discussed this in the planning phase. The plane would now be mostly empty and it would be hours into the siege. There was no way that the government wouldn't take advantage of this attempt to stop him. But Doug was taking this situation one step at a time. This would be an enormous step with potentially fatal consequences.

It was only a few minutes later that the aft stairs were once again dropped and a single man entered with a black duffel bag. Doug didn't even look inside it, so desperate was he to get to the bathroom. He started barking orders, once again directing the people off the plane.

He looked over at Sara and then back at the men exiting, their numbers diminishing by the second. He then explained to her, far louder than he needed to, that he was holding a Deadman's switch and that if anything happened to him, the plane would explode.

Sara flew to the interphone as the last of the hostages were leaving the plane. Doug started laughing as he strolled to the back of the plane. He hoped that the laugh didn't sound as fake as it was.

As the last of the passengers, trailed by the two remaining stewardesses, exited the plane, Doug activated the switch to raise the aft airstairs. As the ramp slowly lifted, Doug could see the assault team in the distance, frozen in place. His laugh was genuine, but now from relief rather than the faux amusement he had been projecting. Moments later, after the door was closed, he headed back to the front of the plane, and the waiting lone stewardess.

When he reached her, Doug asked, "How are you holding up?"

"Terrified."

Doug nodded.

Sara then said, "How about you?"

Doug got up and darted to the lavatory. "Gotta pee so bad!"

A minute later he exited feeling like a new man. Sara was waiting with a fresh cup of coffee.

Doug took it gratefully and started gulping it.

"You look exhausted," she said, pouring herself a cup.

"I know that none of us knew that tonight would be the night, but I wish Stu could have gotten me on a day where I had been able to get some decent sleep the night before."

Sara grinned. "You and me both." She then looked around. It was quiet. Quieter than it had been since all of this started. No quiet whimpering, heavy breathing, muttering of prayers, or even soft snoring from the hard-core passengers who were actually able to sleep.

Doug looked at Sara and could see the fear in her eyes. "Sara, we're almost there. Once Stu gets the captain to take off, we're home free."

"Do you think he'll be able to do that?" she asked, tears forming in her eyes.

Doug forced a smile. "With a little help from me, I'm sure we can pull it off.

A couple of threats later, both Doug and Sara heard a distinct change of the airflow into the cabin. Moments later, a low moan rose from outside. They were starting the engines. Doug's threat of setting off the fictitious C4 had worked.

At once, Doug and Sara went to work taking Doug's bags down from the overhead. He then threw an extension cord down the aisle of the plane. Sara grabbed the end of the cord and plugged it into the standard power outlet in the galley. This outlet was used primarily for cabin servicing when the plane was on the ground overnight. He then pulled a drill and reciprocating saw out of his bag.

By this time, the plane had started moving slowly across the airport. As the plane started its taxi, Sara and Doug were working furiously pulling up the carpet, exposing the metal below. As they did, the whine of the engines increased as the plane started rolling down the runway. Doug and Sara made no effort to find seats. They started drilling into the floor as the plane pitched up and took flight.

Once the first hole was drilled, Doug took out the saw and started cutting into the floor of the plane.

As they climbed, Doug felt the pressure in his ears. It was uncomfortable but made him smile. Stu had convinced the other pilots not to pressurize the plane. This would be critical when blowing the door off of the cargo hold.

By the time they were in level flight, Doug was starting on the last segment of the square that would provide access to the cargo hold. That was when the chime sounded. Both Doug and Sara turned. Looking at the cockpit, both of them ran to the front of the plane.

"What's up, Arnie?" Sara asked, trying to keep her breathing normal. Her eyes grew wide as she said, "I'll ask. Just a minute."

She hung up the interphone and whispered, frantic, "Arnie, the captain. He wants to come back."

Doug muttered, "Shit!" He then thought for a quick moment and said, "Tell him no."

She picked up the interphone and relayed the answer. She looked panicked for a minute, then seemed to deflate with relief. She mouthed, "He's sending Stu."

She then spoke into the handset. "He said, only the flight engineer. If anyone else comes back, he'll blow up the plane."

Doug smiled, nodding. "Good."

Doug threw the carpet back in place, covering the work they had been doing to gain access to the cargo hold. They both moved out of the way as the cockpit door opened and Stu emerged. Closing the door behind him, Stu relaxed, giving Sara a quick kiss. "This bad man hasn't been threatening you, has he, sweetheart?"

"Screw you," Doug said with a grin. Both men greeted each other with a firm handshake.

"What's the status? The boss is getting edgy," Stu said as the trio headed back to continue work on the floor.

"We're on schedule. Have the floor almost open. How about you?"

Stu looked at the location of the work and nodded as Doug resumed sawing into the aluminum floor.

His voice rising above the noise of the electric saw, Stu said, "We're looking good up here as well. You have a couple of hours until we're over the coast of Florida. You've gotta be done by then. I worked on the flight plan and unless you hear differently from me, at 0427 blow the door. That will give us 10 minutes until the drop. I'll try to get back to help, but no promises. Sara. I want you in the cockpit once the explosion happens."

Both nodded. Doug then looked back at the floor and continued cutting.

"0437 is drop-time Doug. You and the money need to be out of the plane by then. Got it?"

Doug looked up and nodded. "Sure." He then continued his work. As he was sawing, without looking up, Doug said, "I'll clean up as best I can, but no promises."

Stu pursed his lips. "Once the door's blown, throw as much equipment overboard as you can."

Doug nodded once again, now without looking up. "I know Stu. We've been over this already."

"Stu, you'd better get back to the cockpit," Sara said.

Stu exhaled and nodded. "I'm just on the other side of that door if you need me."

Sara smiled. "You might as well be on another planet for all the help you can provide without giving yourself away."

The grin Stu returned had no humor in it. "We're almost there. Just keep your focus and this will all be over soon."

"And we'll all be rich," Doug added, still working on the floor.

"And we'll all be rich," Stu agreed.

It was only a few minutes after Stu returned to the cockpit that the floor fell into the cargo hold. Sara then helped Doug down into the exposed opening. As Doug descended, Sara pulled a work lamp out of his bag and plugged it into the extension cord, lowering it below.

Now that Doug had light, he started locating all of his checked bags.

They were easy to find, being loaded last, and he went to work at once with the tasks before him.

As he worked, he glanced up occasionally at Sara. She stood vigil in case the cockpit called. Mercifully, they did not.

The first order of business was to rig the money. Doug removed the parachute pack from one of his checked bags and secured it to the plastic-wrapped pallet. He then attached the rafts that would inflate once the pallet hit the water.

As he worked, he was dismayed how quickly the time was slipping away.

He tried to slow himself into deliberate motions so as not to make errors. Even without coffee, he was wide awake.

Next order of business was to take a car jack and elevate the pallet and then place a series of metal pipes under it. This would allow him access to maneuver and evacuate the money once he blew the door off.

Finally, after what seemed an eternity, Doug called up to Sara who passed his duffle bag down to him. It had not been C4 inside his bag, but det-cord.

He was very careful with the detonation cord as he placed it around the seam of the door to the cargo hold. It was actually very stable, but Doug had always treated all explosives with the utmost respect.

Finally, with the help of Sara, Doug extracted himself from the dark hole.

"How long?"

He was drenched in sweat. The fake tan was holding. He knew that he needed to wash it off the following day, but that was a problem he could focus on later.

Sara grinned and removed her working smock, handing it to him. He wiped himself down as she answered, "Not long. You took a little longer than I expected. I was getting worried."

Doug grinned. As he wiped his face, his hands shook. The fatigue was setting in now.

"Me too."

They both looked at their watches. They had eight minutes to spare. The time moved at an excruciating pace. Finally, Doug nodded. "All right, Sara, you're going to feel this. Head up front. Stu's going to want you up there."

She kissed him on the cheek and searched for words. None came. Doug then smiled. "I know. Me too."

Doug watched Sara as she made the quick journey to the front and then turned and nodded. He nodded back and then whispered, "Fire in the hole."

The explosion was far more violent than he had expected. Doug had experience with det-cord, but not using it on a plane in flight. Even depressurized, the vacuum was obvious.

Smoke was in the cabin now, but it starting to clear almost as quickly as it materialized. The seconds seemed to drag on at an excruciating pace until Doug finally saw the cockpit door open. Doug held his breath as Sara flew into the cockpit. If anyone other than Stu emerged, he was done.

A handful of heartbeats later, Sara was replaced by Stu who shut the door behind him. Doug exhaled and nodded as Stu picked up the interphone, no doubt calling the other pilots to report in. He talked for only a few seconds before he hung up and made his way back toward Doug.

"What the hell did you do to my plane?"

Doug looked down and then back up again. "I think I might have scratched it. I'll buy you a new one."

"Good enough. Let's go get the money."

"Deal."

Stu helped Doug into the cargo hold and then started tossing the remaining tools down to him. Doug tossed the tools out of the gaping hole he had created on the side of the aircraft, and into the Gulf of Mexico below.

Stu looked over at a bag sitting on a seat near the hole in the floor. He hadn't seen it yet, but knew instantly it was the ransom. He grinned, despite himself. He deftly opened the bag. It was filled with crisp new hundred-dollar bills. His grin widened. He pulled out three of the notes and left the rest.

Stu then descended into the cargo hold, joining his partner. This was a risk. Although Sara would do her best to keep the remaining pilots in the cockpit, if they ventured into the cabin, chances were she wouldn't be able to hold them back. But it was a risk he had to take.

As he started down, Doug called up to him, "Be careful. The edges are sharp. I cut my hand earlier."

"Are you OK?" Stu asked with concern.

"We've gotten this far. I'm not stopping now because of a little scratch."

Once inside, they started cleaning up the remaining evidence, throwing everything they could overboard.

Stu glanced at his watch and yelled, "Two minutes!" over the roar of the wind outside. Doug only nodded.

Stu helped Doug on with his parachute and then attached a static line to the cargo net inside. The net would provide more than enough resistance to deploy the parachutes. Once done, both men looked outside as the seconds ticked by. Stu handed Doug the three bills. In return, Doug gave him a questioning look.

Stu yelled over the din of rushing air, "Souvenirs. Give mine to Eric. He'll get it to me later."

Doug took the money with a puzzled expression. "Only three?"

"Sara couldn't care less."

Doug nodded his acknowledgment as he put the bills in his pocket.

"Time!" Stu yelled. Doug lowered the jack and removed it. Using the pipes as rollers, both men pushed the pallet of money out of the door. It rolled easily and disappeared. Both men nodded, and then Doug charged out of the gaping hole in the side of the plane.

Wasting no time, Stu disconnected the static lines and threw them out of the plane, taking a moment to glance outside. He thought he saw two white chutes, but he didn't take enough time to verify whether they were real or imagined. He threw out as much as he could, leaving only a few pipes behind as he was running out of time and didn't want to be caught in the cargo hold.

He found some cargo that he could climb up on and made his way back into the cabin. After throwing the carpet over the floor, he did his best to straighten up his hair as he made his way back to the cockpit.

As he entered, looking frazzled, he made the pronouncement a little louder than he intended.

"He's gone!"

The parachute jerked violently as the static line deployed the canopy above him. Outside it was dark. Very dark. Doug swiveled his head, trying to get his bearings. It was several seconds before he saw the flash of the 727's anti-collision lights fading off into the distance.

As he looked around, searching for the parachute carrying the pallet of money, he quickly realized how cold it was at 10,000 feet. *Well*, he thought, *probably more like nine or eight thousand at this point.*

It was a new moon, and the stars provided little illumination as he searched for the pallet. In the plan, finding a large white parachute was supposed to be easy. He was becoming concerned about how much difficulty he was having spotting the chute amidst the ocean below him.

With almost five minutes of hang time, Doug had thought this would be the easiest part of the plan. However, as the minutes ticked by, his mind was awash with everything that could have gone wrong. Did the chute deploy? Was the money too much weight for the chute? What if he didn't secure the load correctly? Did they just go through all of this for nothing?

As Doug continued to descend, frantically looking for the prize he had worked so hard for, he thought about Stu and became angry. Stu probably wouldn't even care if the money's chute didn't open and everything went to the bottom on the sea. He seemed to care more about *doing* the job than *getting* the money. He was more interested in seeing if he could solve the puzzle. *To hell with that*, thought Doug. *I'm doing this for the money.*

The air was becoming noticeably warmer when Doug thought he saw something in the water, off in the distance. It looked like it *could* be the parachute. But it was in the water, and Doug was still a few thousand feet in the air. *Well, that made sense*, he thought. *The pallet would fall much more quickly, wouldn't it?*

Doug wasn't sure he had found his prize, but he figured he had little choice at this point. He maneuvered his rig towards the disturbance on the surface of the gulf.

As he continued to descend, he pulled out a flashlight and started cycling it on and off, while scanning the surface of the water. He now needed to find Eric.

This task proved far less stressful. Less than a minute passed before he found the answering flashes coming some ways off, in the void below.

When Doug finally hit the water, he was only a couple hundred feet from what he thought was the money. He had expected the warm water of the Gulf to be welcomed after the cold ride down. Instead, he was greeted with what he perceived to be frigid water. His teeth chattered as he went to work cutting his chute loose. Once free from the lines, he started swimming, as the silk descending over him. He pulled for all that he was worth towards the money that should now be afloat thanks to the automatically inflatable raft.

As he swam, the silk settled over him. Doug dove beneath the water's surface to escape the parachute. He didn't want to come all this way only to drown.

The first time he surfaced, he was still under a tangle of cloth and cord. In a panic, he took in as much air as he could and went under the inky water once again. When he broke surface the second time, he was greeted by delicious, salty air. He inhaled deeply and searched for the money. The first couple of seconds he was glad to just be alive, but as the moments ticked by, he started to become frantic. *Where had it gone?* He continued to tread water, searching in the black night, but once more coming up empty.

As he struggled to tread water, his boots impeded his efforts to stay afloat. He stopped for a moment, took a deep breath, and did his best to strip them off as he descended below the water's surface. As Doug worked to free the boots, the salt of the Gulf of Mexico seared into the cut he had gotten traveling between the cabin of the 727 and the cargo hold.

As the first boot released its grasp on his foot, and fell to the depths below, Doug kicked for all he was worth to reach air again. Breaking the surface he took several seconds before he repeated the process. As the second boot was set free, he once more surfaced, just as a wave washed over him. He took in a large mouthful of salty water. Choking and coughing, Doug struggled to locate the raft. As the moments passed, the raft now became the focus for Doug instead of the money atop it. The raft was the only thing that could keep him alive until Eric could find him. If he didn't find it, the chances were almost certain that he would drown.

It was as a swell lifted him high, that he caught sight of what he believed to be the raft and money. It didn't matter at this point. He would take whatever he could. He started to swim again.

The eight minutes spent swimming towards the money were the longest minutes of Doug's life. When he positively identified the yellow raft bobbing on the ocean's surface, Doug cried.

With tears streaming down his face, washed out by the salty water of the Gulf, he broke the water's surface one last time. With trembling muscles, he climbed the mountain of money.

Later, he would not remember how he had scaled the peak. All he would remember was sitting atop the pallet, shivering violently while cycling his flashlight, searching the horizon for a return to his signal.

Eric arrived twenty minutes after a severely hypothermic Doug had found salvation atop more money than either man had ever even conceived.

"Doug!" Eric's voice rang out as the massive yacht cut its engines.

"E-E-Eric." Doug chattered in response.

Eric threw a line to Doug, who caught it on the first attempt. Doug didn't know where the strength came from, but he somehow secured the line, fastening Eric's yacht to Doug's far more expensive life raft.

"H-h-h-ow d-d-do y-y-you l-l-like m-my b-b-b-boat?"

Eric leapt over to Doug and lead him to the Chris Craft. "Oh, my God! You look terrible!"

Doug took Eric's arm as he helped him off the pallet and onto to the stolen yacht. Leading him below deck, Eric draped a blanket around shivering man and sat him down on the couch.

Once Doug was sitting, Eric went to the galley. He had made a fresh pot of coffee to keep them both awake. He now poured a big cup to help warm Doug up.

As Doug sat trembling on the couch, sipping the hot coffee, Eric went into one of the cabins and emerged with a duffle bag.

"You wait here, man. I'm going to start transferring the cash to the boat."

Doug started to stand. "OK, I'll help."

"No, man. You need to stay down here and get warm."

"Eric," Doug protested, "if you're going to move two thousand pounds of money, you're going to need help. Besides, it will warm me up. Part of my problem is I haven't been moving since I got on top of that pile of cash."

Eric smiled and relented. "OK. Go to the cabin on the right. There's a bunch of clothes the previous owner of this magnificent vessel left behind. That will help warm you up. The cabin on the right also has a bunch of bags. After you get changed, bring one out to me. I should have filled this one by then. You can dump the money into one of the cabins and come back outside. When you get back to me, I'll give you another filled one. We'll keep doing this until we've offloaded everything."

Doug nodded and headed as directed. There he found a vast array of clothing and selected the warmest garments he could find.

Minutes later, he made his way off of the Chris Craft and onto the pallet where he gave Eric the empty bag. The one Eric gave him in return felt like it weighed a ton. It appeared that Eric had cut a large hole in the plastic wrap and was busily transferring money off of the pallet and into the now-stuffed duffel.

Doug left with the full bag and Eric went back to work filling the empty one. Below deck, he dumped the money in the far corner of the cabin on the left, the largest on the boat. He then returned to Eric and exchanged bags again.

The next bag was lighter, as Eric hadn't had as much time to fill it as before. This went on for over an hour until Doug realized he couldn't go on like this.

"Eric," he finally said. "How about we switch for a while?"

With a nod, the two men changed places, and the process started anew.

The sun was just cresting the horizon when they finally moved the last of the money to the Chris Craft. Taking his knife out, Eric ripped a large gash in the raft's side. The two men watched what remained, as it slowly sank in the inky darkness of the gulf.

"Come on, let's get going," Eric said as he headed upstairs to start the dual motors.

"Where are we going?"

Eric pointed. "South. I'll drop you off at Key West. You can get cleaned up there and catch a flight back to St. Louis."

Doug looked like the living dead as he asked, "How long?"

Eric cracked a sympathetic smile. "Head below and get some rack time. It'll be hours. We should arrive before nightfall."

Eric didn't need to make the offer twice. Doug headed down to the only cabin left that wasn't overflowing with currency and fell heavily into bed. He was asleep before his head even hit the pillow.

Doug awoke with a start. His sleep had been troubled by a series of bad dreams. As he woke in the pitching boat, everything came flooding back to him. He struggled unsteadily to his feet. It felt as if every muscle in his body had been destroyed. Every step was agony as he slowly made his way topside.

The sun was low in the sky when he reached the bridge of the yacht. There, smiling, was Eric Mansfield.

"You slept long enough, princess."

Hair disheveled and clothing rumpled, Doug croaked out, "What time is it?"

"A little before six. Should have you in Key West in less than an hour."

Doug looked out at the setting sun and could see the faint sliver of land on the horizon. Eric continued, "Once we dock there, you can head into town and get a room. There you can clean up. You can also pick up everything you need to get that shit off your skin. Frankly, you look ridiculous."

Doug forced a grin. "Got the job done, didn't it?"

Eric returned the expression. "That it did, my friend. That it did." They both looked out at the horizon as the boat continued to make its way towards the island off in the distance. Finally, Eric offered, "Why don't you go below and get yourself cleaned up? The head has a shower in it. Also, put together some cash. There are several fifties and hundreds, but not as many as you'd think. You'll need money for your room and ticket back to St. Louis."

Doug nodded, still trying to force himself into wakefulness. He then slowly descended the stairs, wincing with every step as he headed below.

He looked at the boat's small head but decided to first visit the cabin with the money. There he pulled together the cash to get himself home.

Eric had been right. There were ones and fives as far as the eye could see, but the larger denominations seemed to be in short supply. However, after some time, Doug had amassed a fair-sized pile of fifties and hundreds. He counted them out before he put them in his bag. In all, he put together a little over forty thousand dollars.

The plan was: after Doug left the boat, Eric would take the money somewhere offshore and launder it while everyone else waited. Then, after a reasonable time period, everyone would reconvene and split the money four ways. Doug was never thrilled with this plan, since the money would leave his direct control. However, Stu was the one running the show, so Doug had little choice but to trust him. Further, Doug had known Stu for years. In all the time he had known the man, Stu had never been motivated by money. From what he had heard about Eric, this had been the case as well. Stu said all Eric wanted was a boat. As Doug made his way to the small shower in the yacht's head, he couldn't help but think he had gotten his wish.

When Doug entered the small bathroom, he first stopped to take two aspirin. After washing them down with water, he considered the bottle. He then opened it again and took six more.

After a long, hot shower, Doug went into the closet of the ship's previous owner and pulled out what he hoped would be a suitable wardrobe for travel back to Missouri. When he finally returned to the bridge, the soreness had started to abate. He arrived just as Eric had slowed the boat to a few knots as they entered the harbor.

"You look better," Eric commented. He then added with a grin, "But the tan still looks like shit."

"Well, I'll be losing the tan soon enough. How about you? You look terrible," Doug replied.

"I'm fine. Just a little tired. I'll get some sleep soon."

"You going to overnight in port?"

Eric shook his head. "Naw. Just going to take on some more fuel. I've pulled together some cash for the gas. Then going to head out for a while and drop anchor offshore."

"Why?" Doug said with a questioning look. "You can afford any hotel you want."

"Somebody needs to look over the haul. I need to protect your investment." He then added with a look of pride, "Besides, what hotel can beat this magnificent floating palace."

They pulled alongside a dock and Doug helped as they tied up the boat. To avoid suspicion, it was Doug who directed the attendant at the gas pump to top off the tanks. They both decided that it would be best if Doug did this since, although it might be Eric's boat, it was still the 1960s and Eric was still black.

After they finished, Doug helped untie the lines securing the boat to the dock. He watched as Eric and the yacht drifted quietly away, then Eric started its two massive motors. With a low rumble, the vessel—and the millions in it—slowly made their way off into the early evening.

Doug picked up his duffle bag filled with cash and some clothes. It was far more than he would need. Stu would have objected because, if Doug were discovered with a sudden influx of funds, it could raise suspicion and lead back to him. Doug wasn't worried. He would be smart. After work tomorrow, he would head to the bank and get a safe deposit box. No one could ever trace the money back to him.

He then turned and headed off to find a hotel and drug store so he could get this stuff off of his skin.

Chapter Twelve
In the Wind

"You're telling us Sara was in on it?" Paul struggled to get out.

Doug nodded calmly. "Sure. I think that was one of Stu's motivations for pulling the job."

"Why's that?"

Doug shrugged. "Stu was pissed that he and Sara couldn't get married."

Greg started shaking his head. "What are you talking about? Why couldn't they get married?"

"Well, I guess they could, but TWA, like most other airlines, have rules about their stewardesses. If you get married, you either have to quit or get fired. Stu was pissed at TWA for making Sara choose between her job or marrying him. And he was pissed at the government for its hypocrisy."

"How's that?" Paul asked.

"The constitution says you're entitled to the pursuit of happiness, but they stand by as the airline tells the stewardesses they can't get married."

"And that's why he masterminded all of this."

Doug grinned, "It was part of the reason. But believe it or not… I think his main motivation was to see if he could do it. He's always loved a good challenge."

"What about this..." Greg looked at his notes, "Eric Mansfield."

"I don't know him very well. But he and Stu go back to Stu's Navy days. They were on an aircraft carrier together. Stu said they became good friends during his time there. Used to plot and plan all manner of schemes."

"But you said all Mansfield wanted was the boat?" Greg pressed.

"That's what Stu told me."

"But you said he had a boat. A big boat. Where did he get it?"

Doug shook his head. "No idea. Might have saved up and bought it, or he might have stolen it. I really couldn't say."

"Could you describe the boat to us?" Paul asked.

Doug looked up at the ceiling, trying to remember. "It was big, I can tell you that for sure."

"How big?"

"I don't know. I don't know boats very well, but it had to be at least sixty feet. It had three bedrooms and a bathroom. Also, a living room. The bridge was high up. Overlooked everything."

"What was the make of the boat?" Greg asked.

Doug shook his head. "Don't know."

"The name of the boat?"

Doug pursed his lips. "Sorry. Didn't see it."

Paul lowered his voice in a threatening tone and leaned forward. "You're telling me you didn't see the name of the boat, and all you can provide us with is a general description of every large boat out on the water today?"

Doug's expression turned. He looked worried again as the pitch of his voice went up slightly. "I told you, I don't know boats. I didn't look at the name because I was freezing and then working my ass off. After that, I was asleep. I've confessed to everything. Why wouldn't I tell you the name of the boat?"

"Gentlemen," Ryan said, to calm the tension, "my client has been as cooperative as he could be. He's giving you everything he has. I can assure you, he isn't holding anything back."

Greg held up his hand. "You're right, councilor. This is just a lot to process." He turned his attention back to Doug. "What about you? You said Stu did it for the thrill and Eric did it for the boat—or something to that effect. Why did you do it? Was it for the thrill as well?"

Doug seemed to relax, even forcing a slight grin. "For me, it was about the money."

"But it wasn't for Stu?"

"Don't get me wrong. I'm sure he's more than happy to be rich now, but not really. No."

The two feds looked at each other and shook their heads. Paul resumed the questioning.

"What happened with Mansfield?"

"Don't know. He took off."

"With all of your money?"

Doug shook his head. "It was always part of the plan. I didn't really have much to say there. I'll be honest; I didn't like it, but if I didn't agree to it, I knew Stu would find somebody else."

"What about the three hundred dollars you guys took from the ransom?"

Doug shrugged. "Gave Eric two bills like Stu told me to, and I kept the last one for myself. I told Eric to give Stu his when he saw him, but to make sure not to spend it."

"Why?"

Doug shot Greg a condescending look. "Why do you think we left the rest of the money behind? The bills were new and we can count: they were sequential. We knew they're being traced."

"If we're tracing the bills, why take the three hundreds?"

Doug shrugged. "I don't know. It was Stu's idea. Last-minute thing. Seemed like a good idea at the time. Kinda cool."

Greg asked, "Where's your bill?"

"Safe."

"Where?" Greg pressed.

Doug leaned in and whispered to his lawyer. Ryan then whispered back to his client. Finally, Doug said, "Safe deposit box."

Paul leaned in. "Why the hesitation?"

Doug deflated. "I also have some money from the job in there. I took it with me."

"How much?"

"Not much. Only forty thousand or so. It's all I have now."

Paul shook his head. "No, it's all you *had*."

Doug deflated more.

"Where's Mansfield and the boat now?" Paul asked, no sympathy in his voice.

"No idea. He dropped me at Key West and then took off for the Bahamas or the Caribbean. Somewhere like that. Swear to God."

"So, you're telling me you, and your other two accomplices, had no problem trusting a fourth member of your team with everything?"

Doug shrugged. "Yeah."

Paul shook his head. "I don't buy it."

"Why's that?"

"You can't be trusted. You turned on your friends. Why would they be any different?"

Doug looked down and shook his head. He then said, almost under his breath. "They're better people than I am."

The man dressed in all black was flanked by three other men. Behind him, at a safe distance, were two other men. Both wore windbreakers with "FBI" on their back, although one man was actually Treasury.

The man in the lead held up one, then two, then three fingers. Two men beside him slung a round pipe about two feet long into the door. As they did so, they yelled "FBI" as they disappeared into the room.

Paul and Greg entered behind them, both of their guns drawn to the sounds of, "clear, clear" emerging from every room in the small apartment.

They were in St. Petersburg, only a score of miles from where the two men first met. This was the last stop for them as they entered the last known residence of Eric Mansfield. Like Stu and Sara's apartments before, the small dwelling Eric used as his home turned up empty. At first glance it looked like nothing had been cleaned out, but upon closer inspection, it was clear it was abandoned.

It had been like this in every apartment. Stu's home was the first that they entered. On initial inspection it looked like everything was there: clothing, dishes, electronics ... even the bed had been made. However, as they looked closer, they noticed everything of actual value had been removed. There were no photo albums, personal letters or even pictures on the walls, save generic artwork.

They found the same situation at Sara's apartment. At this point it was just assumed that when they started going through Eric's place in St. Petersburg, they wouldn't find anything of value. As it would turn out, they were wrong.

Paul and Greg nodded to the FBI agents who had broken down the door as they left the apartment. Now alone, Paul and Greg started looking for anything, neither expecting to have their efforts rewarded. It was a little surprising when Paul called Greg over a few minutes later.

"What've you got?"

Paul was sitting at a desk with a small stack of newspapers in front of him. "Sara was from San Jose, California. What's the local paper there?"

Greg thought for a minute and said, "I believe it's the *San Jose Mercury News*."

"And Stu's from St. Louis. That paper's the *Post-Dispatch*, right?"

"Sounds about right."

"Mansfield was from Los Angeles."

"No, he's from Watts."

"But Watts is in the Los Angeles area."

"If you're asking if his paper was the *LA Times*, then yes, it is. What are you getting at, Paul?"

Paul pulled out a copy of the *San Jose Mercury News*, the *St. Louis Post-Dispatch* and the *Los Angeles Times*. All were dated April first.

"What do you think it means?"

Paul looked at Greg, shaking his head. "April Fool's Day?"

The two then started pouring through the papers, looking for any clue why three hometown papers would be there.

They were searching for a needle in a haystack, but the needle eluded them until an hour into the search.

"Paul."

"Yeah."

"Have you looked through the obits yet?"

Paul frowned. "No."

"I'll wait."

A minute later Paul muttered, "Shit!" under his breath.

They then opened the last paper, knowing what they would find. All three contained the obituaries of each member of the heist crew. Sara's in the *Mercury News*, Eric's in the *LA Times,* and Stu's in the *Post-Dispatch*.

"What does it mean?" Paul asked.

"You won't like the answer," Greg said.

"Humor me."

"Powell's sending us a message."

"What's that?"

Greg shook his head as he answered. "He's telling us that they may not be dead, but the investigation is."

Chapter Thirteen

Gambling

Outside was everything the interior of the casino wasn't. Outdoors it was a beautiful day. Not a cloud in the sky, and temperatures in the mid-80s with a gentle breeze. There was a serenity there. The predominate sound was the gentle crashing of the waves washing up on the shore. The overwhelming smell was the salt in the air, tinged with the fragrance of artificial coconut from the suntan oil slathered upon the sun worshipers by the pool or on the beach. Indoors it was dank and dark. The only light was produced by numerous 40-watt bulbs adorning the ceiling. A thick haze of smoke hung heavily in the air. The place reeked of the stagnate odor of burning tobacco, mixed with the pungent aroma of body odor, courtesy of gamblers spending far more time in the artificial cave than was decent in a place as picturesque as the island they were now on.

As Stu entered the casino, his eyes struggled to adjust. After several seconds, he scanned the room before his gaze landed on his target. A lone man at a blackjack table with a sizable stack of chips. A smile danced around the edges of Stu's mouth as he moved across the room to join the man.

Taking the empty seat next to the gambler, Stu pulled out his wallet and produced a ten-dollar bill. He laid it upon the table.

"Ten dollars. Changing ten dollars," the dealer announced, and then took the bill, inserting it into a slot in the table. She then produced two five-dollar chips and slid them over to the newcomer.

Stu glanced at the man next to him. Without returning the look, the man beside him placed two twenty-dollar chips in the bet ring on the table. Stu returned his attention to his almost non-existent stack and pushed one of his two five-dollar chips forward. The dealer then laid two cards face down in front of the two men, and one face down in front of her, with the other face up. The face-up card was a six of diamonds.

Stu looked at his cards. He had a five of clubs and a king of clubs. He glanced at the man next to him again. His face was impassive. "How are the cards today?" He asked casually.

The man glanced towards Stu for the first time. The man had black skin and short, cropped hair peppered with grey. However, his physique was not that of an older man. He was very well defined with large muscles and not an ounce of fat. His face held no humor as he glared at the man beside him. It was apparent that he was focused on the game and did not appreciate the question. He growled in response, "I've been getting by."

Stu nodded and said, "What the hell? Hit me."

The dealer placed a jack of hearts face up on the table. Stu threw his cards down next to the jack. Twenty-five.

She took the five-dollar chip as he busted. The gambler next to him laid his cards on the table. "Stand."

He had a seven and a five. The man stood at twelve.

The dealer turned over her card. She had a ten to add to her six. She then took a mandatory card. It was a jack. Twenty-six. She busted and pushed two twenty-dollar chips to the winner.

"Nicely played," Stu said with a grin.

The man next to him kept an expressionless stare. Stu looked into the man's eyes and was sure he saw joy there.

Before Stu could make another comment, the man reached down to a briefcase next to him and produced a stack of one-dollar bills, all US, and laid them upon the table.

"Change these, please."

The dealer rolled her eyes. She didn't need to vocalize anything to convey that he had done this before. She started counting the bills as Stu glanced over at the man next to him with a quizzical look. However, rather than rebuff Stu, the man cracked a smile. Even more surprising, he actually spoke.

"At night I play a lot of poker. Actually, I do better there than here. But it leaves me with a lot of smaller bills."

Stu nodded as the dealer announced, "Changing a hundred." And started stuffing the bills into the slot. When she finally finished, she asked the gambler, "How would you like your chips, sir?"

The man shrugged. "Fifties are fine."

She nodded and slid two chips in front of him. Both he and Stu pushed a single chip forward; the gambler a fifty-dollar chip and Stu his remaining five-dollar chip.

As the dealer started producing the cards, Stu asked, "What's your name?"

The man glanced over and sighed. "Charles."

"Nice to meet you, Charles."

The man exhaled in annoyance. "Charles is my last name."

"My mistake. I usually take Charles as a first name. If your last name is a first name, does that mean you first name a last name, like Miller or something like that?"

Rolling his eyes as he picked up his cards, Mr. Charles said, "It's Stanley."

"Nice to meet you, Stanley Charles, my name is..."

But before he could finish, the dealer announced, "Insurance?" In front of her was a face-down card next to an ace of hearts.

Stanley turned his attention back to his cards and pushed forward a twenty-five-dollar chip. Stu looked at his cards. Two tens. He shrugged and said, "I'm good."

The dealer turned over a king of spades, and announced, "Dealer has blackjack," as she took both the twenty-five-dollar chip and the five-dollar chip. She then returned Stanley's fifty-dollar chip to him.

Stanley took the chips off of the table, moving them to his briefcase.

"Table's going cold."

Stu looked at the lack of chips in front of him. He got up, following the gambler.

"Hey Stanley, I'm kind of new at this…"

"You don't say," he responded before Stu could finish.

"Yeah. Well, I was wondering, could I buy you a drink and pick your brain for a bit?"

As they arrived at the cashier cage, Stanley started removing several chips from his briefcase, saying, "Hundreds please."

The cashier nodded as he claimed the chips and started counting them. He then returned a stack of hundred-dollar bills to Stanley, who placed them into his briefcase.

He looked over at Stu. "You're buying?"

Stu smiled. "As I said…"

The man shrugged. "Why the hell not?"

Stanley followed Stu through the casino and into the hotel lobby. They then continued through the resort until they exited by the vast pool out back. Beyond the pool was a brilliant white Caribbean beach stretched out before them. As they emerged from the hotel, Stu blinked back the brilliance of the midday sun as it assaulted his eyes. He then led Stanley to the poolside bar, where he strode up to the bartender and said, "One scotch and a Jack Daniels. Both doubles, and both neat."

The woman behind the bar took out two tumblers and poured the drinks and handed them to the men. "That will be nine dollars."

Stu nodded and looked at Stanley. "The lady said nine dollars."

Stanley raised his eyebrows. "I though you said you were buying?"

Stu shook his head, taking a sip from his glass. "Just pay the lady, please."

Grumbling, Stanley reached into his briefcase and withdrew eleven old, one-dollar bills.

"Thank you very much," the bartender said with a smile.

Stanley was grumbling as Stu led him to a table at the far end of the pool, allowing them some privacy.

"I though you said you were buying?" Stanley grumbled as they took their seat.

"Take it out of my cut," Stu replied with a grin. Both took a sip from their glasses, then Stu resumed, "So its Stanley Charles now, is it?"

With a shrug Stanley replied, "I like the names."

"Well then, here's to Stanley Charles. May Eric Mansfield Rest in Peace."

The men clinked their glasses together and took a sip. After a moment, Stanley asked, "Where's Sara?"

Stu nodded towards the pool. There was a blonde in a bikini on a chase lounge sunning herself. As the two men looked in her direction, she caught their gaze and waved. Both men lifted their glasses in greeting and returned to their conversation as she returned to lazing by the pool.

"Have you come up with names yet?"

"Working on it."

"Good. I'm not sure 'Stu' will ever be able to show his face again."

Stu gave a shrug. "That's fine with me. How's the money coming?"

"Slow. I've separated a lot of the hundreds and fifties. Also, a respectable stack of twenties. I've opened twenty-three bank accounts across the islands. All have north of a hundred grand. I've been using the casinos to change in the smaller bills. I move around a lot, so it seems to be working."

Stu took another sip from his glass. "Any issues with losing at the casinos?"

Stanley smiled. "I lost a lot at first, but it hardly made a dent in the haul we had. I'm picking up on games now and doing a lot better. Not sure if we're up or down, but it's close either way."

"Good deal. How's everything else going? I know we're asking a lot of you to change the money in. Sara and I'd like to help, but I'm not sure that's such a good idea. If the American government is looking for two men, one black and one white, and a blonde while cashing in hundreds of thousands of ones, fives and tens, then we might garner more attention than we want."

"Don't worry about it," Stanley said with a wave of his hand. "I'm doing fine. When we first met, I told you I wanted to sail the Caribbean on my own boat. Well, now not only have I got my boat, but I've also got a job to do. I'm having fun."

Stu took another sip. "Glad to hear it."

"Have you and Sara figured out where you're going to settle?"

"Still thinking about it. Close on that one as well."

"States?"

"Not sure. Leaning towards Australia."

Stanley nodded. "Not a bad choice. Pretty far from here, though. Still no qualms about trusting me with the money?"

Stu shook his head. "Not before and not now. However, when you merge the accounts, I want only six million in savings and invest the rest."

Stanley nodded. "I figured as much. Still cutting Doug out, eh?"

Stu's face darkened. "The bastard ratted us out. No excuse for that. He can rot for all I care."

"He was always the weak link. I told you that. All he cared about was the money. The challenge was always an obstacle for him. Never the goal."

Stu took a drink but said nothing. Stanley continued, "Still, he *was* the one who pulled off the heist."

"Never would have done it without us. Wouldn't even have conceived the plan if we hadn't been involved. He only played a role. It might have been center stage, but it was a minor part."

"But he played it. Shouldn't he get something?"

"No! He sold us all out. He forfeits anything he might have received."

Stanley held up a hand, trying to calm Stu down. "Relax, man. I was just wondering."

"Well, you don't have to wonder anymore."

"What about the feds? They still looking for us?"

Stu shook his head. "I'm sure they are, but I doubt they'll find much. You're out of the country and its unlikely Sara and I will return. They got my message."

Stanley smiled. "April first?"

Stu shrugged. "I'm sure they understood: looking for us is a joke. We're ghosts now."

Stanley's grin faded as he said, "I'm impressed with the forethought. Putting the four obits in the paper so long ago."

Stu took another drink. "I've been planning this for a while. I had all of you in mind." He gave a humorless laugh. "My biggest concern was we would pick up another member of the crew."

"Nope. Worked out how you planned it. They got the papers. I'm sure they got the message."

"I only left them three papers." Stanley gave Stu a questioning look. Stu continued, "They have Doug. He's still among the living. The three of us are the only ghosts."

Both men sat in silence for a long while, both drinking as Stu thought about Doug's betrayal.

Finally, Stu broke the silence. "You change the name of the boat again?"

Stanley nodded. "Yeah. After I freed the girl, I changed her name from *Bull Market* to *Liberator*. When I heard about Doug's betrayal, I couldn't say for sure if he saw her new name or not. Just to be on the safe side, I'm now calling her *Winnings*. Found a guy in St. Kitts who made everything legal. New papers, new serial numbers… the works. The authorities can pour over my boat all they want. All they'll find is a boat that was purchased by Mr. Charles and used regularly by him."

Stu's humor returned as he chuckled. "I'll bet that asshole stockbroker doesn't even know his boat's gone yet."

Stanley laughed. "I'll bet that asshole Summers hadn't realized his janitor quit yet."

The men clinked their glasses. Both were now almost empty.

"What do you want me to do with the balance?" Stanley asked, returning to business.

"Stick to the plan. Invest it in stable stocks and bonds."

"You need any cash?"

Stu seemed to consider this for a little while before responding, "Maybe fifty to eighty thousand to get us started. You can give me an account number so I can get more if I need it."

"I can give you whatever you want. I'll take you and Sara to Tortola in a few days. From there you guys can catch a flight to wherever you like." He leaned back and closed his eyes and said, "It will be nice to spend time with you at sea again, lieutenant."

Stu grinned. "You as well, Petty Officer."

A few minutes later, the two men drained their glasses. Stanley stood up, after removing a handful of ones from his briefcase.

"Want another?"

"If you're buying, why the hell not?"

Part II

Little Planes
(and a boat)

Chapter Fourteen
A Hot Lead on a Cold Case

To say that John Alexi had been a bad kid would be inaccurate. That phrasing might lead one to believe that he was no longer a child. At fifteen years old, he was far from an adult. However, in those fifteen years he had gotten into more trouble than most adults do by the end of their lives.

John's troubles were even more impressive when one considers that whereas most troubled youths with a long history hail from cities like New York or Chicago, John lived in a small Alaskan Village.

St. Mary's was on high ground beside the Yukon River. Not far below lay the smaller village of Pitkas Point. Together, they barely had a population of 400 people. Almost all were Native Alaskans. And all within that community knew of John Alexi and his shortcomings.

John started chewing tobacco at eight. It wasn't until he was eleven that he had his first drink of whiskey. This feat was even more impressive considering the village of St. Mary's was dry. That is to say, alcohol was strictly illegal. That made it slightly more restrictive than Pitkas, as that was only a "damp" village. Alcohol was legal to possess in Pitkas, but illegal to buy. However, there was a rub: the airport servicing both villages was, technically, in St.

Mary's. That meant that flying alcohol in was illegal. Not that people didn't smuggle it in from time to time. Most of the alcohol in Pitkas arrived illegally. However, there were a few ways to legally obtain it. While St. Mary's and Pitkas were mostly inaccessible by land in the summer, during winter one could make the trek on a "snow machine" (snowmobile in the 'lower forty-eight') to one of the neighboring villages that wasn't dry. But at a mere 30 to 40 miles per hour, this was often a long and arduous journey. Yet to many, it was worth the effort.

Regardless how the family living in Pitkas got the whiskey, when John broke into their house, he rifled through their possessions and found the bottle of amber liquid.

When John took his first drink, he found it foul, and it burned his throat. But he also knew it was illegal, motivating him to take another drink. It was through shear will that he finished that first bottle.

Later that night, John found himself sick and vomiting. Although it really made little sense, John sought another bottle the next day. It wasn't necessarily the high that led him to seek more whiskey (although he had enjoyed that part of it), but that it was forbidden.

When the first bottle had turned up missing, there was no question amongst the residents of St. Mary's whom was to blame. First: John's reputation had preceded him, even at the tender age of eleven.

Second: he was the only child in the village of Pitkas, vomiting all night and reeking of alcohol.

As the years passed, all in the village knew of John and his extracurricular activities. All, except the bush pilots.

In Alaska, because of the lack of roads, most goods were moved around by air. Pilots would come from all over the world to fly light airplanes into and out of the short gravel strips ubiquitous in almost every bush village.

Yet, since the bush pilots came from all over the world (primarily from the lower forty-eight states), they mostly didn't integrate into the community of the Alaskan villages. To a man, none of the bush pilots knew of John Alexi.

So, no one was prepared, late one night, when a shadowy figure broke out a pane of glass in each building serving as offices at the St. Mary's airport.

John was unseen as he crept around looking for money, or better, whisky, lying around the deserted offices.

His efforts in the first building turned up very little. The second building, even less. He made some progress with the third building, finding twelve dollars in one desk. However, the fourth building made his crime spree worth the effort.

As he crept through the building, at first glance it appeared there was nothing worth having. However, he continued to rifle around, looking for some hidden stash of money. He even removed pictures from the walls, hoping to find a hidden safe. This was a silly notion as John wouldn't have the first clue how to gain entry into a safe if he found one. But such ideas were inviting to him, so he continued his search. This, ironically, was how he made his biggest score.

Behind the desk of the third building, John removed a picture from the wall (he had removed 3 others so far), and once again met with disappointment until he looked at the backside of the picture he had just removed. There he saw something that made his heart leap. Taped to the backside of the picture was a crisp, new $100 bill!

John quickly tore the money from the back of the picture. In his haste, he ripped off one edge of the bill. He then took the part that had separated from it and quickly absconded with the haul and made his way home where he went immediately to sleep.

When he woke the next morning, John taped the torn section of the bill back into place. He then headed back to the airport where none knew him. As the bush operators were grousing about replacing the broken windows, John headed to the general aviation part of the field and hitched a ride to Bethel.

From there he could hitchhike on a series of small planes all the way to Anchorage. There, despite his young age, he could fund a bender that would last for three days.

When he landed in Anchorage, hitching a ride across town wasn't difficult. On Northern Lights Blvd., John found a small liquor store. The attendant working that evening was unwilling to sell the bottle of Jack Daniels to the underaged man. However, when presented with the possibility of a hundred dollars, John persuaded the older man that a one for two special would be worthwhile. That was to say, John would buy one bottle for the price of two. The clerk would make a nice profit from the difference.

That night the owner of the small liquor store arrived and saw that several bottles of stock were now missing. But as he collected the profits from that day, everything tallied correctly. He had no way of knowing that half of the bottles the $100 paid for were now tucked away safely in the clerk's car out back. As the owner surveyed the day's take he noticed that besides the smaller bills, there was also a $100 bill. Further, he noticed that a corner of the large bill had been ripped off and taped back in place. The next morning, he went directly to the local bank to make sure it was still good.

When the liquor store's owner showed the bill to the teller, he was assured that both pieces matched, as did the serial numbers. The $100 was valid. The owner made the deposit and went on his way.

As the liquor store owner left, the teller returned to the bill. While examining the serial numbers earlier, he had noticed that the bill in question was over ten years old. This was not unheard of, but it was a little out of place.

Being a good employee, the banker reported the serial number, knowing that nothing would come of the report—after all, it never had in the past. But he did his duty, anyway.

It somewhat surprised him when he was ordered to take possession of the bill until a treasury official could collect it from him later in the day. He was told that, although there was no problem with the serial number, treasury wanted to look over the money for possible counterfeiting. After all, a decade old "new" bill was suspicious. Best not to take any chances.

Twenty minutes later, a man in a dark suit arrived and exchanged a new bill for the suspicious currency.

As the man in the suit (unusual for Anchorage) left the bank, everything returned to normal. Of course, "returned" was perhaps a bit of an overstatement. Nothing had really been out of the ordinary to begin with, had it?

"Director Owens, Special Agent Stephens to see you."

"Thank you, Linda. Show him in."

Paul got out of his chair and crossed the room to meet Greg as he entered. The two men embraced as old friends. Paul's secretary softly closed the door behind them.

"It's been too long," Paul said as he showed his friend to the chair on the other side of the desk.

"I know. What's it been? Two years?"

"I think closer to three. How long have you been in Washington now?"

Greg looked to the ceiling and then answered. "Believe it or not, almost four years."

"And we've only gotten together twice."

"No," Greg corrected him, "three times. Don't forget your 50th birthday party."

Paul snorted. "Hardly counts. All of Washington was there. What happened?"

"We're both chasing career. You've done pretty well for yourself. Deputy Director of Treasury."

Paul nodded. "I'm enjoying it. You've done well too. I heard you're now working directly for Mark Felt. Associate Director at FBI."

Greg smiled. "Yeah, he's a great guy. Strong moral compass."

Paul's smile faded. "We need more of that right about now."

Greg nodded his agreement.

After a moment, Paul said, "Actually, my new position came with a few perks."

Greg looked around. "I hope the office wasn't one of them."

Paul laughed in return. "No, not that. But they have given me some latitude on fishing."

Greg raised an eyebrow. "How's that?"

"Well, a few weeks ago a very old fish washed up on shore. My new position gave me the clout to throw a few lines in the water and see if there was anything worth going after."

Greg now leaned in and lowered his voice in a conspiratorial tone. "What did you find?"

"One of the bills from the ransom."

"There were only two unaccounted for."

"I know."

"That's the first lead in almost a decade."

"I know."

"All right. Now *I'm* hooked. Where'd you find it?"

"Anchorage, Alaska."

Greg looked crestfallen as he slumped back in his chair. "Alaska? Oh hell, Paul. That could mean anything. No way you can trace a single bill back to its owner there."

"Really?"

Now Greg re-engaged. "You found something?"

"Oh, ye of little faith. Would I have dragged you halfway across town if I hadn't?"

"What did you find?"

"I'll admit my first reaction on finding the bill was elation. That was probably the best ten seconds of my life. Followed directly by the letdown of my life when I realized what you just did: Alaska's far too large to trace a single bill back to its owner. And even if I did, there's little chance that it would turn up anything. Another dead end."

"So, what happened? Why am I here today?"

"Fate intervened."

"How so."

"Three days after the news, I was at a reception on K Street and the Secretary was there…"

"Which one?"

"My boss. Simon. Secretary of the Treasury. Anyway, we've met a few times and I'm friendly with the guy and he introduces me to another gentleman who asked what my most interesting case was. Well, I started telling him about some old operation when Secretary Simon leans in and whispers, '*What about the good one*?'

"I look around the room and there's hustle and bustle everywhere; lots of ambient noise. So, I lowered my tone and the Secretary and his friend lean in and I tell them about *our* case."

"What happened?"

Paul leaned back and looked out of the window before continuing. "I told them how we found

Mansfield's place and the obits on everyone and how we relegated the case to the cold files.

"The Secretary then asked if there had been any fresh leads since moving the case into storage. I told him, ironically, the first fresh lead turned up earlier that week. But it was a thin one. One in a Million chance really, and not worth pursuing. The chance that it would pay out could never justify the cost."

"And?"

Paul grinned. "He asked me to elaborate. I did. He told me to let him worry about the money. He wanted me to follow the lead."

"No!"

"Oh, yes. I even told him I wanted my old partner back. He told me to start my fishing. If I got any nibbles, he would see to it I got whatever I needed."

"And?"

"You're here, aren't you?"

"Holy shit, Paul! You found Powell?"

"I've got a line. We traced the money back to some low life who comes from one of the villages out there. Never even would have found that if it wasn't so bizarre that such a character had had a hundred-dollar bill on him."

"Do you have Powell?"

"We think we might. We have a lead. I'm putting my pieces in place right now. I want confirmation before we act. We let this guy slip through our fingers once before. It won't happen again."

Greg leaned in. "Paul, you know we're going to have a problem with the statute of limitations."

Paul nodded. "We've thought of that. We may not get him on the theft, but air piracy doesn't have such constraints. Regardless, if we get the guy, we'll find something and make it stick."

Greg got up and paced the room a couple of times, lost in thought. He finally looked back at Paul. "What kind of timetable are we looking at here. I still have my caseload I'm dealing with."

"This thing will move fast. I want to get my people in place, but that shouldn't take very long. I don't see this going more than a couple of months. And this isn't like last time. We'll be running everything from here. We won't have to be on site. But even from here, it will be worth it. You know, closure."

Greg stood and extended his hand. "Closure would be nice. This bastard's been hanging over my head long enough. Let's put this one to bed. Once and for all."

Paul stood and accepted his hand, shaking it firmly. "Agreed!"

"Great! Now, first thing's first," Paul said as the two men settled back into their chairs. "I think we need to get somebody physically up there to do some recon before charging in. What do you think?"

"I totally agree. We need boots on the ground." Greg leaned forward, his fingers steepled as he pondered the situation. A few moments later, a smile crept across his face.

"You have an idea?" Paul asked.

"I think I might. I know a guy. A pilot. Might be just the guy that can get us in close. Close enough to monitor Powell until we're ready to make our move."

Paul leaned back in his chair. "Just tell me what you need. I have the full backing of the Secretary. Whatever it is, we can make it happen."

Chapter Fifteen
The New Pilot

The speed of the propeller rendered its opaque blackness, invisible. Spinning at 2400 revolutions per minute, the small slice of blade was overtaken by the larger, empty void comprising the disk which provided propulsion for the small Cessna aircraft.

All of this, however, went unnoticed by the young man flying the plane. Since his teenaged years, Eric Johnson had spent the better part of his life in, or thinking about, airplanes. The fact that the propeller was in front of him was a million miles from his thoughts. His thoughts were instead on the vast, open land on the other side of the rotating disk. The vast emptiness of the Alaskan landscape.

Eric was not from Alaska. He was from, culturally, as far from Alaska as one could get. He had been born and raised on an island. Not a remote, deserted island. Nor was it a primitive, uncultured island (although in Eric's mind it was). Eric had been born on the island of Manhattan, in the great City of New York. And he hated it. Ever since he could remember, Eric felt a crush of humanity, as a sea of people swarmed around him.

He was the only son of two working parents. His father had been a police officer with the NYPD, and his mother a secretary working for a Wall Street firm. The pressures of two working parents resulted in very little time for family life. Not that they neglected him. His parents made time for their son whenever they could, but the oppressive expense of living in New York City forced both to spend far more time earning a living, rather than living a life. This resulted in solitude for young Eric. Solitude, while growing up amidst a sea of humanity.

It wasn't until Eric turned sixteen that he found an escape from that which suffocated him. It was at his high school, PS110, in his junior year, that Eric attended a career fair. A career fair that produced the most unlikely of results—it resulted in him finding a career.

Eric had been meandering from booth to booth when he saw a table with a man in a dark suit, white shirt and black tie. Upon the sleeves of his jacket there were four golden stripes, and on the man's head was a white hat. But the coup de grâce of the ensemble were the golden wings on the man's breast. The imposing figure whom had so completely captivated young Eric's attention was a Pilot for Pan American World Airways, there to spread the gospel of aviation.

Eric was afraid to approach the man at first. Something about him seemed celestial. As if Eric was only a mortal, daring to scale Mount Olympus, and converse with the residents whom occupied the mythical peak. So struck by this man, Eric turned to seek more obtainable pursuits, when the man... this *airline captain...* singled Eric out and beckoned him closer.

Eric hesitantly yielded to the call as the pilot asked the question that would change the course of the young man's life: "Have you ever felt free?" This was a concept that Eric could not grasp. It wasn't until the pilot told him that the greatest freedom he would ever experience was found above the earth, rather than being tethered to it, that Eric's entire outlook on life changed.

This simple question sparked a conversation. A conversation that sparked a friendship that would forever change the course of Eric's life.

Three days later (on a Saturday) Eric and Captain McCarthy were sitting in a Cessna 150, taking off out of a small airstrip in New Jersey.

It was in that instant, as the plane broke ground and climbed into the sky, that Eric truly understood the question Captain McCarthy had posed earlier. For the first time in his young life, Eric felt free. Free from the crush and free from the onerous planet to which he was born.

At seventeen, Eric was the only student in his school with a pilot's license. At eighteen he had obtained his commercial pilot's certificate.

Eric's mentor encouraged him to pursue a job with the airlines. Captain McCarthy had dreamed of one day having his protégé sit next to him in a Pan Am Clipper. Eric, eager to please his friend, tried to follow that route. He spent a little time in formal education. A couple of years attending classes in a junior college, but at twenty he sadly realized that formal education, much like city life, was not for him. Much to the dismay of both his parents and Captain McCarthy, Eric left school. All knew that without a college degree, a pilot without military experience would have a hard time finding employment with an airline. However, Eric realized that an airline career would ultimately be as stifling as living in the city. He wanted to recapture that feeling of freedom he felt on that first flight. And he knew that he would never be happy in New York, or any big city near it.

Eric started by moving west. He had romantic dreams of finding employment as a crop duster, or other jobs where a pilot could fly in total freedom. Dreams that came in sharp contrast with reality.

It took almost six months of working various odd jobs (jobs that did not include flying) before Eric found his way to Alaska. It was in Alaska that Eric found the frontier he had been seeking.

Eric had been in Alaska less than a month before he talked his way into a job flying for a shuttle service between Anchorage and the fishing destination of Kenai. Although this was a brief flight (typically a 28-minute flight in a Cessna 206), and very repetitious (he often made the round trip five times a day), it provided him with valuable experience flying in Alaska.

After a little more than a year, Eric moved on to a bigger plane... if only slightly: The Piper Cherokee 6.

And with the new plane, he also left the big city of Anchorage, and moved to a remote village: Dillingham. As villages go, it wasn't as rough as some on the Yukon/Kuskokwim Delta, but it was a far cry from the civilization of Anchorage. It also paid more. After less than a year of working for this new airline, Eric earned enough money to buy his own plane.

In most areas, owning a plane would seem a wild extravagance. However, as with most things in Alaska, what holds in the lower forty-eight does not apply there. In Alaska it is common to find that many families own a plane, but not a car. This was the case for Eric.

Eric had bought a used Cessna 150, similar to the plane he had first learned to fly in. The Cessna was a small single-engine plane with high-mounted wings and two seats. With only a one hundred horsepower engine, it was limited in its speed and endurance. To most looking at the plane, they only saw a small, cramped machine good for nothing more than basic flight instruction. However, to Eric, this was the most beautiful device ever created. It was one hundred horsepower of pure freedom! It was enough to get him around the wilds of central Alaska and opened the entire world to him. It was Eric's means of escape. Whenever he felt the gravity of the planet threaten to crush him, and his soul along with him, he needed only to board this plane and he could escape and find genuine happiness.

It was when Eric finally achieved his goal of aircraft ownership, that he dared sever his ties with his current employer and head deeper into the Alaskan frontier. He had a dream and little more. But for Eric, that was enough.

He looked out of the window on the clear summer's day, and he could see a dirt landing strip floating in the distant hills. Few, even in Alaska, would know of the village of St. Mary's. Fewer still in the rest of the country could even grasp the concept of its existence. But Eric knew it. But more important than the village, Eric knew of a pilot who lived there. A pilot named Jake Roth. A pilot who was said to be the best bush pilot in all of Alaska.

For hours, the constant whine from the propeller remained unchanged. The land passing below the small plane was unchanged as well. The only changes were that of the needles showing the level of the fuel in the wings of the Cessna. Once steady on the *F* for full, they were now bouncing around the *E* for empty. Yet Eric remained unfazed. He knew his plane. And besides, his destination was now just within sight.

Eric made a slight correction on the yoke, then called on the common traffic air frequency.

"St. Mary's traffic, Cessna two-six-November turning final, landing St. Mary's."

Now, for the first time in what seemed forever, the sound of the engine changed. As Eric eased back on the small knob serving as throttle, the pitch dropped.

Also, before him, the invisible propeller now darkened slightly as the revolutions of the disk slowed.

The day was pleasant, and the pilot gave no thought as the wheels of the plane made rough contact with the hard-packed dirt and gravel of the runway.

Unconsciously, Eric turned the plane and headed to one of the small buildings on the far side of the field.

Eric maneuvered the plane across the mostly deserted ramp until bringing it to a stop in front of a series of buildings. Once he had found his parking area, he pulled the red knob next to the throttle, and the engine shuddered and then stopped. The steady drone of the motor and propeller were now silent. Silence enveloped the pilot as he removed the large green David Clark headsets which encased his ears, protecting his hearing from the constant drone of the Cessna, save the ticking of the motor as it cooled.

Eric pulled the latch, popping the door open. Even though it was a beautiful summer day, the air was still cool and crisp. In the small cockpit of the plane, the temperature on the flight had been a comfortable 75 degrees. The air that rushed in to greet Eric was a cool sixty-five, made all the cooler by the ten-knot wind blowing across the ramp.

Eric swung his legs out, stepping onto the hard-packed gravel comprising the runway and ramp of the airport. After hours of flight, it felt good to emerge from his small cocoon and stretch. His muscles were far more fatigued than he realized. He unconsciously pulled off a red baseball cap and ruffed his hair, matted to his head after hours under the cap. After replacing the hat, he allowed himself a few brief moments to rejoice in the pain that greeted his tired muscles before heading purposely toward the weather-worn building under the gnarled sign of Y/K Air.

The airport was unlike any commercial field located anywhere in the 'lower forty-eight' states. On the far end of the field there were a series of five small bungalow-style buildings built one next to the other. All the buildings were old and dilapidated, with peeling paint and what appeared to be years of filth and dirt crusting them. The buildings were also built on stilts, raising the actual structures a little more than a foot above the ground. Each building had stairs, made of battered pine, leading up to the doors. Above each building was a sign, exhibiting the operator it served. The names of *Yute, Hagelands, Chami* and *Y/K Air* were old and weathered. It was obvious that they had seen many seasons out here, with little attention to up-keep. The last building had the sign *Northern Central*. Unlike the other signs, it appeared to be brand new. Further, the building below it seemed far cleaner than the other structures. The first three buildings had one pane of glass missing in each, with plywood covering the gap. In the building identified as Y/K Air, there was a clean pane of glass in the same position as the plywood in the other buildings. Of the four structures, that pane of glass was the only clean window in the place.

Beyond the five offices was a small hangar, large enough to house only small, single-engine planes. Beyond that were three rows of various aircraft, secured to the ramp with linked-chain tie-downs.

On the other side of the buildings, set farther back, was a large fueling station. The ramp next to it was sizeable enough to house a jet aircraft. Eric had been in Alaska long enough to know that some larger operators served small communities like this with 737s or DC-9s, but he had a difficult time imagining anything larger than a twin-engine prop plane coming into the tiny village.

As Eric moved across the ramp, to anyone looking out at him, they might be somewhat puzzled by the sight. Eric looked the part of a bush pilot. He wore a ball cap, a gray jacket over an old tee shirt. Blue jeans and tennis shoes completed the ensemble. His clothing was faded and worn, and while not dirty, they weren't exactly clean either. Under the red ball cap, blonde hair protruded in all directions. His hair was neither long nor short. Just the right length to fit in with those whom he shared a profession in this area.

Yet, he didn't quite fit in either. While most in the area looked worn and weathered by the harsh Alaskan environment, Eric looked different. If anyone were to take a closer look at the young man, the word that would best describe him would be... pretty.

Eric had a thin build and fair features. He was clean shaven and had sparkling blue eyes. In his youth, he had never had much trouble finding a date. However, he found little in common with the girls in New York. Although there were several first dates in Eric's past, after spending hours of listening to Eric expound upon the virtues of flying, there were few second dates. Eric's biggest motivation with girls tended more to the challenge than the companionship. He was drawn to women who were deemed unobtainable. For Eric it wasn't the date, but the challenge of proving that he could do what others before him had failed to achieve.

Eric walked down the row of old, dilapidated buildings, studying each one. The airport was silent, as it was later in the day. Most of the planes were out making their last runs or put away for the evening. The only sounds were the wind blowing and the crunch of gravel under his feet. When Eric arrived at the fourth building, he wondered if this was the correct one, or if it was abandoned. Reaching for the door, he found it unlocked.

When Eric pulled open the door, it moved easily. The hinges were well oiled and didn't make a sound. As he took a few tentative steps inside, he found the room dark. There were no lights on. The only illumination provided was from the bright sunlight outside that filtered into the room through the dirty windows.

However, despite the low light, the room was actually rather inviting. In the far corner of the room was a large rug next to a now-dormant cast-iron stove. The walls were lined with several bookshelves, and an assortment of pictures of airplanes. At the center of the rug was a large, low-sitting circular table. Around that were six over-stuffed, black leather chairs. Across from the chairs was a large, dark couch. During his time in the Alaskan bush, Eric had found most of the furnishings to be rather old and worn. Everything here seemed well cared for and in good repair. Rather than a bush operator, this building felt more like an insufficiently lit ski-lodge.

As Eric looked round, his eyes adjusted slowly to the semi-light. He was slightly surprised to hear a woman's voice.

"May I help you?"

Eric turned left, to the direction of the voice. There he saw someone only in shadow sitting at a large desk.

"I'm sorry. I'm looking for Jake." Nothing. "Jake Roth."

"I knew which Jake you meant." The voice was unquestionably that of a woman. Eric could not see her through the darkness, but her voice sounded cold and distant.

Eric blushed despite himself. "Of course you did. Is Mr. Roth around?"

Now there was a laugh. It was if someone had thrown a switch. Her laugh was light and pretty. The coldness of her voice only a moment ago seemed to give way to a friendlier tone. "Mr. Roth? I think you had it right the first time, son."

"OK. Jake then. Is he around?"

"Oh, I'm sure he's around somewhere."

Eric fidgeted uncomfortably. "Well, I was hoping to see him."

"Maybe I can help you. Do you need something delivered? Or are you looking for a charter?"

"No, ma'am. I'm a pilot and was hoping to talk to Mr., uh, Jake about…" he trailed off.

"Sorry son, but we don't need any more pilots."

"But you have three planes." Eric moved more boldly into the room, towards the silhouette he was talking with. Behind him, the door slammed shut. Ignoring the bang, he continued, "I know you have two other pilots besides Jake, so I was hoping that I could serve as a floater. Someone to give the guys a break on their days off."

The woman struck a match. The sudden flash of light startled Eric momentarily. The light also illuminated the woman's face. She was pretty, but older than him. She looked to be in her mid-thirties. She had blonde hair pulled back in a ponytail. Her face was not what Eric had expected from their brief conversation. From her initial tone he had expected someone hard and weathered, but she appeared pretty and somewhat delicate. She looked out of place in this wilderness.

The light from the match quickly dimmed to a faint illumination and then produced a red glow as the flame contacted the end of the cigarette.

After a few glowing red beacons from the tobacco, she waved the match out and took a long drag before answering.

"You're welcome to wait, but I don't think he'll be interested."

Eric searched for the right words. He didn't want to offend the woman, but he wasn't about to give up either.

"I don't mind waiting. When will he be back?"

She waved her hand. "Hell if I know. He left an hour ago with a load going up to Unalakleet. But, he had his fishing pole in the plane as well so, who knows."

Eric nodded. "OK. Well, if it's OK with you, I'll just go fuel my plane and wait around then."

"We have gas here. Pumps around the corner."

"Great," Eric said with an enthusiasm he did not feel. "How much a gallon?"

She laughed. "Honey, we have the only gas pump in the area. Unless you can make it to Bethel, you'll pay whatever I say."

Eric nodded uncomfortably. "Sounds like a good point. I guess I'll just bring my plane around and fuel it."

"Good idea. When you're done, you're welcome to wait in here."

Eric nodded as he backed out of the door. "Great. I'll do that." He then stumbled as he made his way back outside.

The sun hadn't even begun to set when Jake finally arrived. Sunset at this time of year wouldn't be until a little before midnight. However, it was late enough in the day that Eric was nodding off as he sat in the large, comfortable leather chair in the dimly lit building.

"And who is this?"

The voice had an edge to it, but somehow there was no menace behind it. Even as the voice startled Eric out of his drowse, there was a kindness that was hard to pinpoint.

Eric looked up and saw a man dressed in blue jeans and a Pink Floyd tee shirt standing over him, looking down.

The man's hair was shaggy and covered his ears and collar. He looked to be in his mid to late thirties, but it was hard to tell. He had a rather youthful appearance, however there were a few telltale signs of age, such as small lines about the eyes and touches of gray in his jet-black hair. He also had a beard. However, rather than being shaggy and unkempt (like the beards of the other pilots Eric had worked with), Jake's was neatly trimmed and short. The beard was also jet black with touches of gray taunting the man's age.

Eric sat up and said, "Mr. Roth?"

The man glanced over at the woman still sitting at the desk and then back at the young man before him. Eric's eyes had adjusted to the dim light in the building. He also realized that outside illumination wasn't only thing lighting the room. Now, a few dimly lit bulbs were shining overhead. As he looked at the pretty woman still behind the desk, he saw her roll her eyes.

Eric cleared his throat. "I mean, Jake?"

The smile was easy and Jake fell into another oversized leather chair beside Eric.

"So, Jen here tells me you want to talk."

"Yes, sir. My name's Eric. Eric Johnson and I want to fly for you."

Jake gave Eric a sad smile and a shrug. "Only have three planes. And I already have two pilots. Including me, we have a full boat. Sorry."

"I understand that, but here's what I'm thinking: You have three pilots and three planes, but that would mean that no one gets any time off. If I were to fly for you, you could set up a schedule that could rotate guys, providing some downtime, while increasing the time your current planes are in the air. It's a total win/win. It would work out perfectly."

"Eric, I like your enthusiasm, but it wouldn't work out. I know it sounds like a great idea, but I'm barely getting enough business to keep my planes flying as much as they are. I only have a few mail contracts, and passenger travel is sporadic. It's enough to make ends meet, but that's about it. And that's summer flying. In the winter, business really dries up."

"But it's summer right now. Maybe I could fly for you until the end of the season."

Off in the distance, across the room, Jen struck a match. Her face illuminated as she lit a cigarette.

Both men turned and watched her until she waved out the flame. Once the cherry of the burning cigarette started floating under the dim light of the two bulbs, the two men faced each other again.

"Eric, there are lots of places here that would be happy to have a young man like you flying for them. There's a new operator that just opened up next door. They only have one pilot and one plane, but I'll bet they'd be thrilled to have another body join them. I'd be happy to tell them we've talked, and that I think they'd be lucky to get you."

Eric exhaled, tired from the long day's flight and from the long evening of waiting. "Jake, I don't want to fly for them. I could get a job flying anywhere."

"Anywhere?"

Eric waved his hand. "Well, enough places that I wouldn't be sent packing back to New York. Yes, I wanted to fly in Alaska. And I have. I've done well up here. I've already spent a couple of years flying in the bush, and somehow I've managed *not* to bend any metal." Eric sneered, "When it comes to finding a job,

I don't need your charity. I can find a job by myself. I wanted to fly for you because everyone says you're the best." At this comment, Jen rolled her eyes and started to shake her head. Undeterred, Eric continued. "I wanted knowledge. The upstart next door can't provide that. You can. Or, at least, I thought you could."

Jake looked at the woman smoking across the room and then back at Eric. He then leaned back in the large chair and chuckled.

"What?"

"It just seems like a unique approach to getting hired, that's all."

Eric, wearing a confused expression, shook his head. "What are you talking about?"

"Well, usually when someone's looking for a job, they come in, meet the boss and then kiss his ass. Now, don't get me wrong. You started off strong. I felt really bad when I told you no. But usually, what happens next is the candidate in question—that would be you—then politely accepts the rejection, hoping to keep any potential job opportunities down the road open. You know, instead of tearing into the boss, therefore killing any chance for future employment."

The color drained from Eric's face as the meaning of Jake's words sunk in. "I killed any chance I might have had. Didn't I?"

Across the room, Jen started laughing as she stubbed out her cigarette. "You would have, if my husband had any sense about him."

"Excuse me?" Eric said.

"Jen's always yammering on that the only reason I kept pursuing her was because she kept shooting me down. She now thinks that just because you started berating me, that I'm now going to offer you a job. However," Jake glanced across the room at Jen and shot her a warning glance, "she would be wrong." He then looked back at Eric. "You do understand that don't you?"

Eric's expression was one of bewilderment. "Honestly, I'm not sure, sir."

Jen called out, "Eric, if you're going to work here, one thing I won't have you doing, is calling that man 'sir.' Words like that will go straight to his head."

Jake stood up and stared across the room. "Look Jen, I won't have you showing me that kind of disrespect. Especially in front of an impressionable young man like this."

Jen stood as well. "And I, Jake, am the one that cuts the checks around here. So, If I say the boy's our new pilot, then the boy's our new pilot."

Eric watched in utter confusion as the two continued to go after one another, not knowing what to think. Finally, Eric stood, inserting himself back into the conversation. "Jen, I appreciate what you're trying to do for me, but if there isn't enough flying…"

"Eric, you stay out of this," Jake cut him off.

"But you said…"

"Eric, as your boss, don't make me tell you again."

"Boss?"

"Which one?" Jen asked.

Jake shrugged. "Leon?"

"Of course, Leon, you idiot. I knew Leon. I meant what airline."

Jake held up his finger and started to say something and then stopped himself momentarily. "Good point. Yes, well, I was thinking Wien. Leon wants to move, but not too far away. Anchorage isn't that far. And they fly out here, so we would still see him occasionally. I can call Steve. He owes me a favor."

Eric said, "Excuse me?"

"He is a chatty little one, isn't he?" Jen said.

Jake shrugged. "I'll give him the benefit of the doubt and go with 'inquisitive.'"

Eric opened his mouth again, but Jake cut him off. "We are discussing which one of my pilots to get rid of, so you can work for me. I was serious when I said that we didn't have enough business to employ a fourth pilot."

"Jake, I want the job, but I don't want…"

"Relax there, Ace," Jen said. "You're not causing anyone to lose their job. And we aren't discussing '*who to get rid of.*' We both knew it would be Leon. We were discussing where Leon is going to go. Leon's been antsy for a while. Want's to fly jets, but we don't think he wants to leave Alaska. Jake here thinks Wien Air Alaska would be the best place for him. Don't worry, you're helping someone move up, not out."

Jake said, "Eric, sit."

Eric and Jake settled back into their chairs and Jen came around to join them. She took a seat on the large couch across from the two chairs.

"Eric, if you're here for money, you've come to the wrong place. Almost every other bush operator out here pays better than me. If you're here for experience—you said you wanted to learn from me— I can help you out there. However, in all honesty, I'm really not any better than most of the other pilots out here. However, if—and I mean *if*—you're here to have fun... well, we might have a fit."

"Look, Eric," Jen said, "Jake thinks of this place as his personal toy shop. He keeps just enough business to cover the bills. Unlike most of the other operators, we fly here as little as possible, not as much as we can."

"But why...?"

"Eric, do you like flying?"

Eric looked Jake in the eye. "More than anything."

"And you're going to have an entire lifetime of it. Why burn yourself out now? We're lucky guys: we found what we love and get paid to do it. You seem like a nice young man. Jen likes you. If nothing else, that would be enough for me. But I also like the way you stood up for yourself."

"Bullshit," Jen said under her breath.

Jake turned to face her. "Excuse me?"

"You heard me. I said bullshit! You liked that he said you were the best pilot out here."

Jake seemed to reflect on this for a few moments. "I wouldn't use the word 'liked.' I think it would be more accurate to say, I respect the boy's judgement."

Jen rolled her eyes. "Whatever."

"Anyway," Jake said, returning his attention to the young man next to him, "are you still interested in working here?"

"Are you serious? When do I start?"

Both Jake and Jen started chuckling again. "Go tie down your plane. I'll get a permanent spot for it tomorrow. You can come home with us and spend the night in our guest room. Leon will be out of the pilot's house, probably in a week or three. Like I said, I'll make some calls tonight. Once he's gone, you can take his place."

"I don't want to put you out."

"Really? If you're not staying with us, where will you sleep?"

"I have a tent. On a summer night like this, that's more than enough."

"I've heard about some guys doing that. But there are three problems." Jake held up a finger. "The mosquitoes might carry you away overnight." He held up a second finger. "If you're going to work for me, I want to get to know you." Then he held up a third finger. "Jen is a wonderful cook—I can't even joke about that one—that's how good she is. How could I live with myself knowing I've deprived you of a wonderful meal? It's the least I can provide you with when you see what I'm going to pay you."

A look of concern washed over Eric's face. "Just how bad *is* the pay?"

Jake and Jen started laughing anew. "We can talk about it over dinner tonight."

Greg had been in the office for only fifteen minutes, drinking coffee and going over some reports when the phone rang.

"Stephens," he answered.

"Greg, its Paul. I just got word. We're in."

Chapter Sixteen

Alaska

The house was not what Eric had expected. Just after Eric had finished tying down his plane, Jake and Jen swung around in their jeep. Eric pulled a small bag out of the back of the Cessna and threw it in the back seat, taking the seat beside it.

"Is that all you have?" Jake asked.

"I like to travel light." Eric answered with a shrug.

"Oh, you're going to love the pay here then," Jen said with a wink.

Eric was catching on to the sense of humor of the two and took the comment with a chuckle. Even Jake's comment, "She's not kidding, sport," didn't break his good mood.

The drive from the airport to the village was longer than most drives would have been in the region. In St. Mary's, the airport was miles from the village. In most Alaskan villages, the runway was longer than the village itself and usually ended in the outskirts of the buildings.

In St. Mary's, you had to take a long dirt road a few miles through the rolling hills until you arrived at anything habitable.

As Eric looked out of the dirt-caked windows, he saw a series of old buildings. It looked more like a ghost town one would find in an old western movie than a place people were living in the twentieth century.

Finally, near the center of town, Jake pulled into a short driveway and shut down the jeep. He followed Jake and Jen as they opened the doors of the vehicle and emerged into the dusky Alaskan evening.

The house was not large. It looked about the size of the apartment in which Eric grew up in Manhattan. The building was brown, and the paint was peeling in several areas. The building also stood atop stilts, elevating the structure a foot in the air. As Eric looked around, he saw that every building in the area was constructed the same way. This was because of the silt which comprised the Yukon/Kuskokwim Delta. There was not a solid foundation to be found. The winters were harsh and the elevated construction helped protect them from the elements.

Eric followed Jake and Jen up a short flight of worn, wooden steps as Jake opened a black door. Unlike most of the buildings, the door looked like it had been freshly painted.

Inside, Jake flipped a switch. Eric had expected more dim lights like he had experienced in the office at the airport. Instead, the house was bathed in a warm, inviting glow. As Eric followed the couple into the house, everything looked pristine. Eric had been in Alaska long enough to know what to expect from most dwellings there. The furnishings were usually ancient and long past their shelf life. Typically showing their age, and their exposure to the harsh environment Alaska fostered. However, in this house, everything looked shiny and new.

"That will be your room, there," Jen said, motioning to a door on the right side of a short hall.

Eric followed Jake, who led him to the door. As he followed, he took in everything in the small house.

Jen split from the two and headed to a beautiful kitchen and ignited a burner under a teakettle.

"I'm going to make some tea. Would either of you like tea or coffee," she asked.

"I'm good. You, Eric?"

Eric shook his head. "No. I'm kinda wiped."

Jake smiled as he opened the door to the spare room. "I don't doubt it. It sounds like you had a long day. Why don't you just settle in and get some sleep? We can talk tomorrow morning over breakfast."

Eric nodded as he entered the room. Jake switched on the light. Inside was a large, inviting queen-sized bed. The walls looked like they had a fresh coat of paint and were adorned with pictures of various planes.

"The bathroom is at the end of the hall. If you need anything, Jen and I are in the room across from this one. Plan on breakfast at seven."

Eric nodded and said, "Thanks, Jake."

Jake smiled. "Not a problem. See you tomorrow. Sleep well."

Eric woke to the sound of a door slamming shut. Moments later he heard several loud voices. Eric blinked several times as he looked around the room. Slowly, the events of the previous day came flooding back to him and he regained his bearings.

It took Eric a few minutes to muster the energy to roll out of bed. Once he did, he quickly pulled on his tee-shirt and jeans. Dressed, he glanced at the clock on the nightstand. It was five minutes after seven.

As Eric emerged from the room, his hair askew and bare footed, he was greeted by Jake's voice, overpowering the conversation in the room.

"I believe I said breakfast would be at seven."

Trying to find his footing, Eric offered lamely, "I'm not really all that hungry."

In protest to his lie, his stomach gave a loud grumble. From across the room, Jen said, "Would you please give the boy a break? He came all this way so he could kiss your ass. The least you can do is give him a meal." She turned to Eric and added, "How do you like your coffee?"

"Cream and sugar, please."

"You're going to need to learn to take it black if you're going to work for this asshole."

Eric turned and saw two men across the room. One wasn't much larger than he was. He was dressed in a tee-shirt with a blue button-down shirt, the top button opened. He had a boyish face, but it was apparent he was older than Eric, but younger than Jake. He was clean shaven and wore an amused smile. The other man, the man who had spoken, was by far the largest of the men in the room. He had dark hair and deep-set eyes. He also had a bushy beard which made him look menacing.

"So," the man spoke again, "you're the little piss-ant who took my job." Eric stood frozen in place as the entire room fell silent. The large man then moved closer to Eric, who stood immobile.

"Do you know what you've done to my life? Do you?" He moved inches from Eric and looked down on him. He must have been at least a foot taller than the boy. "Now," he said, as his face broke into a wide grin and he pointed at his beard, "I've got to shave this thing off!" He then took Eric in an embrace as everyone in the room started laughing.

"You must be Leon?" Eric offered, still unsure of what to make of the situation.

Still grinning, Leon released Eric and took his hand. "And you must be Eric. So glad you're here. I'd love to warn you off about this joker," he motioned to Jake, who gave him a 'who, me?' look, and continued, "but he hasn't gotten me the job with Wien yet."

"Leon, look, I never meant to take your job. As I told Jake last night, I just wanted to be a floater pilot. Someone who could take up the slack while you guys took days off."

The last man in the room approached Eric and took his hand in a firm handshake. "I'm Charlie and don't worry about it. Jake doesn't work like that. In fact, Jake doesn't work much at all, isn't that right, boss?" In response, Jake just gave another 'who me?' shrug. "But the good news is he doesn't make us work too hard either. But all this clown over here…"

"That would be me," Leon said.

"… keeps talking about is flying jets. He thinks it will be an easier gig than what Jake has us doing. So, I guess it's a win/win all around. Or at least it is for now until Leon the jet jock finds out what he's lost here and comes crying for his old job back."

"Not going to happen, Charlie. Not going to happen."

As the men spoke, Jen came over to Eric, who still looked somewhat unsure of the whole situation, and gave him a cup of coffee. She led him to a large table with five places set. As she did so, Jake started bringing over dishes of eggs and potatoes.

"He's a bright kid," Jake said. He set the food on the table and started scooping eggs on his plate. As he did so, Jen crossed the room and brought another plate with bacon and sausages. "He said that I was the best pilot in the area and that he wanted to learn from the best."

As Jake spoke the entire room—save Eric—groaned. Jen said, "I told you, Eric, that those words would come back to haunt you."

"Haunt *him*?" Charlie said, now filling his own plate, "They're going to haunt *all* of us!"

"Not me!" Leon said, waving a hand in the air. "I'm going to Anchorage to fly 737s for Wien."

"We know!" the room said in response.

Undeterred, Leon picked up several strips of bacon from the serving plate.

"Eric," Jake said, after taking a bite of eggs, "As you can see, we're more or less a family here."

"A dysfunctional family," Jen added.

"True. A dysfunctional family, but a family, nonetheless. We want you to feel welcome and at home. I've done the whole 'working for a living' thing, and frankly, it sucks. I find it far more rewarding to play for a living. I don't believe in long hours and I'm not much of one for high stress. But, if flying is a game, like any game, it is only fun if you push yourself. I like you. More importantly, Jen likes you. And the boys here seem to think you're OK too. So, we're going to give this a go. Leon the Jet Jock and Charlie will fly their regular schedule, and you'll be with me until we find a class date for Leon. Today we'll get off to a bit of a late start because I have a few calls I need to make, but the boys will pick up the slack. There'll be plenty of time for us to fly this afternoon. How does that sound?"

Eric took a sip of coffee and asked, "Will I be in a ground school?"

Jake shrugged. "You said you flew the 206 already, if I remember correctly."

"I did."

"OK. Good enough then. I deem ground school complete and you passed with flying colors. If you'll pardon the pun."

"Just don't screw up the checkride," Leon added. "I haven't gotten hired with Wien yet."

The room continued to laugh as Eric ate his breakfast.

"Easy on the throttle," Jake said as the Cessna 206 rolled on the gravel strip of Kotlik.

"I am being easy on the throttle," Eric replied in his defense.

"No, you're not. You're running up the power."

"Yeah, I am. How else would you get the plane moving?"

Jake eased on the brakes, halting the plane's motion. "OK Eric, my plane."

Eric took his hands off of the controls and raised them in the air. "Fine, your plane."

Jake took the throttle and fully closed it. The propeller in front of the plane was moving at its slowest speed. Jake then released his feet from the brakes. The plane remained static.

"See how we aren't moving at all?" Jake asked.

"Yeah," Eric replied in frustration.

"Now watch this." With his hands off the throttle, Jake started moving the yoke forward and aft repeatedly. As he did, the small plane's elevator moved up and down, causing the plane to pitch slightly up and down. After a few moments of doing this, the plane started rolling slowly. As the plane started its slow crawl down the gravel runway, Jake keyed the mic. "Kotlik traffic, Cessna Two Kilo Mike back-taxiing Kotlik."

As they continued to roll down the runway, the plane slowly picked up speed. Not once did Jake's hand touch the throttle.

When the plane reached the end of the strip, Jake made one more call alerting area traffic that they were departing and took his hands off of the controls. "Your plane, Eric."

Eric sighed in embarrassment. "My plane." Smoothly adding power, the plane started its roll down the rough runway. A little more than halfway down the strip, Eric eased back, and the plane broke ground.

They were now three days into Eric's employment. Things were moving forward smoothly. Leon had been given a class date of the following

Monday at Wein, and Eric had been flying with Jake, learning the lay of the land, until Leon departed.

A few minutes later they leveled off at a thousand feet.

"You said you wanted to learn from me."

Eric nodded. "I did."

Jake grinned. "Eric relax. It's OK that you don't know everything. If you run up the power the vortex from the prop will suck gravel into the blades, damaging them. If you pump the yoke, it will break the plane free and it will roll on its own."

"I should have known that."

"Why? Because of your years of experience flying on gravel strips?"

"I've been in Alaska for a while now."

Jake laughed. "A while? You've been here what? A couple of years? I've been here for a decade and count myself as wet behind the ears. Give yourself a break."

After a few minutes of silence, Eric asked, "What more do we have today, boss?"

Jake shrugged. "I think we're pretty much done for the day. Its Friday, and we don't have any more deliveries that I'm aware of. Also, you have a busy schedule ahead of you.

"I do?"

"Sure. Tomorrow is the block party."

"The what?"

"Block party. Every month we try to get together with all the pilots in St. Mary's and relax in a non-work environment. It will also be a good way for you to get to know the other guys working in the area.

"What else?"

"On Sunday you have to move. Leon will be leaving for Anchorage. Your spot will be open."

"In the pilot house?"

"Well, Jen and I aren't going to let you stay with us forever."

Eric rolled his eyes. "I'm moving a duffel bag next door."

Jake nodded. "See, a full day. We don't want to overdo it."

Eric chuckled as he continued back home.

A minute later Jake pointed at the Yukon River below them. "There's a straight stretch. How low are you comfortable going?"

Eric glanced over at his boss. "Lower than you'd be comfortable with."

Jake arched an eyebrow. "Oh, really?"

Now the hint of a smile touched the corner of Eric's expression. "Yeah, really."

"Show me."

Eric smoothly eased back on the throttle until the plane was at idle speed. The altimeter slowly unwound. Nine hundred. Eight hundred. It was at two hundred feet that Eric stole a glance at his boss. Jake's expression was serene.

Eric returned his attention to what lie ahead of the plane. The Yukon River was now prominent in the window as the tallest of the trees crept above the plane on either side of them. Below, the river flowed at an imperceptible rate, the water calm and glassy.

Eric thought of stealing another glance at Jake, but thought better of it. He was now below fifty feet and this maneuver would take all of his attention. If Jake didn't like it, he could call Eric off. Jake said nothing.

They were so low now that they couldn't see above the tree line. They were mere feet above the water and still losing altitude.

It was seconds later that the tires contacted the surface. A spray erupted from the calm water below them as the tires rode along the liquid. They continued like this for a few seconds before Eric added power and the plane left the surface of the river, climbing into the sky. It was a handful of seconds later as the tree-line fell away from them and the 206 ascended into the still air above them.

As they were passing through five hundred feet, Eric looked over at Jake. His expression was unchanged. He seemed to be taking in everything around him.

"Well?"

Jake shrugged. "Well, what?"

"Was that low enough?"

Jake nodded, grinning slightly. "I'll admit, I wasn't sure you'd touch the water."

Eric tried to keep his expression neutral, but a grin slipped through. "I wasn't sure you'd let me."

"Kind of bold move, though; touching the water with your boss next to you. Kind of displaying a recklessness that you might want to keep away from the guy signing your paycheck."

Eric shrugged. "You said you wanted low. I gave you low."

Jake looked out of the front of the window as they leveled off at a thousand feet. "Did you know you could make it?"

"I was pretty sure I could make it."

"Pretty sure?"

Eric shrugged. "Better than vaguely hopeful."

Jake leaned back in his seat and nodded. "Fair enough."

The planes that Jake used for the airline he had dubbed Yukon/Kuskokwim Air—or Y/K Air for short—was the Cessna 206. The 206 was a six-seated plane, allowing for five passengers and one pilot.

With a high wing and a 300-horsepower engine, it was exceptional for the environment. When Jake was establishing the airline, he knew the plane would be perfect for the operation and bought one at once. Initially, he started by carrying whatever he could. This was usually an almost equal mix of passengers and cargo. However, over time, Jake felt that the plane was better suited for the cargo side of the business and focused on maximizing his loads in this area of the operation. It wasn't long before Jake realized that mail would be an ideal way of providing a steady revenue stream. He then concentrated on getting a mail contract. It was the airline's second year of operation that he secured his first deal with the United States Postal Service. With the postal contract in place, he then started drawing down on his efforts to attract passengers and opted instead for more mail and freight. Not that he didn't carry passengers, he did. But as the years went on, unlike other airlines operating in the area, human cargo became less and less with the Y/K Air operation.

Another difference between Y/K Air and the competition was Jake's rule of having weekends off. It was common for small bush carriers to have Sundays off in the winter when the flying slowed down. There were even a few outfits that kept Sundays off year-round. But Y/K Air was the only airline in the Delta that didn't fly both Saturdays and Sundays on a year-round basis.

This was a new experience for Eric, whom had worked almost nonstop since he arrived in Alaska. On

Saturday morning, as Eric glanced over at the clock hands showing 8:45, he gained a new appreciation for Jake's work ethic. He could not remember the last time he had slept in that late.

After Eric finally dragged himself out of bed, the rest of the day was spent at a comfortable pace. With Jake, Jen, Charlie and Leon, he enjoyed a hearty breakfast of French Toast, bacon, eggs and fresh cinnamon rolls. They laughed good-naturedly as everyone teased Leon on how he would not be eating this well or sleeping in this late once he started with Wien.

Leon knew that there was a great deal of truth in the teasing he was receiving. He would now be on reserve for years, just waiting to be called out for a flight. He also would have little to no control over his schedule for the foreseeable future. Despite this, he had a hard time containing his excitement. While he would make more money, that had almost nothing to do with his excitement. It was the opportunity to fly jets that had Leon over the moon. In two days, Leon would start ground school, learning to fly the Boeing 737. It would go faster and higher than anything he had ever flown before. No amount of teasing could wipe the smile from the pilot's face.

The rest of the day was spent either reading or chatting as the rest of the world went on around them.

At four o'clock Jake rounded everybody up, telling them they would depart in ten minutes for the block party.

"Who all will be there?"

"Pretty much everybody. All the pilots based out of St. Mary's."

Eric made a face and asked, "You're saying that pilots for airlines we compete with are inviting us into their homes?"

"I'm sure you noticed, the flying up here goes fast and heavy during the week. Someone decided a few years ago that every so often one of the guys should host a party and invite the rest of the pilots. We don't spend much time with the native Alaskans who live around here, so things can get kind of lonely. The block party reminds us we're not alone and have friends."

"But they're the competition," Eric protested.

Jake grinned. "Sure, but at the end of the day we're all friends. The companies may compete against one another. It doesn't mean that the pilots have to."

"But Jake," Eric said, lowering his voice, "You own the airline. You are the company."

Jake shrugged. "I'm a pilot first. Come on, get a move on. We leave in ten."

The walk to the neighboring house took less than five minutes. The crew of five arrived carrying a large platter of finger food. When they showed up en masse at the front door, Eric felt they were invading enemy territory as they rang the bell.

The pilot who answered was a short, overweight man with thinning hair. On his face he wore an angry expression as he threw open the door and stuck a finger at the departing member of the crew.

"Leon!" he growled, leveling a cold stare at the man standing beside Eric. "I can't believe you're hijacking my party. Here I thought it was my turn to host the monthly gathering, and this asshole over here," he motioned to Jake, who put on his innocent "who me?" expression, "goes and gets you a job with Wein. Now, before I know it, it's a 'farewell Leon' party."

Both men stared at one another with steely eyes for several seconds before they both cracked up laughing and embraced as old friends.

"I'm sorry to do this to you, Deke." He then motioned over to Eric. "But it's really this guy's fault. He had a job flying Cherokee 6s in Dillingham, but he had to come out here."

Deke took Eric firmly by the hand, pumping it in a warm handshake. "I'm Deke Elliot. I run the operation here for Chami."

"It's great to meet you. I'm thrilled to be here."

"Working for this joker, I'll bet you are. Saturdays off? Really? He's making the rest of us look bad."

Jake held up his hands in protest and said, "I wouldn't have to take Saturdays off if you weren't so good at procuring contracts. You guys are getting so much flying out here, it's all I can do to keep my birds in the air just during the weekdays."

As they entered the house, Eric said, "Chami? You're a few hangars down from us, right?"

"That I am," Deke said, closing the door behind them. He led the group into the deserted house.

"Are you the owner?"

"Hell no. Not all of us can own our own airline like Jake and Jen here," he said as he ushered them into a large open room. Jen set the tray down on a table, already heavily laden with food and drinks. "Chami is one of the larger operators in the area. We have operations here, in Bethel and in Aniak. We have only five planes here, and about the same in Aniak. In Bethel our fleet size is eight."

"Impressive operation."

Deke smiled broadly. "I like it. We also get a hell of a lot more flying than this slacker here."

Jake held up his hands in defense. "Hey man, we can't all be as good as you guys."

The fifth member of the group then said, "Yeah, and you need to watch what you say. Jake takes pride in being a slacker. Any more comments like that, and we won't have any flying at all."

"Hey Charlie. How ya doing?"

"Good. Eric's a good kid. I think he'll make a good roommate."

Leon shook his head. "I'm not even out and you're measuring for drapes."

As Eric looked around the house, devoid of human life, save the six of them. He puzzled where everyone was. Deke must have caught the expression on Eric's face and responded to the unasked question.

"Since Jake's the only one out here who doesn't fly on Saturdays, his crew's always the first to arrive." His grin broadened. "But don't worry, there'll be a big crowd here before you know it. Now try this."

Deke went behind what was obviously a makeshift bar and dispensed brown liquid from a keg into six plastic cups. Once done, everyone gathered the drinks and held the cups in the air as Deke said, "To Leon!"

Everyone repeated, "To Leon!" and took a long drink.

"It's good," Eric said.

"St. Mary's is dry, so we can't have beer up here. But no one really says anything once it's in your house. But since the land the airport is on is dry, we can't even fly it in. The solution, you may ask? I make the stuff myself."

Eric took another drink. "Too bad you can't sell it. You'd probably make more selling this stuff than flying."

Everyone held up a cup in agreement and took another drink.

They slowly settled into seats across the room. Charlie, Leon and Jen were talking and laughing as Jake took a seat at the far end of the room, taking everything in. Deke motioned Eric over, and they went to the couch and had a seat.

"Seriously Eric, it's nice to have you up here. You'll like St. Mary's. The weather's a little harsher than Dillingham—in the winter, at any rate—but it's a great place. You'll like the people. I have to admit, I'll miss Leon, but he's wanted to fly jets for a while. This will be a good fit for him."

"If he's wanted to fly jets, why hasn't he left?"

Deke nodded across the room. "Because Jake's a great guy to work for. He gives his pilots one hundred percent of his support, and he doesn't work them too hard. He's also a fun guy to be around. Jake's been looking for a reason to kick Leon out for a while now. It just turns out you were the excuse he needed."

As they talked, the doorbell rang, and all turned to the hall leading to the front door.

"I've got it!" Charlie said and went to greet the new arrivals. He let in six people from Hagelands Air. As the party grew, Deke turned his attention back to Eric and continued, "Don't get me wrong: it's not out of disappointment or disapproval that Jake wanted to see Leon move on. It's just, Jake knew he'd be happier there than here. And look at Leon. He doesn't seem too broken up to me." Leon was across the room talking animatedly to the new arrivals.

"Do they know he's leaving?"

Deke laughed, "They probably knew within minutes of Jake deciding. It's a small village. News travels fast out here."

Pondering the words, Eric looked across the room at Jake. He seemed happy in the far corner, taking everything in as the room came to life. His face wore a slight grin. As their eyes touched briefly, Jake and Deke raised their glasses. Deke returned to Eric.

"Do you know much about him?" Eric asked.

"Jake? Hell no. Not that that means much up here. There are just as many unwilling to tell you anything about themselves as guys who don't mind sharing. But I know the kind of *man* he is."

"And what kind of man is that?"

"Well, I already told you the kind of boss he is. But as good as that might be, he's a better friend. If I ever need something... anything... often Jake's the last one I want to call."

A quizzical look came over Eric's face. "Why's that?"

"Because he's the first one who'll arrive. If you need him, and he's doing something else, it has to be a big something else for him not to drop everything and be there for you."

"When did he come out here?"

Deke nodded. "Now that's a good question. Let me see. Well, Jake and Jen have been here longer than most. Not as long as me, mind you, but longer than most. I'd have to say almost a decade or so."

"And he started the airline?"

Before he could answer the question, the doorbell rang again. It was Charlie who once more answered it. This time it was a group of seven from Yute Air. They all followed Charlie into the room where Leon was holding court.

Deke then returned his attention back to Eric. "I'm sorry, what was the question?"

"I asked," Eric said a little louder as the din of the room continued to grow, "Did Jake start the airline?"

"Aren't you staying with them? What do you guys talk about, anyway?"

Eric shrugged. "Not their past. Whenever I bring it up, both Jake and Jen steer away from the subject. I guess that's why I'm so curious. At first, it was just to make conversation. Now, I really want to know."

"Well, it's true. The best way to keep a secret is to tell it. Because if you tell it, it can't be that good a secret, can it?" They both took another drink of beer. Then Deke continued. "Yeah, Jake started the airline. Showed up with a 206 and he and the missus bought a place—but you'd know that since you're sleeping there now—and set up shop. At first Jake flew a lot. Really humped for the business. So much so that a little more than a year later he bought another plane and hired a pilot. He also bought another house so the guy he hired would have a place to live."

"He bought another plane and another house? Where does he get the money?"

Deke shrugged. "Like I said, he busted hump. Had a ton of flying back then. He even brought on a third guy. The three of them rotated through the two planes. Then, suddenly, he bought a third plane and everything slowed down. Well, it was good news for the rest of us. The sonofabitch was taking all our flying. But with Jake there, he seemed to settle into a rhythm."

"Was it always Leon and Charlie flying for him?"

"Naw. They've only been there a couple of years. Jake likes to cycles through pilots. Most can't handle the pace."

"I thought you said Y/K doesn't fly much?"

"That's it. Most pilots in Alaska want a steady rush. Not all the sitting around shit Jake does."

As he said this, Jake came across the room and settled into a chair across from the two men. He was holding three cups.

"I brought refills. I also thought I should cut you off before you give this young lad all of my secrets."

Eric started to protest. "Jake we weren't..."

Jake held up a hand, "Eric, its fine. I was getting bored. So, who else is coming to the shindig tonight?"

"Everyone's almost here."

"What about the new guys?"

Eric looked over at Jake. "New guys?"

"I told you when I first met you that a new operator's setting up shop next door."

"Yeah, they'll be here," Deke answered.

"What kind of operation do they have?" Eric asked.

"Good God Eric, I just hired you. Don't tell me you want to jump ship already." Eric started to respond, but before he could get a word out, Jake raised a hand, silencing him. "Relax, I'm just kidding. It's small. Just a couple of guys and a plane. But that's how most start out here."

"What kind of plane?"

"Cherokee 6."

"The Cherokee 6 is a good plane," Deke said. "That's why half of the planes we operate are the six. It's got outstanding performance, and it carries one more passenger than your 206 does."

"Hey," Jake said, glaring at his host, "I like the 206." He then continued more seriously, "What are your impressions of the new guys, Deke?"

"Seem nice enough. Only one's a pilot, though. The other's the office manager or something. Hell, Jake, you should know more than I do. They moved in next door to you."

"Yeah, but I'm out flying all day."

"Shiiiiit."

"All right. I'm around a bit. They seem fine. New, but settling in. They'll be fine once they get their footing."

"There are four operators out here, right?" Eric interjected.

"Five now with the new guys." As Deke spoke, a knock came from the front of the house and the door opened. "Speak of the devil. I'll be right back, boys."

Deke got up and crossed the room to meet the two new arrivals.

"Does this party happen often?"

"Every month."

"It's nice that everyone can come together like this."

Jake looked around at everyone in the crowded room, talking together animatedly. He nodded and said, "And necessary."

Eric gave his boss a questioning look. "Necessary?"

Jake smiled. "I like Dillingham. I'm sure when you got there after Anchorage, it was the most remote place you'd ever been. And I'll bet you felt cut off from humanity there, even though a village like Dillingham is far larger than St. Mary's. I would imagine you would have done well with a party like this." Eric seemed to consider the words and nodded. "It's even more remote here. And more tribal. Make no mistake, that's what we are: a tribe. We're the only pilots up here. We're also some of the only white people up here. They call us gussics. There's an invisible barrier between us and them. Don't get me wrong, I know—and like—a lot of the people who live in the villages. But we'll never be one of them. Just like they'll never be one of us. And I'm not talking about race. We fly. I don't believe that makes us any better or worse than anyone else. But it sets us apart. The men in this room may be our competition out there, but they're also our allies and our only friends. That's why we like to get together at least once a month and keep that bond strong."

"You said you don't really know the new guys."

As if on cue, Jake nodded to Deke and the two men he was leading into the room. "They've been here barely a week, and both of them are at the party. It's how we survive." Jake looked at Eric and smiled. "You're a good kid. We're going to have a lot of fun. I'm looking forward to working with you. I don't want you to be inhibited about anything with me. We're family now. If you have a question, ask. I'll give you a straight answer."

Eric smiled. "Thanks boss."

Jake returned the smile. "Anytime."

"Since you're making the offer: when did you and Jen first come to Alaska?"

Jake wrinkled his brow in concentration. "Good question. Long story. I'll tell you another time."

The following Monday morning, instead of heading to the Hoover Building, Greg cut his drive short and ended up at the Treasury building, just beyond the White House.

When he entered Paul's office, his friend was already there with coffee and muffins.

"I was going to go with donuts, but with you being a cop and all, I thought it might hit a little too close to the mark."

"Nice," Greg said as he closed the door behind him and picked up a blueberry muffin while taking a seat. "What's the latest?"

"I just got word. We have positive contact."

"You've positively identified him as Powell?"

Paul looked out the window, a slightly embarrassed look flashing across his face. "Not exactly positive, but we're pretty sure. There are some physical differences, as expected. He now has a beard, and a little more grey in his hair. But most everything else fits. Height. Build. Even his weight doesn't seem to have changed that much."

Greg took a bite of muffin before asking, "Then what's holding you back?"

"Look, even his history fits. He's calling himself Jake Roth now. But the thing is, although we have a birth certificate and social security number, Jake Roth's history only goes back a little more than a decade."

"Again, what's holding you back?"

Paul exhaled. "The money."

"What about it?"

"My forensic accountants have been all over this Jake Roth's history, and we can't find a trace of it. Not only are the bank records of Jake and Jennifer Roth clean, but they aren't living the lifestyle of millionaires. They seem to have dropped out of nowhere with enough money to buy a small plane and start their airline, but that's it. Their airline now has three planes, but by all accounts, the other two came only after Jake worked his ass off, earning enough to buy the additional two airframes. They don't have a house that's any better than anyone else's. They don't take extravagant vacations. They don't own anything remarkable. They pay their taxes. They make a small profit from the business but live within their means. They seem to fit the descriptions of Stuart Powell and Sara Gray, but the lifestyle just doesn't fit. If you had eleven million dollars, you would spend at least some of it, wouldn't you?"

Greg took a drink of coffee and let this hang in the air before responding. Finally, he said, "So are you thinking of calling off the raid? Do you want to take more time?"

"No," Paul sighed. "We've invested enough in this that I want to go forward. Once we have him in custody, we should be able to figure out if this is our guy. Besides… I have a feeling."

Greg nodded. "That, my friend, is probably the best reason to proceed. Someone as intimately involved as you can usually trust their gut. What kind of time frame are you looking at?"

"I want to do this quickly. Within the next two weeks. I've got my resource in place. I want to give it a little more time to see if I can glean anything new, but I don't want to leave the fish on the hook so long that it's able to get away."

Greg nodded. "I agree."

Chapter Seventeen

Fishing

The weather hit Bethel before it hit St. Mary's. Bethel was a village on the Kuskokwim River, 88 miles south of St. Mary's. It was also the largest village in Central Alaska. It had a long, paved runway (almost unheard of in the region) and over a thousand residents. It had a gas station, two general stores, and even some paved roads. Bethel had a hospital, a school and, in some areas, running water. There was little doubt that Bethel was the center of commerce in the region.

Yet, despite how modernized the airport was (not only was it paved, it had an operating Air Traffic Control Tower), weather was still an ongoing battle. And as the weather rolled in, all at the airport knew a long day lie ahead for them. The Instrument Landing System, or ILS, on the field allowed an airplane equipped for an instrument approach to land in weather as low as a 200-foot ceiling and half-a-mile visibility. Usually, that was enough to get most planes into the airport. But not always. Today was such a day.

As the pilots flying the Wien Air 737 approached the Bethel airport, the copilot tuned in the frequency that would provide the ATIS. ATIS (or Automatic Terminal Information Service) provided weather, and other pertinent airport information to the pilot's landing there. As the copilot wrote down the weather report being transmitted, the news was not encouraging.

"What've you got, Steve?" the captain asked.

"Not good boss. One-eighth mile and indefinite ceilings."

"Great," the captain muttered.

As if on cue, the radio transmission came across: "Wien 601, Anchorage Center. We are showing the Bethel airport currently unable to accept traffic. Ready to copy holding instructions?"

"Great," the captain muttered again.

"Anchorage Center, this is Wein 601. We were looking at the weather as well. This wasn't in the forecast. How's the rest of the area looking?"

"Wein 601, Aniak's down as well. However, St. Mary's still looks OK. I can't make any promises on how long it will hold, though."

Steve looked over at the captain, waiting for an answer to the unasked question.

"This weather wasn't forecast and we don't have a lot of fuel for holding," the captain said. "I'm thinking, let's go to St. Mary's and drop the load there. Then we can fuel up and get back to Anchorage."

Steve nodded his agreement and transmitted, "Anchorage Center, this is Wien 601. We think we'd rather just go to St. Mary's before the weather gets too bad."

"Roger Wien 601. Standby for a new clearance."

Eric was maneuvering onto final approach into St. Mary's as he slowly advanced the pitch knob next to the throttle. The volume inside the small cabin increased as the pitch of the propeller changed until Eric eased back on the throttle. As he did, the drone of the engine died off to a constant whir and the plane leveled its wings aligned with the runway. As Eric rolled out, he saw the Wien 737 sitting on the ramp as a forklift approached the side of the plane.

Planes like this were familiar to Eric. In fact, he had seen the combination freighter/passenger planes (called 'combies') several times in Dillingham. He had also seen a couple in Bethel over the past few days. However, he had not yet seen a plane like that in St. Mary's. He had been told that Wien Air Alaska and Alaska Airlines made a stop into the village once a week, but he had yet to behold the sight himself.

As he touched down, his eyes kept going back to the plane on the small ramp. It looked mammoth compared to the small Cessnas and Pipers.

After landing, he taxied clear of the runway and over to the ramp in front of the Y/K building.

As he got out, he was met by his coworker.

"Charlie, what's up?"

"Weather to the south has gone to hell. Wien diverted here. They're taking on Jet A and leaving us a shit ton of cargo to deliver."

"To Bethel?"

"No. That was the hub. Most of this crap's going to the outer villages. Going to keep us all busy for a couple of days, though. I hope you're ready to work."

"Hell yeah! Where's the boss?"

"Inside with Jen. They're working on the contracts."

"Are we going to be able to get the business?"

Charlie shook his head. "That won't be a problem. Everyone out here will be assholes and elbows for the next couple of days. Jake's just dealing with boss shit. Nothing that concerns us." Charlie then motioned his head. "Come on, let's head inside and get some chow. As soon as the jet's out of here, we're not going to have time to eat."

"Sounds good," Eric said as he followed Charlie into the building.

It took two days, with every operator in St. Mary's constantly flying, to deliver the cargo from the diverted Wien flight.

The sun was still bright in the sky, even though the hour was bearing down on dinner time. Eric had just finished a delivery as he headed into the office for his last flight of the day. As he entered the dimly lit room, he found Charlie lounging with Jake and Jen.

"What's up, guys?" Eric said, weariness touching the edges of his speech.

"I vote Eric," Charlie said enthusiastically.

"For what?" Eric replied.

"I've got a load to Kotlik and two loads for Quinhagak," Jen answered.

Eric shrugged. "I don't mind going to Kotlik."

Charlie's shook his head. "Of the two of us, I'm the senior pilot. I say, you take the Quinhagak load. I get Kotlik."

Eric looked puzzled. Quinhagak was the far more desirable of the two trips since they were paid by the minute. Every minute they were in the air resulted in their pay. From St. Mary's, Quinhagak was almost four times the distance as Kotlik, thus paying four times as much.

"What's the catch?" Eric asked suspiciously.

"The catch is," Jake answered, "I have my fishing poles and we aren't coming back until we have tonight's dinner."

"I love salmon," Charlie said, "but not enough to spend all evening with Jake to get it."

Jake glared at Charlie, who started to laugh. He then said, "Just for that, you don't get any tonight."

Charlie glanced over at Jen, who motioned for him to calm down. "You'll be fine," she mouthed.

"And don't you go taking his side either," Jake scolded his wife. He then turned. "All right Eric, you're with me. I've got two poles and a cooler that needs filling. My plane's already loaded. Let's go load up yours and we'll be on our way.

Less than twenty minutes later, the tires on Eric's 206 stopped their vibrations as they left the rough gravel of the St. Mary's runway.

A few minutes later, Jake's 206 joined up on his right wing. Both planes leveled off at 500 feet and turned south to Quinhagak.

An hour and a half after they took off, both men found themselves on the bank of a river running by the small gravel airstrip, casting lines into the water.

"This is the life," Jake said as he watched his line lazily drift down the river, waiting for a target to take the bait.

"How long have you been out here?" Eric asked, not for the first time. However, to his surprise, Jake answered.

"Ten years, give or take." He then seemed to consider the answer. "Ten years. My God, where does the time go?"

Eric chuckled. "I was just starting high school ten years ago."

Jake looked at him, shaken from his thoughts. "Are you trying to make me feel old?"

"No, just making an observation."

"Have you always wanted to be a pilot?"

Eric nodded solemnly. "Pretty much. When I was sixteen, I met a pilot for Pan Am. He took me under his wing," he glanced over at Jake and grinned, "no pun intended." Jake dismissed the comment with a wave of his hand, and Eric continued. "Well, Captain McCarthy wanted me to go to work for Pan Am. He didn't have any kids of his own, and I think he saw me as a surrogate son. He dreamed I would one day fly beside him."

"What happened? Why aren't you flying jets for Pan American?"

Eric's expression darkened. "Part of me wishes I could. He was a great friend and changed my life. But that just wasn't for me. I couldn't handle school, so I dropped out. I slowly made my way across the country until I ended up here." Both men were quiet for a long time as they continued to make several casts. Finally, Eric spoke again.

"But you know what?" Jake looked over at Eric without saying a word. "It all worked out for the best. Look at me now. Fishing with the boss and flying a 206 in the coolest environment imaginable. How do you beat that?"

Jake smiled and cast his line again. "I can't think of anything better."

Eric threw out another cast, a little beyond Jake's. "How about you? Have you always wanted to be a pilot?"

"I guess so. I always wanted to fly and make a career of it. But it wasn't always what I hoped it would be. But this..." Jake looked at the sparse surroundings and started reeling in the line. "This is what it was supposed to be. Jumping in my plane, eking out a living. Casting a pole whenever I want to. This is better than just about every other option out there. Once upon a time flying gave you a sense of freedom. Opportunities like that are few and far between these days."

The two were quiet for several minutes as they continued to fish. Finally, Eric tried to push his luck. "What kind of flying did you do before Alaska?"

Jake turned and scowled at the younger man. Eric quickly turned and looked back at his line in the water.

"You know I don't like to discuss my past. Hell, I've never even told anyone how long I've been out here. Why should I trust some kid who's been flying for me less than two weeks?"

Eric shrugged without looking at his boss. "Honest face?"

Jake grunted and cast his line again. "Must be something like that. Navy."

Eric was dumbfounded. Not so much by the answer, but because an answer came at all. He completely forgot his line, which floated downstream, making its way to the shore. Jake then continued. "Don't look so stunned and keep fishing." Eric quickly reeled in his line and cast it out again. "After college I joined the Navy and just missed Korea. I then went to work for the airlines—and don't bother asking which one—and found it torture. I then quit and Jen and I took the money we were able to scrape together and bought a plane and started our own business."

"You saved up enough to buy three 206s from a Navy salary?"

"I was able to get some money together from my time at the airlines as well. I also didn't start with three planes. I started with only one. But I busted my ass the first few years and scratched up enough to amass the spectacular fleet you see before you today." Eric looked out to the two 206s sitting on the airstrip 100 yards away. Jake caught his glance and added, "Don't act too impressed: You own your own plane too, don't you?"

"Sure, a two-seater Cessna 150. A far cry from a 206."

Jake cast his line again. Eric followed suit. "I had years to save for that first plane. You've been flying for a living, what? Two years?" Eric nodded. "And in that time, you've been able to find employment with two airlines and saved enough to buy a 150, complete with autopilot."

"I wouldn't say, 'complete with autopilot.' It only has a crude altitude and heading hold. Hardly worthy of the title 'autopilot.'"

Jake shrugged. "That's more or less what the 727 had." Eric started to ask a question, but before he could form a sentence, Jake continued, "What do you need an autopilot in a 150 for, anyway."

Eric shrugged. "Alaska's a big place. If I'm flying, it's probably for hours. If I was instructing, sure the autopilot would be pointless, but when its three hours from Anchorage…"

Jake nodded his acknowledgement and cast his line into the river again.

Greg arrived in Paul's office Monday morning. This had become his normal routine. They were making excellent progress on their case, and both were excited to see it through. It was far from the only unsolved case either had, but it was the one with highest profile (even if, ironically, almost no one knew about it). It was also well on track to being closed. The excitement was palpable.

"Anything new?" Greg asked, taking his seat, passing a box of donuts to his friend. Paul took the box, and in exchange, passed a cup of coffee to Greg.

"Our data collection is going better than expected. I can't offer one hundred percent yet, but I'd be willing to say we're in the 80s. Perhaps even the 90s."

"The spy's paying off?"

"Like gold. We're getting more information than we ever expected."

Greg took a bite from a glazed donut and asked, "Like what?"

"Our target, Jake, used to fly for the airlines. We think there's a good chance he had a military background."

"Doesn't that cover just about every pilot out there?"

Paul conceded the point. "It does. But there are other things: his age. His wife. As far as we can tell he's been living in Alaska for almost ten years. The timing would line up with that of the hijacking. Also, where did a guy like that get the money to buy three planes and start a business?"

"Haven't we been over that one? He started with only one plane and worked his way up from there."

Paul nodded. "Still. A brand-new Cessna 206? That's a lot of money."

"Not to poke holes in your theory, but what about his lifestyle?"

"We've also been over this already."

"Is he living like a guy that stole eleven million dollars?"

Paul wouldn't let it go. "He could be laying low. He's got to know we're onto him."

"I've been thinking about that. Why would he? He has to know the statute of limitations has passed. Why not start spending?"

Greg fished another donut out of the box. "He's not stupid. He'd know this would be a priority for the government. Look, Paul, I'm on your side. It's just,

I've been here before. So close. I just don't want you to set yourself up for disappointment."

Paul nodded. "I've set the sting for a week from today. Next Monday morning. What are your thoughts?"

"I think it's a good plan. If it's him, you'll have him, and can sweat out the truth. If not, well... we'll know that too. Are you still planning on using the air piracy charges as justification?"

"It's about all we have left."

"Do you think he'll give up the money?"

Paul took a long drink from his coffee cup. "I don't know. We'll have to deal. But I don't want him getting away scot-free."

"The wife will be your best leverage."

"That's what I was thinking. A reduced sentence for both might compel him to give up the money." Paul then grunted out a half-laugh. "It's not like he's spending it, anyway."

Greg took another bite from the donut and nodded. "Good, the sooner we wrap this thing up, the better."

"Why? Is this starting to interfere with your other cases?"

Greg took another bite of donut and answered, "No, it's expanding my waistline."

Chapter Eighteen

Revelations

The sky was dark and overcast with low ceilings (only 800 feet, but more than good enough for bush operations). However, the temperature was pleasant at 70 degrees with a light, cool breeze. Eric rolled to a stop in front of the Y/K Air building and popped open the door to his 206. Stretching his tight muscles, he emerged from his metallic cocoon.

Eric's first week flying for Jake had gone forward as promised: light flying with little pressure. Although everyone had told Eric that this would be the pace working for Y/K Air, it still felt unnatural. But over the past week, he was settling into the routine. Jake turned out to be an even better pilot than Eric had hoped for. His friendship with Charlie also developed faster than Eric could have imagined. Even his relationship with Jen had developed at an amazing rate. She was less of the boss's wife to him, and more like the big sister he never had. Jake had been correct: they were not coworkers, but a family. However, Eric still could not shake the feeling that he was getting away with something. The job was better than anything he had ever dreamed of. It seemed too good to be true; too good to last.

It was Friday afternoon, and Eric was in a fine mood. The weather had been challenging enough to make the week interesting, but not so bad as to scare him, or worse... ground him.

As Eric left his plane behind, he proceeded to the office whistling and tossing an orange from hand to hand, as he went to get his next assignment.

As he was climbing the stairs, his foot missed its mark, and he stumbled slightly. Not enough to fall, but enough to send the orange sailing under the building next door.

This building, like most in the bush, was built raised off the ground.

Whereas this served as the foundation for the building, as well as protecting the structure from the weather, today all the architecture did was to serve as an irritant to Eric. He swore silently as he watched his orange go rolling under the edifice. Focused, and determined to get it back, Eric hopped over the railing that led to the front door of the Y/K building and crawled under the structure of the new airline that had just opened up.

Eric slowly made his way under the building, wriggled into the darkness, searching for his snack. There was filth and silt everywhere, covering him. Yet, Eric was determined and refused to give up, venturing deeper underneath. Finally, triumph! He saw the orange sitting in the half-light, resting against a rock, taunting him. Eric grinned as he reached out, snatching the fruit from its resting place. It was just as he started to wriggle back out from under the building that he heard the voices above him. They were muffled, but clear enough that Eric could make out what they were saying.

"I just got off the phone with the Director. He's sending a team in on Monday morning."

"FBI?"

"No, we're keeping it all in-house."

There was a pause as footsteps fell over Eric's head. Years of collected silt rained down on him. He struggled to stifle a sneeze.

"Are we looking at everyone there?"

"No, right now, just the Roth's."

"What about Drake and Johnson? They've got to have some level of involvement, don't they?"

"What are you talking about? Eric Johnson's only been there a couple weeks. And I don't think Drake's been there more than a handful of years. The robbery went down almost a decade ago."

"I still think we should grab the other two."

The hairs on the back of Eric's neck prickled up at the mention of his name. He strained to hear more. It sounded like the owner of the first voice fell into a chair. Even under the floorboards, Eric could hear the old springs give above him.

"I'm not sure what value it would add by grabbing them."

"What about leverage?"

"We're going to have the guy's wife. How much more leverage do you think we need?"

There was a lengthy pause.

"Listen, I'll talk to Washington about it. I'm calling to check in again in a few hours. I'll let them make the call."

"Fine. I'm ready to get the hell out of here. This place is a dump."

"Flying's good though, isn't it?"

"I usually fly a Lear Jet. The guys up here are welcome to their Cherokees."

"Speaking of flying. Don't you have a flight?"

Eric could hear the second man grouse as his footsteps fell across the room.

"Four more days. We're out of here in four more days."

Eric heard the door slam and looked out. Beyond the structure of the building, Eric could see a set of feet walk over to the Cherokee 6 across the ramp. As the feet disappeared, climbing into the small plane, Eric wriggled his way out from under the building.

A few minutes later, covered in dirt, Eric burst into the office.

In a voice, far calmer than he felt, Eric said, "Jake, I need to talk. Could you come out to my plane, please?"

"Eric, what's the…"

Eric held up a hand, silencing his boss. He then shot him a glance that stopped Jake in his tracks. The tenor in his voice changed slightly as he asked, "What's wrong with your plane?"

Realizing he was playing along now, Eric said, "Fuel gauge seems to be sticking. I just filled it, but I'm still showing empty tanks."

"Well then," Jake said, rising and coming across the room to meet Eric, "Sounds like we should take a look at it."

Eric held open the door. Jake exited and Eric followed him. As they left the building, the Cherokee 6 belonging to the Lear Jet pilot next door, roared down the runway and left the ground.

Once clear of the building Jake shot Eric a look.

"Yes," Eric replied to the unasked question. "I think we can talk now."

"Why couldn't we talk in there?"

"I think the guys next door are spying on us."

"The new guys? Northern Central? Why would you think that?"

"I was heading in just a minute ago and dropped my orange. It rolled under the Northern Central building. I crawled underneath to get it back and heard voices. They were talking about arresting us, or something."

Jake arched an eyebrow. "Are you sure you heard them correctly?"

"I'm sure I heard the word FBI."

This stopped Jake momentarily. He turned and looked over at the building next to his. He then looked at Eric and continued to the plane. The two men opened the door to the small Cessna and climbed inside.

"Jake, what the hell's going on?"

"That's a long story. What else did you hear? What makes you think they're bugging the building?"

Eric looked at the gas gauge while he answered. "I'm not sure they're bugging the building, but they said something about the FBI, so I just assumed..."

"Good assumption. Did they say when the FBI would be coming?"

"They said they weren't."

"What?"

"They said something about keeping it in-house. I don't know what that means, but they said someone would be arriving on Monday morning. Jake... what the hell's going on?"

"I told you; it's a long story." He then looked around the deserted ramp and added, "and it sounds like time just got short. Here's the plan: your gas gauge is broken. The plane's grounded. I'm also done with my flying for the day. You, Jen, and I will head back to the house. I'll pick up Charlie later, after he's finished up. I'll explain everything on the way to the house. OK?"

Eric shook his head in resignation. "Fine. But tell me one thing: did you do it? Did you break the law?"

"I keep telling you, it's a long story. I don't want you to judge me until you've heard everything. But the short answer: Yes. Several years ago, I stole some money. Jen played a part in it as well."

"You stole some money? So, what? Why are they talking about the FBI?"

"You said they weren't using the FBI."

"But they *said* FBI. You don't just throw around the word FBI unless it's serious. How much did you steal?"

Jake shrugged. "Somewhere around eleven million dollars."

Nate Deckland had been with the Treasury department for ten years. However, this was his first undercover assignment. He had been looking forward to it and was actually enjoying himself. He had been read in on the details of the case, as had Martin Lake. Marty, however, was not as happy to be there. The assignment was "offered" to him, and he knew that if he was to continue to advance as a government pilot, he should accept it.

Nate was single and enjoyed being out in the Alaskan wilderness. He also knew that when this case broke, even if the details were kept classified, internally it would be high profile. Playing his part in the operation could lead to promotion.

Marty had two small children and a wife who hounded him mercilessly when he was away. She was remarkably unsuited to be a pilot's wife. The assignment to Alaska caused him no small amount of strife on the home front. Although the chance to fly in rural Alaska would be a dream assignment for most pilots, Marty's wife made it a nightmare scenario for him.

Marty was off on a delivery, fulfilling a small mail contract Treasury had secured to maintain the cover. Nate remained in the Northern Central Building, monitoring the bugs set in both the Y/K's office and the Roth household.

Forty-five minutes ago, Jake and Eric walked into the office and announced to Jen that Eric's plane's fuel gauge was broken. He then told his wife that he and Eric were going to head home and invited her to join them.

At first, she had refused, but after an uncomfortable silence, she did an about-face and said she would like the afternoon off. This sudden reversal of position got Nate's radar up, and he moved over to the bug in the house. The large reels of the audio tape were slowly turning, recording every word at the residence in St. Mary's, when Nate heard the telltale sign of a door opening.

"Listen, there's really nothing to this," Jen's voice was saying as she entered the house.

"What the hell is wrong with you two? You broke the law." Nate pressed the headphones closer to his head, not wanting to miss anything.

"Eric, this isn't a big deal."

"Yes, it is Jake. They said they were going to bring in the FBI."

"No," Jake's voice answered, "They said they *weren't* bringing in the FBI. That means they don't have anything."

"Eric," it was now Jen speaking, "the statute of limitations is long since passed. Even if they wanted to arrest us, they couldn't."

There was a long pause. Nate pressed the headphones tighter to his head. He looked over to ensure the reels were still turning. They were. This was the smoking gun they had been looking for. However, he was growing concerned about their apparent knowledge. From the conversation, there was little doubt that they knew they were suspects and under surveillance. How could they have learned that Treasury was interested in the couple?

Finally, Eric said, "Jake, I'm not sure I can do this."

"What? There's nothing to do. You fly the plane, you get paid."

A long exhale. "You're both criminals."

"Eric…" It was Jen.

"Listen," Eric interrupted her, "I need some time. I need to get out of town for a bit. Drive me back to the airport. You need to pick up Charlie, anyway. I'm going to spend the weekend in Anchorage. I'll head back on Monday. If you're still here, maybe we can talk then."

"Where else would we be?" Jake asked.

"I don't know," Eric answered sarcastically. "Jail? Or perhaps you both might take off again, running away from what you've done." At this comment, Nate quit breathing. However, what he heard moments later allowed him to relax, if just a bit.

"We're not going anywhere, are we, Jen?" Silence. Nate took it for the nodding of a head. "They have nothing, and frankly, I'm getting sick and tired of living like this. Fine, let them come. They'll find me here waiting. This is my house and I'm not going anywhere. And to tell you the truth," Jake said, his voice rising, "I'm getting a little tired of your ingratitude."

"*My* ingratitude?"

"Yes. You said you wanted to fly for me. I said no. You then pressed. If I'm to be honest, you impressed me. So, I let one of my pilots go to make a space for you. I've given you a job, a place to stay, and fed you. Who the hell are you to question me and what I've done?"

"How much did you steal?"

"That's irrelevant."

"Damn right it is. One dollar or one million dollars. Theft is theft. You know what, don't bother looking for me on Monday. I hope they nail you to the wall."

"Jake," it was Jen's voice.

"You drive this little bastard to the airport. He's dead to me. If you need me, I'll be in my room."

A few moments later there was the sound of a door slamming.

"Listen, Jen…"

"Eric, I think you've said enough. Let's go."

"Can I at least get my stuff from the pilot house? It isn't much and won't take long."

"Fine. Let's just go."

There was the sound of the front door closing and then silence. Nate looked over his equipment. Still recording. He couldn't help but to suppress a smile. He would definitely be promoted over this. He then looked over at the phone. He should have plenty of time to call Washington before they arrived at the airport.

"Paul Owens." It was just after eight at night in Washington DC.

"Director Owens, this is John Duskas from the office. I have a call from an Agent Nate Deckland in Alaska."

Paul nodded. "Go ahead; put him through."

"Yes, sir."

There were a series of clicks and then the sound of breathing on the other line. "Mr. Deckland, what can I do for you?"

"Sir, it seems there's been a development."

Paul sat up a little straighter and his blood ran cold. "Don't tell me Roth got away."

"No, sir. But I believe they're aware of our presence."

"How so?"

"The new guy, Eric Johnson, must have overheard something. He told both Roth's about us."

"And what was their reaction?" Paul asked in a voice barely above a whisper.

"They said that they were tired of running. That they weren't going to hide from us."

"Do you believe them?"

Nate shook his head. "Not sure, sir. But Johnson was pretty upset. He and Roth had a big blow-out. Roth stormed back to his room and his wife, Jen, took Johnson back to the airport. Johnson said he needed some time away, then decided that it would be a permanent split."

As he talked Nate spread the blinds. Outside, he saw the Roth's Jeep pull up. A man got out wearing an olive grey flight jacket and a red hat. Nate recognized it as Eric's. The man kept his head in the car for a minute, then pulled out a duffel bag and headed to the small Cessna by the Y/K building.

"I can see Johnson now. He's leaving Roth's car. It looks like he has all his stuff, sir. I think he might actually be leaving for good. Do you want me to stop him?"

Back in Washington, Paul thought about the ramifications of stopping the boy. He didn't believe that Stu/Jake was just going to roll over. But he didn't want to spook him in acting too quickly.

"Here's the plan: Let the boy go for now. I don't want to waste our limited resources on him. We'll try to acquire him later, but he's only been there a couple of weeks. Odds are he doesn't know anything. I think Jake and Jen are poised to make their move. It's Friday now. I've already got a team in Anchorage. I'll see what I can do on pushing the timeline up a couple of days. I want you and your partner to continue monitoring them. I'm not sure how fast I can pull this together, but I think I should be able to get something going by early tomorrow. OK?"

"Yes, sir." Nate watched as Eric threw his duffel bag in the back of the plane and then climbed inside. The propeller turned a couple of times before catching. Nate hung up the phone and watched as the small Cessna taxied across the ramp to the end of the runway. When it added power for take-off, it wasn't like the 206s or Cherokee 6s. The tiny Cessna was quiet and lifted quickly into the leaden Alaska sky before making a turn off towards the distance.

Nate then turned his attention to the Jeep. It hadn't moved.

"Hey Marty, you on frequency?" Nate said into the microphone on the desk. Marty was still out delivering the mail. He waited a minute to see if he could reach the pilot.

He received nothing for his efforts and continued to watch the jeep. In the distance, he could make out the shape of Jen Roth. As he watched her, he put the headphones back on his head, listening to the bug in the Roth's house. There was nothing. Perhaps Jake had just gone to sleep. He had sounded upset. Nate then looked back to the jeep. No change.

It was almost twenty minutes later when the droning of a distant engine broke through Nate's headphones. He tried the radio again.

"Five-Five Tango, you on frequency?"

The reply was scratchy, but audible. "What's up, Nate?"

"Marty, we just got a special delivery. How long until you can return?"

"Twenty minutes or so." That meant that the airplane Nate was hearing wasn't Marty's. Nate looked out of the window. The plane was a 206, not a Cherokee 6 like they flew.

"Understood.   Get back here as quickly as possible."

His transmission was answered with two rapid clicks of the mic.

A few minutes later, the 206 touched down. The paint scheme denoted it was a Y/K plane. It had to be Charlie. Nate made a note of it.

As the 206 taxied toward the Y/K building, Jen got out of the car and pointed to the far hangar where the 206s were tied down for the night. The pilot nodded. He goosed the power, and the plane made an abrupt turn towards the other two Y/K planes.

Jen followed the 206 to the ramp and met up with the pilot there. As he emerged from his plane, she started talking to him. He nodded and went about securing the plane for the night. As Nate watched, he wished he had a listening device and could hear what they were saying.

"Charlie. Tie down your bird. You're done for the night," Jen said as she approached him.

Nodding, Charlie immediately started taking the chains anchored to hooks in the ground and attached them to the eyebolts on the wing and tail, securing his plane. As he did so, he asked, "What's up."

"A lot."   She then looked around, her eyes lingering at the building beside the Y/K office a few moments longer than all the others. "I don't want to go into too much now, but a lot of things have changed."

Charlie hesitated for a moment, then resumed. "Good change or bad change?"

"Just change. Look, we're being watched and," she glanced around again, "I think the office and homes are bugged."

Trying to keep his expression natural, Charlie asked, "Why?"

"It's a long story, and unfortunately I don't have time to tell it to you now. But here's the short version: Jake and I committed a crime when we were younger and, well, the chickens have come home to roost."

Charlie finished up with his plane and joined Jen as she started towards the car.

"We're not going to the office?"

"No."

"Because they're listening?"

Jen looked back at the building besides theirs and said, "No, they already know what they want to."

Charlie glanced over at the Y/K office and then back at her as they came to the jeep. She got in the driver's side as he opened the passenger door.

"What do they have?"

"Enough."

"Enough what?"

"Just enough. Let's leave it at that."

"Jen," Charlie asked with concern on his face, "Are you OK?"

"No," she said, and started the car. They headed down the dirt road from the airport to the tiny village of St. Mary's.

"What's wrong? What did you do?"

"They'll be coming to arrest us. I have to leave tonight. I can't stay."

"What about Jake," Charlie asked in almost a whisper.

"Jake will be fine. He always is. But I have to leave. Charlie, I know it's a lot, but I have a favor to ask you."

"Anything."

"I want you to spend the night at our place tonight."

"OK. Why?"

"I'm going to sneak out. I have a plan, but I don't want anyone to know about it."

Charlie nodded. "OK, what's the plan?"

Jen smiled. "I just said, I don't want anyone to know about it."

Charlie nodded without humor. "Got it. What d'ya need from me?"

"Stay at the house. Keep an eye out. I'm sneaking out tonight around midnight." Hurt was in her eyes as she added, "You won't see me again after that. Ever."

The full gravity of the situation hit Charlie. His reply came out as a horse whisper. "OK."

Jen smiled kindly again. "They're going to be watching the doors. I know that. But Jake and I put in a trapdoor in the living room years ago. It opens up under the house. From there, I can sneak out. The house was only built with the front and back door, so they shouldn't be watching the sides of the house."

Charlie nodded dumbly.

"I don't know when they'll come, but it will be soon. They'll detain you. Just answer honestly. Don't try to protect anyone. Jake and I know what we did. We're not looking for forgiveness. And we don't want anyone else to get into trouble because of our sins. Just be honest and you'll be fine."

"What about Jake? And where's Eric?"

They continued down the dirt road as Jen filled Charlie in on everything that had transpired earlier and where the two men were.

Chapter Nineteen
Taking Prisoners

The sun was just below the horizon at midnight. Outside everything was dark, but not black. Alaska was in a state known as 'continuous twilight.' Although it was dark out, the sky was a deep sapphire blue, but not dark enough to unveil even a single star.

Outside, the temperature was cool. Even though it was midsummer, the temperature was only in the mid-50s.

Jen was as quiet as she could be, not making a sound, as she moved the rug in the living room. She then silently opened the trap door leading under the dwelling.

As she worked, Charlie silently helped her. Once the door was open, Charlie glanced towards the closed door of Jen and Jake's bedroom. Jen grimaced and shook her head. Charlie returned the expression and nodded.

Jen looked down into the void beneath and leaned over, giving Charlie a soft peck on the cheek. His eyes were welling as she descended into the opening. Tears were running freely down her face.

As her feet found solid ground, the muted light above her vanished as Charlie replaced the trapdoor.

Wasting no time, she crawled towards the side of the house. After a quick survey, she darted out, staying in shadows, and made her way across town.

Not five minutes later, she was tapping on the window of an old, dilapidated building. Nothing. A few more taps and then a thin line of light pierced the darkness, illuminating the woman's face. This sudden change terrified her, but she knew there was nothing that could be done.

A moment later the thin line of light erupted in a full shower of illumination as the blackout curtains were parted. Jen was staring at a very tired looking native Alaskan. A moment later, the window raised. Before the man could say anything, Jen spoke in a horse whisper. "Peter don't say anything. We're being watched, but I think I was able to slip away without them seeing."

"Jen, what are you doing?" the man in the window asked in a halting Alaskan accent.

"I'll explain later, but I need a huge favor."

The man looked back into the room and then back at Jen. "What do you need?"

"I need you to take me to Marshall. You have a boat. We could slip down to the river and be at the village before morning."

"Peter, what is it?" a female voice asked in the same halting speech pattern as Peter's.

"It is nothing, Martha. It is just…"

"Don't tell her it's me," Jen whispered forcefully. Then added, "For protection."

Peter nodded and turned back to the room. "It is a long story. I will tell you everything in the morning. But I need to go out now."

Jen heard Martha ask, "Why."

"A friend needs help. I will tell you in the morning. I will call you before mid-day. Now go back to sleep. I will be fine." He then looked back down at Jen and said in a whisper, "I will meet you out front in a few minutes."

Jen nodded, and headed around the building, lurking in the shadows, alert for any sign that she was being followed.

True to his word, a few minutes later, Peter opened the door to his house and emerged into the night. Dressed warmly and carrying a fishing pole, he whispered, "You stay in the darkness. If anyone is watching, they will just see a fisherman getting an early start."

Jen nodded and followed him for several minutes. Finally, they crested a small hill and were no longer visible from St. Mary's. It was a long walk until they reached the neighboring village of Pitkas Point. From there it was only a few more minutes until they reached the shore of the Yukon River and Peter's boat.

Jen did her best to help get the small craft ready, but knew the best thing she could do was stay out of Peter's way. After a few more preparations, he directed her silently into the small craft and shoved off into the river, jumping into the boat as the current took it.

Seconds later, Peter started the boat's motor. It was not loud, but it pierced the oppressive silence of the night like an explosion. Jen knew for sure that every light in the village would come on immediately and FBI and Treasury agents would come storming over the hill as the motor roared to life. Yet somehow, inexplicably, none of this happened. Peter just adjusted the power, turned the tiller, and started up the river.

"You said that you want to go to Marshall. Is someone looking for you?"

The chill was made even worse by the river. Jen's cheeks were already rosy. So much so that Peter could not see her blush. But she made no pretense and nodded. "Yes. Government men."

Peter nodded. "Then we should go to Russian Mission. The village is further down river than Marshall. They may check Marshal or Mountain Village, but I do not think they will go much further."

"Good thinking. How long will it take?"

"Several hours, but it is still early. You should be able to make the first flight out to Bethel or Aniak. From there you can go to Anchorage."

Jen nodded. They continued for a long time, with the droning of the motor lulling them to sleep. More to stay awake than anything else, Jen asked, "Do you want to know what I did?"

Peter seemed to consider this for a long time before answering. "Martha and I have known you and Jake for many years. I do not know who you were before we met you, but we know who you are now. If you need my help, I will give it freely without condition or explanation."

Jen smiled, grateful for this friendship. Another pang of regret shot through her mind as she realized she would lose yet another friend.

"Thank you, Peter."

Peter just smiled in response as he navigated the Yukon.

"Peter," Jen said after another long while. Peter looked at her in response. "When they ask, tell them the truth. But don't tell them I told you I was running away. Just tell them I asked for a ride up the river." The term gave Jen an involuntary shudder. She then continued, "Don't tell them anything that could get you or Martha in trouble."

Peter smiled as he continued to maneuver the small boat. In the distance, the sun crested the horizon. Yet the newly risen sun provided very little light, and the droning of the motor finally won out. Jen drifted off to sleep as Peter continued to drive.

The C-130 Hercules touched down hard on the gravel runway of St. Mary's. As the four-engine plane reversed the pitch of its props, slowing the plane, a huge plume of dirt was kicked up. As the Herc continued down the runway, it soon disappeared from sight.

Nate stood in front of his little building as the C-130 emerged from the dust cloud, its engines whining loudly as the plane taxied to the ramp.

The plane didn't have any markings on it. It was just plain white with a small registration number on the empennage and a small American flag beside it. Despite the lack of livery, there was no doubt in anyone's mind that the plane now sitting on the ramp was not a Wien or Alaska Airlines plane. Just one look and it was obvious this plane was owned by the government.

When the back door of the four-engine turboprop was lowered, six men descended the ramp. All dressed in identical black outfits. On the back of each black uniform, there were big block letters in white denoting "Treasury." Each of the men also carried an assault rifle and had a duffel bag slung over their shoulders.

As the blades of the four engines slowly spun to a stop, Nate, now wearing a blue windbreaker with yellow "Treasury" emblazoned on the back, approached the first man exiting and extended his hand.

"Nate Deckland."

"Steve Hanson. We were told there were two of you?"

"Agent Lake's in the village, watching the house. No movement yet."

Steve nodded as the others fell into position behind him. As they walked, Nate continued. "We only have one vehicle. And it looks ready to be condemned, but standard for what you find around here."

As Nate was talking, two jeeps were backed out of the rear of the C-130. Both looked pristine.

Steve looked over his shoulder at the vehicles being unloaded and then back to Nate. "It's OK. We brought our own rides."

Nate nodded and continued. "We'll head into the village—about a ten-minute drive from here—and then I'll let you guys do what you do.

The two men started walking toward the two jeeps. As they walked, Steve asked, "What's the tactical situation?"

"Three people in the house. Two men, one woman. One man has worked for the suspects for several years."

"We were told there was a second pilot in the suspect's employ."

"He left yesterday. I talked to Washington. They said that since he had only been here a few weeks, we should let him go."

Steve nodded. "Good enough. I want you and Agent Lake to stay back. I don't want either of you entering the building until we've cleared the area. Understood."

Nate nodded, all business. "Understood."

All the men from the plane, and Nate, boarded the two jeeps, leaving the dilapidated car Nate had been driving over the past few weeks, behind. The vehicles drove for several minutes as Nate continued to pass along as much information as possible to the team until they crested the hill and St. Mary's came into sight. A few minutes later the two cars came to a halt and the men silently exited the vehicles.

It was now late in the morning and the village was awake and active. Several men, women, and especially the children watched, but no one said a word.

Marty ran over to the assault team and filled them in.

"Still holed up inside. No talking. However, I've been picking up breathing and movement."

"Very good. Stay by Agent Deckland. We'll take it from here."

Marty nodded and moved towards his partner, who handed him a blue windbreaker. Marty put on the thin Treasury jacket as the assault team prepared to go to work.

The team moved silently as all in the village slowed and settled in to watch the show. A few minutes later, using only hand signals, the team breached the front door, using a hand-held battering ram. They descended into the room like locusts, all the while shouting "Treasury!"

Nate and Marty watched from a distance, guns in hand, but looking rather non-threatening as muffled shouts of "clear" escaped from inside the building. Finally, they heard a barely audible, "Treasury! On the ground! Hands behind your back!"

Moments later, the same litany was repeated. Nate and Marty waited for the third call to come, but it never did. Finally, Agent Hanson emerged from the front door, beckoning the two agents outside to enter.

As Nate and Marty walked into the house, Steve said quietly, "We have two males. One appears to be in his early-thirties, and the other in his mid-twenties. There was no woman."

Nate and Marty looked at each other and then at Steve. Nate said, "Roth should be pushing forty."

They entered the room and saw the two men on the floor. They recognized both instantly.

"That's Charlie Drake and Eric Johnson," Nate said. He then turned to the men on the ground and addressed them directly. "Where's Jake and Jen Roth?"

Charlie looked at Eric beside him and seemed to suppress a laugh as he said, "I don't know."

"Me either," Eric said with the same expression on his face. "We've been here all night. Haven't seen either of them."

Nate picked Eric up off the ground and threw him violently onto the couch in the center of the room. Despite the abuse, his expression did not change. "Bullshit! I saw you leave yesterday! What the hell's going on here?"

"I didn't leave. What are you talking about?" As Eric talked, Charlie looked up from the ground with a grin on his face. Something then seemed to occur to the younger pilot, and he said, "Oh, are you talking about yesterday afternoon? I loaned my jacket and hat to Jake, but I've been here."

"Do you think this is funny? We're federal agents! I don't think either of you have a clue just how much trouble you both are in! Were the hell's your plane?" All the Treasury team circled around them, listening to the show.

"Jake wanted to borrow it. Well, I've been flying one of his planes for the past few weeks, so who was I to say no?" Both Eric and Charlie started giggling.

Nate raged at him, "Don't screw with me, you little shit! I heard you fight!"

"How could you hear that?" Eric asked, trying to put on a more serious face. Charlie, however, kept snickering. All eyes turned to Charlie. Nate looked like he wanted to shoot both men. Eric continued, "I guess we had a little fight, but I was really emotional at the time. We made up and I let him borrow my plane."

"You made up? After fifteen minutes?"

"What can I say? I've never been one to hold a grudge."

"Where's Mrs. Roth?" Steve asked.

Charlie looked up at the newcomer and said, "No idea. She left last night. Said she was going out. Hasn't been back since."

"Bullshit!" Marty said. "We've been watching this place all night."

Charlie, still on the ground, twisted his head and looked over at the Treasury pilot. "Apparently not very well. Look all you like, Jen's not here." Both men started laughing.

Nate yelled, "Shit!" and flung his arm violently, sending some knick-knacks on a table, flying.

Steve looked at him and asked, "What now, sir?"

Nate exhaled. "Get them in the jeeps. I'll call Director Owens and let him know the situation. Put these two on the plane and we'll let Washington deal with them.

Paul closed his eyes. Not from frustration or anger, but weariness. Greg was in the office with him.

"Thank you, Agent Deckland. And Agent, don't blame yourself. These people are experts at disappearing." Silence. "Yes, I understand." Silence. "I want you and Agent Lake to remain there through the weekend and close shop. Once you have everything in hand, you can take the plane back to Anchorage." Silence. "No, I'm going to keep Mr. Johnson and Mr. Drake in Washington for the time being. I want to see what we can get out of them." Silence. "Don't worry about it. We'll talk on Monday or Tuesday. Thank you, Agent."

Paul hung up the phone with slow, deliberate motions as the man across from him spoke.

"Got away again, huh?" Greg asked.

"You know, when we found that damned bill, I thought it was a stroke of luck. I didn't realize we were just opening an old wound best left undisturbed."

"Short version?"

"They got away... again."

"OK," Greg replied with a humorless grin. "Little longer version."

Paul sighed. "Jake/Stu switched places with the kid. Took his jacket and hat, got in his plane and flew away while we were watching. Don't know what happened with the girl. Our guys said they were watching the place, but apparently not too closely. She somehow disappeared."

Greg coughed. "They do that a lot, don't they?"

Paul pinched the bridge of his nose. "Yes, they do."

"Next move?"

Paul shook his head. "The two pilots are being brought here. They're loading them on the plane and heading back to Anchorage. From there they'll be put on an Air Force C-137 and taken to Andrews. I don't see any reason they shouldn't be here by tonight. I figure, don't let them sleep on the plane and keep them awake all night. Might loosen their tongues."

"Think so?"

Another humorless grin. "No, but what have we got to lose?"

"The first thing I want to make clear to you Eric—may I call you Eric?" There was a nod. "Very well. The first thing I must tell you, Eric, is you have the right to counsel."

"What do you mean 'counsel'?"

"You have the right to a lawyer."

Eric looked up at his questioner. The man was wearing a suit, but the tie was loosened. He looked to be a little tired, but nothing like Eric was.

When Eric and Charlie had first been arrested by the Treasury Department, it had all been a thrill. Eric loved that his new mentor had trusted him with the greatest secret of which he had ever heard. Even more so, Jake himself had offered to make Eric a part of the eleven-million-dollar heist. Eric was giddy ever since Jake and Jen had left him alone at their house.

Later, when Charlie had shown up, Jen had offered him a role as well. Both Eric and Charlie were like schoolboys again, pulling one over on the authorities. The height of excitement was the big reveal when the feds had found not Jake and Jen in the house, but their two employees. Both had laughed and enjoyed the thrill of watching the federal agents realize that they had been made fools by Jake Roth.

And then came the plane ride to the lower forty-eight.

Eric had never been so tired in his life. Try as he might, he hadn't been able to sleep a wink the night before the raid. Following the arrest, he and Charlie were brought directly from St. Mary's to Anchorage. They were then transferred from the C-130 to a military jet transport plane, and brought to Washington, D.C. As soon as they landed in Andrews Air Force Base, they were put in a holding cell. The entire time they were separated and kept awake throughout the entire journey. Both the thrill and the joy of the adventure quickly evaporated into a distant memory.

When Eric was shoved forcibly into his holding cell, he thought he could at least finally get some rest. However, he found sleep elusive there too. All night there was a great deal of noise (intentionally caused), and he was denied sleep for the second night in a row.

On Sunday morning, Eric was transferred from Andrews to Washington, D.C. At that point, he had no idea what had happened to Charlie.

Eric, who once was so cocky and sure of himself, now wore the exhaustion heavily. The mention of a "lawyer" seemed to evoke a new emotion: fear.

"Am I under arrest?"

The man across the table from him seemed to consider this for a moment before answering. "For the moment I'll say, no. But that could change in a heartbeat."

"Can I leave?"

The man gave Eric an empty smile.

Eric continued, "If I can't leave, then what's the difference?"

The man exhaled and explained. "You are not under arrest. There is no record of your being here. We have done this for *your* benefit, not ours." This, in fact, was not the entire truth. Treasury wanted to keep the entire affair as contained and off the books as possible; they still wanted to conceal the truth of the missing eleven million dollars. So close after Watergate, the last thing they wanted was another story of a government cover-up to leak out.

"How does it benefit me?"

"There's no record of your being here. Once this entire affair is behind us, you can move on with your life with a clean slate.

"If I'm not under arrest, why would I need a lawyer?"

"Eric," the man said patiently, "This is a messy affair. Some of these waters might be hard to navigate without help. I want to make sure that both our interests are represented."

Eric seemed to ponder this for some time before answering. "If it's all the same to you, I didn't do anything wrong, so I don't believe I need a lawyer."

The interrogator seemed indifferent with the answer and continued. "All right. Then why don't you tell me about Jake and Jen Roth?"

"He's a pilot, and she runs the office."

"You know what I mean."

Eric held up his hands and gave the man an innocent look. "I really don't."

"The robbery."

"I don't know much more than they committed some robbery and got away with it. They then moved to Alaska and started an airline."

"And you know nothing else?"

Eric held up his hands again. "Sorry."

The interrogator stood and walked to the mirror at the back of the room. He seemed to study himself for a few minutes. He then returned to the seat across from Eric.

"Eric, look; you seem to be a nice young man. You have your entire life ahead of you. Why are you protecting these people?"

Eric didn't respond.

"Do you even know why we're after them?"

Eric looked up and met the man's eyes. He then looked down again. "The robbery?"

"The robbery." The interrogator suppressed a laugh. "You think we've gone to all this trouble because of a robbery. I'll tell you what they *really* did: They hijacked a plane. An airliner. Do you remember the TWA 727 that was hijacked about ten years ago?"

"I was just a kid," Eric muttered.

"Well, they threatened a lot of people, stole a plane—pretty much destroying it in the process—and made away with a lot of money."

Eric looked up again. "How much?"

"Does it really matter?"

Eric shrugged. "Might. You're still after them."

"It's not about the money."

Eric straightened slightly. "Then why am I talking to Treasury and not the FBI?"

"What makes you think I'm Treasury and not FBI?"

"Because everyone running into the house was screaming 'Treasury' and not 'FBI.' That, and the guys at the place next to Y/K Air said they didn't want to use the FBI. I might not be all that old, but I'm not stupid either."

The interrogator shook his head. "There was some money involved. There was a ransom—and not an insubstantial amount—and we paid it. So fine: it's about the money; but not *just* the money. The money's not the real point. The point is: they took a plane. How would *you* feel if *you* had been the pilot? Or your buddy, Charlie?"

Eric looked down again.

Several long seconds passed before a tapping came from the one-way mirror. The interrogator looked up at the glass and then back at Eric. He hadn't moved. He looked almost comatose.

The interrogator shook his head and got up. "I'll be right back, Eric."

He left the room and met the men on the other side of the glass.

The interrogator opened the door to the viewing room on the other side of the one-way mirror. As he entered, he found two men waiting for him. On the other side of the glass, Eric folded his arms and lay his head down in an effort to get what little sleep he could.

The interrogator closed the door softly behind him. When he did, the shorter of the two men in the room asked, in a whisper, "What do you think?"

"Director Owens," he replied at the same volume, "I don't think he's a bad kid. He seems bright. I just think he fell in with the wrong crowd."

Paul looked to the man beside him. "Greg?"

"I agree. The hijacking seemed to rattle him. I think a little more time and he'll tell us what he knows."

Paul snorted. "And what if he doesn't know anything?"

Greg shrugged. "Then we won't be any worse off than we are now."

Paul looked at the interrogator.

"Give me some time, sir. We'll get something out of him. But I think he's spent for today. Let's try him tomorrow."

"I agree," Greg added.

"OK," Paul conceded. "Take him back to his cell and bring in the other one, Charlie Drake."

The interrogator nodded and left the room.

Chapter Twenty
The Reckoning

Monday had produced little more than Sunday, but cracks were now starting to show. When Eric was brought back into the interrogation room on Tuesday, it was all he could do to just hang on. He was now deeply sleep deprived. He had also been held in solitary confinement.

Charlie's treatment had not been nearly as harsh. This was primarily because Charlie had accepted the invitation of counsel. Once given a lawyer, his treatment had improved almost immediately.

Meanwhile, Eric was still refusing a lawyer, insisting he had done nothing wrong. On the first day of questioning, all had taken this as a good sign; that Eric would cooperate. It also freed them of restraint, giving them the ability to question him more aggressively.

By Monday, Paul and Greg's attitude was changing. They discussed the ramifications if allegations of being denied counsel were claimed. They made sure that the interrogator was emphatic in letting Eric know that counsel was absolutely within his rights. Again, he refused. He also seemed closer to cracking.

By Tuesday morning it was decided that if he didn't take counsel, on Wednesday they would assign a lawyer to him. It never came to that.

"Eric," the interrogator started. "are you sure you still don't want a lawyer?"

"I told you, I didn't do anything wrong."

"You know, Charlie has taken us up on our offer."

Eric glared. "I'm not Charlie. I haven't done anything."

"And Charlie has?"

"You'll have to take that up with Charlie... or his lawyer," Eric added unkindly.

The interrogator nodded. "Eric, I know you did nothing. But I also know that you know something." Eric looked down and muttered. "What was that son? I didn't quite hear you."

Eric looked up again. "I said, I don't betray people's trust."

The interrogator's heart skipped a beat at one more indication of a crack. However, Eric never saw the slightest change in his demeanor. This man was a professional.

"I'm not surprised. From the beginning of our time together, you've struck me as an honorable young man."

Eric frowned and looked down again. The interrogator continued to press. "That's why we're so keen on finding Jake. He committed a crime and needs to answer for it."

Eric looked up again. "How so? What will you do to him?"

The interrogator shrugged. "He'll be brought before a judge and jury and put on trial. Then they'll decide his fate."

"Will he go to prison?"

The interrogator shrugged again. "I would expect so."

"How long?"

"I don't know, son. Sorry."

"And what about Jen?"

The interrogator shook his head. "She was complicit. She'd serve time as well. But not as much as Jake, I'd expect. She didn't plan the thing out, but she would have to answer for her role in the matter."

Eric put his head down on the table and muttered, "I'm so tired."

The interrogator shook his head. "Eric, just give me something. Please, anything. You don't belong here."

Eric fought back tears, "As soon as I say anything, you're going to put me in prison."

The interrogator shook his head. "No, Eric. That's not true."

"Then why have you been so insistent about me getting a lawyer?"

"So we *wouldn't* put you in prison. We know you didn't mean to do anything. Just tell us something and we'll let you go."

Eric shook his head. "Jake told me about you, about the government. How I can't trust you."

"Eric, I can have a lawyer here in five minutes. We can draft a letter of immunity. Nothing you say will be held against you. You'll be free to go and all of this will be over."

Eric looked resigned. "What do I have to tell you?"

"Everything you know."

Eric looked down again. "I don't want to betray my friends."

"Eric," the interrogator said sternly, "where are they now? I can't answer that. But I sure as hell know where you are. You're far from home, alone in a cell with me. You're here while they're somewhere out there, free. Does that sound fair to you? Does that sound like the actions of a friend?"

Eric appeared to battle with himself, before his shoulders slumped and a look of resignation washed over his face. "Fine. I'll talk to your lawyer."

"Don't I need a contract or something?" Eric asked the man beside him.

"No Eric," his lawyer answered. "They've already agreed to the terms. They have to honor their deal. I'll make sure they do."

Eric nodded. "What do you need?"

The small interrogation room was now crowded with not only Paul and Greg present, but Eric's lawyer and his interrogator. "First," Paul asked. "Do you know where Jake is?"

"Yes."

All in the room inhaled sharply. None had expected this answer.

"Where?" Greg asked, almost jumping across the table.

"Before he left, we worked out a flight plan. Jake was heading to Nassau. Jen would meet him there later."

"How was he going to get there?" It was Paul again.

"Fly."

All in the room deflated. "He's long gone... again." Greg muttered.

"Why do you say that?" Eric asked innocently.

Greg offered him a sympathetic smile. "The Bahamas are massive. If he went to Nassau, he could be anywhere. It's unlikely we'll be able to find him in the chain. Unless you know where in the Bahamas he's going after Nassau."

Eric shook his head. "Sorry. Once he gets there, I don't know where he's planning to go."

A moment passed before the interrogator asked, "What do you mean, 'gets there?'"

Eric shrugged. "Just that. After he arrives tomorrow, I don't know where he's going."

Paul leaned in. "Arrives tomorrow?"

Eric shook his head. "I could be wrong. Sorry. I thought today was Tuesday."

"It is."

Eric shrugged again. "We worked out the flight plan. The 150's a small plane and not very fast. But it's enough to get him out of the country. It'll just take longer than a faster plane would. What time is it?"

Paul looked at his watch. "Ten in the morning."

Eric looked at the ceiling and then back at the man across from him. "Should be somewhere around West Palm Beach or Ft. Lauderdale within the next hour or so. If he stuck to the flight plan, that is."

"In your plane?" Greg asked.

"Yes. But we changed the registration numbers. Just in case you guys were looking for him."

"What's the new numbers?"

"123JR… for Jake Roth. It was his idea. Said you guys wouldn't be able to put it together,"

Greg was out the door to find a phone. The rest of the room erupted in conversation. As they talked, Eric asked his lawyer, "Did I do OK?"

"You did fine, son," the man answered. "You'll be out of here soon and on your way home."

Lt. Commander Tony Rogers, United States Navy, sat in the ready room at the Jacksonville Naval Air Station, when the call came. It wasn't often that a call for a fighter intercept arrived. In fact, it was so rare that not only had Rogers never participated in an actual intercept; he didn't even *know* anyone who had been given such an assignment. When he received the order, he lost no time in readying himself.

As he exited the building, on to the tarmac, Rogers joined up with another man in an identical flight suit.

"I just got the call. What's up, Tony?"

"Interception. There's a Cessna that's approaching Ft. Lauderdale any time now. We're to get him to land there where he'll be met by the authorities."

The other man whistled. "Cessna? What kind?"

Rogers cracked a grin. "You're going to love this one, Scott. 150."

Scott stopped. Two steps later Tony joined him and looked at the man. "A Cessna 150?" he cracked a grin. "Against a phantom. Holy shit, Tony. We'll scare him out of the sky if we can get slow enough."

Tony grinned and the two men started again across the ramp to the waiting jet. "Yes we will, my friend. You can count on it."

Minutes later Tony Rogers and his Radio Intercept Officer (or RIO), Lieutenant Scott Lewis, were climbing the steps into the two-man cockpit. It was less than half an hour after the initial call, when Rogers was pushing up the throttles in the F-4 Phantom fighter jet. The plane started rolling slowly at first. He was departing from a runway and not the deck of an aircraft carrier. The first thousand feet came slowly. But with each passing second, the plane gathered more and more speed. In less than a minute the plane was doing over 200 miles per hour and climbing into the clear Floridian sky.

As the moments ticked by, the plane climbed higher and higher. He was told that the intercept was to happen somewhere between West Palm Beach and Miami. Rogers continued his climb in an effort to conserve his fuel. The F-4 was an amazing machine and struck an imposing sight to any who viewed it, but it went through fuel faster than a politician goes through money.

As Roger's Phantom reached its apogee, he eased back on the throttle and started his long descent to the southern Florida region. As he did so, he keyed the mic.

"Jax Center, this is Pitbull 6 out of NAS Jax for intercept."

"Roger Pitbull 6, we have been advised."

"Copy. Do you have any targets over?"

"Roger Pitbull 6, we have six targets operating in Visual Flight Rules in the area with negative squawk."

"Copy Jax. Please provide vectors to the first VFR target."

Jacksonville Air Route Traffic Control Center then gave Rogers a heading towards a plane just north of West Palm Beach. As he approached the first plane, Tony slowed his massive jet to the minimum speed possible without his F-4 falling out of the sky. Although the slowest speed he could manage would be significantly faster than the light single-engine plane now ahead of him, it would be slow enough to make a positive intercept, letting the aircraft know his intentions.

"What have you got, Scotty?"

"Looking. Give me a second… There! Got it. Low and slow. Low wing. Looks like a Piper Cherokee."

"Shit." Rogers then keyed the mic. "Jax, first target is a no-go. Requesting vectors to the next target."

After receiving the information, Rogers maneuvered the jet further down the shoreline.

A few minutes later, Lewis's voice came over the radio from the backseat. "I have it, Tony. Two o'clock low. Looks like a taildragger. I make it as a Cessna 170."

"At least it's a Cessna." Keying the mic, Rogers communicated the information to Jacksonville Center and then received instructions to find the next plane.

"Hot damn, Tony. We've got a match! Cessna 150 eleven o'clock low."

"Good eyes, Scotty. Making my pass now." Rogers pulled back on the throttles and the plane started a slow descent as it rapidly overtook the Cessna ahead of them. As they were just about on top of the smaller plane, Lewis's voice came over the radio again. "Sorry Tony. Number's don't match."

"Dammit. I thought we had him that time. Calling Jax... again."

The fourth plane was a Piper Cub. They were now 0 for 4. It wasn't until the fifth plane that they hit pay dirt.

Traveling off the shore of Ft. Lauderdale at five hundred feet was a Cessna 150 matching the color of the plane in question. Rogers then deftly maneuvered his massive jet to make a near pass of the smaller prop plane.

"What have you got, Scotty?"

"123 Juliet Romeo. That's it!" Lewis said excitedly.

Rogers turned his plane again, making a sweeping circle to come up beside the small 150. As he did, he tuned his VHF radio to 121.5 MHz and transmitted.

"Cessna 123 Juliet Romeo, this is the United States Navy. You are ordered to bring your aircraft around to a heading of zero-niner-zero and proceed to Ft. Lauderdale International Airport. Over."

There was no response. Before he could get off another transmission, even at its slow speed, the F-4 sailed quickly by the small Cessna. Rogers jerked his hand violently, sending the Jet into a sharp left turn. The Cessna quickly disappeared as the Phantom proceeded in the opposite direction. He then turned the plane again at a sharp angle and rolled out directly behind his target. He was closing fast and keyed the mic to make another transmission when suddenly, the Cessna exploded.

"Oh, shit!" he exclaimed into the active microphone.

"Pitbull 6, say again please," came a transmission from Jacksonville Center.

"Jax, please be advised, the bogie has been destroyed."

"Say again, Pitbull? You fired upon and destroyed the target?"

"Negative Jax. We were on the target's six and it just exploded."

"Copy. Do you have any sign of survivors?"

Tony and Scott looked down at the wreckage, starting to settle on the surface of the water below.

"Do you have anything Scotty?"

"Just debris. No movement."

"Did anything seem out of the ordinary in the plane?"

"Not from where I was sitting. One pilot. It looked like he was flying from the Right seat. Do you think that means anything?"

"Nothing I can think of." He then keyed the mic again and transmitted to Jacksonville Center, "Negative Jax. I see no sign of survivors. However, I'd advise notifying the Coast Guard, just in case."

"Roger that Pitbull."

Scott's voice then came over the internal radio, "Tony, we've been up here for over half an hour now."

Rogers looked at his fuel gauge and started a climb as he keyed the mic to Jacksonville Center. "Jax, Pitbull 6 is bingo fuel. I am RTB at this time."

"Copy Pitbull. We show you return to base."

The Phantom continued to climb as they left the burning wreckage behind on the ocean's surface.

The color drained from Paul's face as he listened on the phone. His office was filled. Numerous people were interested in seeing how this would play out. All were expecting a favorable outcome, but the expression on the Deputy Director's face belied the truth of the situation. He slowly, robotically, hung up the receiver.

Even before he said anything, by his look alone, everyone in the room seemed to deflate. Finally, it was Greg who asked, "What happened?"

"He's dead."

"How?"

Paul shook his head. "They sent a fighter jet to intercept. It was coming up behind him and the plane exploded."

Everyone in the room went crazy asking questions. Paul just sat at his desk, catatonic. Finally, Greg's voice rose above the others. "The military shot him down?"

Paul shook his head without expression. "I honestly don't know."

"What do you mean, you don't know?" someone asked.

Paul answered without looking at the questioner. "The crew says they did nothing, but there appears to be multiple eyewitness reports of a fighter jet shooting down a civilian plane."

"What's the military saying?" someone else asked.

Paul shrugged. "They're saying it isn't true. The plane hasn't landed yet, but the pilots are reporting that they didn't fire. They're saying all of their armament will be accounted for and the gun footage will prove they didn't fire."

"Good God! Gun footage?" someone said.

"Totally standard. Doesn't mean guns were used," someone else said.

Paul just stared at the room around him, seeing nothing. This entire affair had been a mess from the very beginning. The hijacking. Catching what they thought was a lucky break and getting the hijacker. Then thinking they were luckier still to find it a part of a bigger conspiracy, only to have the rest involved slip away. He remembered his elation, thinking the bill found just the month prior, was a lucky break. A break that would allow him to close the case that had been dogging him all these years, only to have it end like this. Even now, there was no definitive answer: was the plane shot down or did something go wrong with the Cessna itself? Paul no longer cared. He let the people chatter in his office. It no longer mattered. Soon they would all be gone and all of this would be behind him. He was ready to get on with the rest of his life.

It was two weeks after the explosion when Paul's intercom buzzed.

"Yes, Janet, what is it?"

"Director, I have a Mr. Mills on the line. He says he's the attorney for Sara Gray."

Paul recognized the name at once as the woman who would eventually change her name to Jen Roth: Jake Roth's wife.

"Put him on."

A moment later, after a click, Paul said, "Mr. Mills, how can I help you?"

"Mr. Owens. I am calling on behalf of Sara Gray, aka Jennifer Roth, Jake Roth's widow."

"Yes. Again, what can I do for you?"

"Well Mr. Owens, as you can imagine, my client is quite distraught over the loss of her husband and would like to put this entire affair behind her."

"I'm sure she would."

"She has engaged my services to see if we could work out a solution to our mutual satisfaction."

Paul grimaced. "No problem. Please let your client know she's welcome to come down here, surrender herself and stand trial for her crimes. If exonerated, she won't have to worry about me again."

"Very nice, Mr. Owens, but I thought perhaps that we could reach a more… realistic solution."

"Really? And what might that be?"

"I propose that you close the case permanently on the hijacking of TWA798 and dismiss the warrants on all suspected to be involved."

Paul leaned back in his chair and grinned. "And why would I do that?"

"Because right now you're facing a lot of trouble. Trouble that you could make go away by ending this witch hunt."

"Mr. Mills let's be clear: Your client and her husband hijacked a United States flag carrier, and inflicted damage to said carrier, to the point where it was irreparably impaired. They stole millions of dollars from the United States Department of the Treasury and then fled justice. And you are now telling me that *I* am the one in trouble?"

"First, Director, let *us* be clear: all the charges you just laid out are far-fetched and unsubstantiated as it pertains to my client. Further, you have the man who *actually* committed the crime, behind bars.

"However, what we *do* have is a record of you relentlessly levying charges against my client and her late husband. Charges so outlandish, that they felt they had to flee, for they certainly would not have received justice from you.

"Then, after years of pursuit, you once again picked up their trail, sending them again on the run. Now, luckily, my client was able to evade you and your agents. Sadly, her husband was not so lucky. Rather than let Mr. Roth... or Powell, if you'd prefer... escape your grip again, you ordered the United States Navy to murder Mr. Powell in cold blood."

"That is a very creative story, Mr. Mills, except we didn't shoot down Mr. Powell's plane." Paul opened a drawer in his desk and removed several sheets of paper, referencing them as he spoke. "An inspection of the F-4

Phantom that conducted the intercept showed that it returned with all armament intact. Film footage from the gun camera further substantiates the fact that Mr. Powell's plane was not fired upon but exploded on its own."

"Yes, sir. I will grant you that the government has done an excellent job of covering its tracks. However, you have left a few things out."

"Enlighten me," Paul said.

"First and foremost, there are hundreds of eyewitnesses who saw the fighter plane in question shoot down Mr. Powell's Cessna."

"Yes, and for everyone who says they saw the plane shot down, I can produce two who claim that nothing of the sort ever happened."

"I'm sure you can. However, that doesn't explain the fact that the plane just exploded. I'm sure you know, just as I do, that planes don't just blow up like that. A Cessna of that size couldn't possibly hold enough fuel to make an explosion anywhere near the size of the one reported."

"Your client is welcome to present herself in court and tell that story."

"Mr. Owens, if you don't drop this entire affair, she will do worse than that. She will present herself to the court of public opinion."

Paul leaned back again, feeling a headache coming on. "How so?"

"I have told you the story my client will tell. Now ask yourself, how will the public see her? Especially when held up against the background of a president who resigned in disgrace. Shot down by a pilot who, for whatever reason, didn't feel as though he got enough action in Viet Nam. I ask you, sir, when held up next to crimes such as these, how can you justify a farfetched theory leveled against a grieving widow?"

The headache was getting worse. Paul wished this case had never found its way to him. "What are you looking for?"

"Not much, really. My client has already left the country and has no intention of ever returning on a permanent basis. However, she would like the ability to visit her family. An arrest warrant hanging over her head makes that difficult. She would like you to drop the charges against her and Mr. Mansfield, the man accused of driving the..." he chuckled, "Getaway boat, in the robbery."

"Is that all?" Paul exhaled.

"No. We would also like to see Douglas Moore released from prison."

Paul shook his head. "Sorry, can't do that one. Ford might pardon Nixon, but I promise you, he won't pardon a self-confessed hijacker."

"Mr. Owens, he doesn't need a pardon, just a release. He's already been in prison for almost a decade. I'm sure most of his time has been served. Surely, you can cut the few remaining years off his sentence."

Paul exhaled and weighed everything in his mind. Was this fair? Was this justice? He wondered if this would free him from a burden he had borne for far longer than he ever thought he would. At first it had been fun. He had been younger. It had been a game. A game against a brilliant opponent. Despite loss after loss in this case, he had continued to advance in the government: advancement that allowed him to do good, solid work. Work that helped make the country a better place, despite Viet Nam and Watergate. He thought back on the career behind him and the career that still lay ahead. The time for games was now over. He made his decision. Even in death, Stuart Powell would get his way. Paul Owens informed Mr. Mills as much. The game was finally over, and he had lost.

Epilogue
The Perfect Vacation

The wheels of the Land Rover crunched the pea gravel on the long driveway leading up to the giant estate in St. Maarten. Although there were tall walls surrounding the grounds within, it was obvious that the house behind the barriers was enormous.

The car stopped briefly as a set of wrought-iron gates opened slowly, permitting entrance. Once fully open, the Land Rover continued through the gates and past the fortifications. Once clear, the gates began to close.

In front of the house, at the end of the lengthy drive, the vehicle's driver and front passenger doors opened. On the driver's side, an attractive blond in her mid-thirties emerged. On the passenger side, a young man in his twenties exited. They both walked around the vehicle, meeting in the front, and proceeded toward the main entrance of the building.

"Ocean front?" the young man asked.

"Of course."

"Pool?"

The woman smiled. "And a hot tub."

The young man smirked. "Of course."

The front door of the main building opened and a well-tanned man in his late thirties greeted them. He wore short pants and an open shirt. In his hand he held a tumbler filled with an amber liquid. He greeted the younger man with a hug, not setting down his drink. He then went over to the woman and gave her a long embrace and a kiss.

"What's in the glass, scotch?"

The older man looked at the drink and took a pull. He then seemed to consider what he had just ingested before answering. "Macallan. Eighteen-year-old, I believe."

The younger man grinned. "Shouldn't you be drinking a Mai Tai with a little umbrella?"

The older man took another drink, paused, and considered. "Nope."

"I'd like a Pina Colada, please," the woman said. "With an umbrella."

"Eric?" the older man answered.

"Actually, Macallan 18 sounds good to me. No umbrella necessary."

The woman shook her head. "Pilots."

"Follow me. I'll show you the pool. You can wait there while I get the drinks."

As they walked, Eric asked, "So what do I call you? Jake, Stu… Boss?"

"Let's stick with Jake."

Eric looked over at the woman next to him and nodded. "Jake and Jen, it is."

The trio came into the house through a large front door. Jake and Eric continued through the house to the pool out back, as Jen said, "I'm going to get changed. We have a bathing suit in your size if you're interested, Eric."

Eric looked down at his legs. He was already wearing short pants and a tee-shirt. "Maybe later."

"Suit yourself."

"He just said he doesn't want to suit himself," Jake replied."

"Not funny," Jen said in a singsong voice without turning around as she headed off to a room in another part of the house.

"How do you want your drink? Neat?"

"Rocks," Eric answered.

"Lightweight."

Jake led Eric out back to the massive pool. As the two emerged behind the house, Eric saw a black man with grey hair lounging by the water. He appeared to be in his fifties and was wearing Bermuda shorts and sunglasses. As Eric and Jake came out to the pool, the man got up and approached them.

"You must be Eric," he said. "Good name. I used to know an Eric once. I'm Stanley. You brought my friends back to me. For that, I can't thank you enough."

"Stanley, I've heard a lot about you," Eric said, taking Stanley's hand in a firm grasp.

"I'll be back in a minute with our drinks," Jake said, as he left the two.

"Come on over and I'll show you around," Stanley said as Jake returned to the house.

"Nice place," Eric said, taking it all in. The back of the house held a large sitting area, home to an Olympic sized swimming pool, with a rock wall climbing up one side. From the top of the rock wall, a waterfall cascaded into the pool. Beyond it was a white sand beach with a pier leading out into the ocean. Floating next to the dock was a seaplane.

"Nice boat," Eric commented.

"Flying boat," Jake said, coming out with the drinks. Jen was by his side dressed in a bikini carrying a tumbler of whiskey for Stanley and her drink complete with umbrella, while Jake also carried two drinks: one with ice and one without. "Scotch for the young man, and Jack for the old pirate."

Jen handed Stanley his drink as Jake handed the other drink in his hand to Eric. "I'll let you boys talk while I take my drink over by the pool."

"What do you mean, 'flying boat?'" Eric asked as Jen walked away.

"It's a Grumman Widgeon. To the layman it might be a floatplane, but to the more educated, it's a flying boat."

"So noted."

The three took seats around the pool and settled in. Each taking a drink, Jake said, "How are you and Stanley here getting along?"

"Well. Good guy."

"Did he tell you his last name?"

Stanley rolled his eyes. "Good God Jake, let it go already."

"It's Charles. Stanley Charles. He has two first names. Isn't that bizarre? Don't misunderstand—it's not like he got to choose his name... oh, wait a minute, he did! And Mr. Charles here came up with two... first... names!"

"How long did you have to put up with him in Alaska?" Stanley asked.

"A couple of weeks. How long were you guys in the Navy together?"

"Long enough that I should have known better than to fall into this joker's schemes."

"Seriously," Jake continued, undeterred, "Two first names. I'm Jake Roth, not Jake Aaron or Jake Ralph. Two first names."

Despite their efforts, Stanley and Eric couldn't help but to grin at the good-natured ribbing.

Finally, Eric asked, "How'd everything play out after you left us?"

Jake shrugged. "More or less, as planned. Several days of flying, fighting like hell to stay on schedule. There were a few times the damn winds were screwing me up so badly, I didn't think the plan would work. Saturday, I really fell behind. I had to make an unexpected stop for fuel. That meant twenty hours in the air that day. I only got four hours sleep that night in the hammock."

"And the explosives?"

"That wasn't a problem," Stanley said. "I just met Jake here at the airport with five pounds of C4."

Eric's eyes widened. "Five pounds of C-4? How in the hell did you pull that off?"

Stanley chuckled, "It's amazing what two thousand dollars can get you."

"I wasn't military like you guys were, but isn't five pounds a lot?"

With a grin, Jake said, "Admittedly, I overdid it a bit. But it was quite the show. You should have seen it. Even from Washington, I'll almost bet you could."

Eric grimaced. "Not from the hole they had me in."

Jake's smile faded. "I'm sorry about that. I know that week must have been rough."

Eric shrugged it off. "Could have been worse."

"Well, your timing was perfect. I had Stanley over here, and Jen spread out with about twenty miles between them. Both were watching the plane through binoculars, holding identical detonation switches."

"How did you know the fighter would arrive on schedule?" Eric asked.

"I know the intercept procedures and figured they'd send a fighter. It's what they do. I knew if you could hold out, we'd be home free."

"When did you bail out?"

Jake took another drink before answering. "A little north of Palm Beach. I also had a transmitter and binoculars. I doubt anyone saw the parachute."

"I'm just glad that the pilots couldn't see inside the cockpit or the game would have been up," Stanley added.

Both Jake and Eric turned to the older man. It was Jake who said, "Undoubtedly they did."

"What, see inside the cockpit?"

"Of course," Eric confirmed.

"How could they? I was aboard the Midway. I know how fast an F-4 is. It had to have at least a hundred mile overtake on your Cessna."

"And I'm sure it did. But that doesn't mean that they couldn't sneak at least a quick glance."

"In that case, didn't it seem suspicious that there was a plane flying along the coast without a pilot at the controls?"

Eric grinned and took a drink. "It would have been suspicious, but we planned for that."

"How so?"

Jake picked up the story again. "I piled up everything in the seat next to me. Duffle bag, trash… everything I could find. I then put Eric's jacket on it and the ball cap on top. At close inspection it would be painfully obvious what I had done. But to a pilot streaking by at two hundred miles an hour, it would look like a pilot at the controls of the plane."

Stanley nodded as Jake explained this. Then something dawned on him. "Wait, you piled everything next to you, right? Then wouldn't the pilot they saw be in the right seat, not the left?"

Both Jake and Eric shrugged. "Yeah. So?"

"Wouldn't that look suspicious?

"Why would it?" Jake asked.

"Well, you fly a plane from the left seat, don't you?"

Eric gave another shrug. "Usually. But you can fly it from either seat."

Stanley refused to give up the argument. "It would be the perfect excuse for the government to argue something fishy was up."

Jake smiled, shaking his head. "If they made that argument, it would look like they were really grasping at straws. I doubt the pilot or his RIO even mentioned it in their report."

The words hung in the air for several seconds before Stanley continued. "So, you were just floating in the water?"

"I had an inflatable raft. I wasn't out there long before the plane disappeared from sight. Once I lost it, I started making my way to land. I was only about a mile out."

"I could have picked him up in my boat, but Jake here thought it was more important to have me on the beach."

Eric chuckled. "I'll bet you're glad I had the autopilot now."

"You know it. I could have maybe gotten away with just trim, but I doubt it would have worked. That autopilot was a lifesaver."

Eric took another drink. "What was the plan if the jet hadn't shown up?"

"Stanley here. That's why I was willing to be out there all alone without him. If the fighter hadn't intercepted the Cessna by the time it passed him…"

"I would have blown the whole thing sky high." Stanley and Jake touched glasses and drank.

"It wouldn't have been as convenient an excuse," Jake continued, "but it would have worked."

"What about the eye-witnesses? As I hear it, a lot of people swear they saw the jet shoot a missile at my plane."

Jake shrugged. "That was easy. Once Jen blew up the plane, while standing on a crowded beach, she started screaming, 'Oh God, that fighter just shot a missile at that little plane.' Once she said that, masses of people around her started swearing they had seen the same thing." Jake then grinned. "I'd imagine some even really believed it. You'd be surprised how powerful suggestion can be."

"Just as well Jen got the honor, rather than me," Stanley said. "I would have made the call, and it probably would have gotten the job done. But a white woman screaming her head off is more credible than an old black man."

Jake brushed it off. "It would have worked either way, Stanley. They wouldn't have been looking at the color of your skin. They would have been looking at the big fireball over the water. I doubt there's a person on the beach who "saw" the explosion who could tell you who the first person to make the claim was."

All three men looked to Jen. She was now out of her lounge chair and climbing on to the small diving board at the far end of the pool. She then made a beautiful dive and started swimming laps.

All three men were staring at her when Jake glanced over at Eric and Stanley. "Eyes off my wife, you two."

Both men grinned and took drinks from their glasses. As Jen swam her laps, Jake looked out on the horizon. There was a cruise ship slowly making its way from the island, heading out to sea.

Watching Jake, Eric said, "What is it, boss?"

"You know, I've never taken a cruise. Not for fun, anyway. I spent six months on a carrier when I was in the Navy. Stanley here spent even more time on the water than I did. I would imagine that one of those ship's..." He motioned to the boat heading out to sea, "would be a lot more fun."

"Amen, brother," Stanley agreed.

"I'd expect so." Eric said as all three watched the boat in the distance. "I've never been on a cruise either."

Still watching the ship slowly make its way across the water, all three took another sip of their drinks at the same time. Jake then said, "Lots to do on those ships. I hear there's gambling, artwork... lots of interesting stuff."

Eric nodded. "Lots of interesting stuff." He took another sip of scotch and asked, "What's going to happen to Y/K?"

Jake shrugged. "Left it to Charlie." He grinned. "It was in my will."

"So, you're not returning to Alaska?"

"Naw. What's the point? Soon it's going to be cold and dark. And we already bought this place here."

"Why didn't you buy a place like this in Alaska?"

"What do you mean? I had two places in Alaska."

"Yeah, but not like this. The places there were nice, but nothing much to look at. This is amazing."

"They were looking for us then. They aren't looking anymore. Case has been closed."

"So, you did it for the money."

Jake shrugged again. "I did it because I was bored. I did it because I figured out how to do it. Didn't do it for the money, but it was nice. It was enough to let me buy three 206s and two decent places in St. Mary's. The rest was invested."

"What about you, Stanley?"

"What about me?" Stanley answered.

"What did you do after the heist?"

With a dismissive wave of his hand, Stanley said, "I spent a long time wandering the Caribbean laundering the money. I'd travel from island to island, gambling and opening up bank accounts."

"So, you didn't make any large purchases either?"

With a grin, Stanley said, "I had my boat. I was traveling from place to place, dropping millions in the casinos. I'll admit it was fun at first, but if you do anything long enough, it becomes work. I still have enough ones to keep you set at any strip club for several lifetimes."

"You were at it for years?"

"Stanley came here almost immediately and bought a place," Jake said. "He's the reason we settled in St. Maarten. He earned an equal share but hasn't been living too extravagantly."

"Got a nice place down the road. Nothing too fancy. Not anything like this. But it has a nice pier for me to park my boat."

Neither of us wanted to draw attention," Jake continued. "They have extradition here. However, he's looking for a nicer place now that the heat's off."

"I have my eye on a nice estate just down the beach. Not an adequate dock, but that's easy enough to build."

"And Doug? The guy who did the hijacking?"

Stanley's expression turned sad. Jake looked angry. Jake looked at Eric momentarily and then shifted his gaze out across the water at the cruise ship growing smaller in the distance. "I'd bet we'd have a great time on a ship like that." The words hung in the air for several seconds before he continued. "I got him out. That's more than he deserved."

"Why?"

"Because he ratted us out. If he'd stayed put and kept his mouth shut, I would have had him out of there within a week. But he sold us all out." Jake shook his head. "Sometimes I wonder if I did the right thing in forcing Owens get him an early release."

Stanley put his hand on Jake's shoulder. "I know you're still angry Jake, but you did the right thing. Believe me."

Eric added, "At least he has to live knowing that he lost all that money."

"I guess there's that."

Jen came up to the edge of the pool and pulled her arms out, crossing them and propping her head up, looking at the men before her. "What are you guys talking about?"

"Nothing much," Jake answered. "Planning a vacation."

"Oh, that sounds like fun. Have you told Eric your plan to replace his plane?

"Oh, yeah." Jake turned back to Eric. "Look, I'm sorry I blew up your plane, but I was wondering if you'd be interested in replacing it."

Eric shrugged, "Another 150? Seems kind of small now, doesn't it?"

"My thoughts exactly." Jake then looked out to the Widgeon tied up to the dock. "I was wondering if you might take half of her as repayment."

Eric's eyes lit up. "I... wow. But what would we do with it? Just island hop?"

Jake looked to the sky for a moment, considering the question, and answered, "Sure, we could do that. But I'm still too young to retire. Maybe we could also start our own little airline."

"*Our* airline?"

"Fifty/fifty."

"Eric looked around at the house and asked, "Where would I live?"

"I'm sure you'd earn enough to buy a place. But until then, I have a great guest house. And you're welcome to the scotch."

"You're welcome at my place as well," Stanley added. "Just as soon as I complete the deal. And there's also my boat."

"Who are you kidding?" Jake said, "You'd have him stay at your house and you'd stay on that stupid boat."

Stanley's expression darkened, "Don't you go calling my boat stupid. And it's a yacht, not a boat. Remember that."

With a laugh, Jake said, "Whatever, Mr. Stanley."

"It's Mr. Charles, not Mr. Stanley."

Shaking his head, Jake said, "Two first names."

All four started laughing.

Returning to the airline, Eric asked, "What will we call it? Island Air?"

Jake shrugged. "I don't know. We'll think of something."

"Great! When do we start?"

"Calm down there, Eric. Haven't you learned anything from me or Stanley? I did the airline thing with TWA and got bored. Even Mr. *Charles* here got bored with years of gambling, hopping from island to island. You have your entire life ahead of you to fly. Just take it easy and enjoy the moment."

Eric nodded as the grin slipped from his face. He took another sip from the tumbler. Jake drained what remained in his glass as he looked off into the horizon. The ship had now almost completely disappeared into the distance. As they watched, Eric asked. "Do you think it would be fun to take a cruise?"

Jake finally pulled his eyes away from the ship and looked at his wife. His eyes then went to the two men beside him. After several seconds of contemplation, a mischievous twinkle sparkled in his eyes as he replied, "I think it would be more fun to take a cruise *ship*."

Acknowledgments

One of the many reasons I wrote this book was because I was raised in the aviation industry. Before I was born, in the 1960s, my mother worked as a stewardess—not a flight attendant—for United Airlines. I grew up hearing stories of what it was like for her in the early days of commercial aviation in the sixties. Many people today are unaware that certain things like "weigh-ins" and prohibiting stewardesses from getting married or having children was a condition of employment back in those days.

I tried my best to represent the times, both socially and technically, and if by doing so I inadvertently offended anyone, I apologize. We live in a very different world today. However, I felt it important to capture the mood and feel of commercial aviation and the social climate of the country as a whole during that era.

When my mother was forced to leave United Airline because she married my father, Jim, she had two children, me, followed by my brother Mark. While Mark did not follow our mother into a career in aviation as I did, he did develop a deep love for flying.

When I reached age fifteen, my mother re-entered the world of aviation working for World Airways. By the time I was eighteen (and well on my path to becoming a licensed pilot myself), my mother was furloughed for the third time with World (an event very common in aviation. I too was furloughed for over a year). My mother, however, landed on her feet and was given the opportunity to return to United Airlines thanks to the Supreme Court decision in the case of McDonald v United Airlines. The Supreme Court deemed that it was unconstitutional for the airlines (most of them were doing this back then, not just United) to tell someone whom they could or could not marry.

Although the character of Sara was prohibited from marrying in the book, that was actually not the policy at TWA. I took some literary license because of my family history. TWA did prohibit their stewardesses from having children though.

After graduating from college, I was fortunate enough to have friends who looked out for me and helped me to find employment in Alaska as a bush pilot working for MarkAir Express. I was employed there for nearly four years before they went bankrupt. After MarkAir Express, I worked for TWA as a flight engineer on Boeing 727s. I worked for TWA just shy of four years before going to work for the major US airline where I am currently employed as a captain to this day.

Although my time at TWA had cost me time and seniority at my current airline, I am grateful to have been part of aviation history that has long since passed. I also tried to share much of that experience here in these pages. However, more than anything, I tried to tell a good story.

I would like to start off by thanking my mother, Danealia (Deni) Mineta. Without her influence, who knows what career path my life would have taken. She and I will always share a special bond because of the paths our lives took in aviation.

I would also like to thank my stepdad, Norman (Norm) Mineta for his love and support. His own story in aviation is unique. The advice he has given me throughout the years is unparalleled.

I also want to thank my dad Jim Brantner and my stepmom, Winifred (Wynne) Brantner. Without their love and support, I don't know if I could have made it as far, and as quickly as I did. They sacrificed so I could get a top-notch aviation education at Embry-Riddle. I have no doubt this is in large part why I am where I am today.

I need to thank my editor Christopher (Chris) Rottiers for spending hours and hours poring over my manuscript, making it suitable for public consumption.

I also want to thank my dear friend, amazing author, fellow Embry-Riddle alumni and fellow TWA alumni, Wes Oleszewski. Wes has been so successful as a writer, that he gave up his career flying planes, to be a full-time author. If anyone has read any of Wes' books, you'll know why. Wes has been a great friend and mentor and introduced me to my editor, Chris. He is a true and supportive friend.

I also want to thank Melanie Johnson and Jennifer (Jenn) Foster at Elite Online Publishing. These two ladies are a part of why you are reading this book today. As little as I may know about punctuation and grammar, it towers over that immense vacuum that is my knowledge in getting a book to market and helping to get it to readers like you.

Finally, I want to thank my wife Kelly, and my daughter Madison. They continue to stand behind me as I try to balance my life as a writer, pilot and family man. I could not have done any of this without their unwavering love and support. I am truly blessed.

Please visit www.robertmbrantner.com for a full list of my titles and links to my other works.

About the Author

Robert M. Brantner is currently working as both a captain and a line check airman for a major US airline. He started his flying career as a bush pilot in Alaska, which later led to a job as a pilot for Trans World Airlines. He spent four years with TWA before he landed his dream job, working for the airline he flies for today.

Bob was born in Southern California and attended high school there before heading to Arizona for college. After graduating from Embry-Riddle Aeronautical University, he moved to Alaska when he got his first flying job as a bush pilot. During his time in Alaska, Bob first tried his hand at writing, penning a memoir on his experiences flying Cessnas in the untamed Alaskan wilderness.

All throughout his flying career, Bob has continued to write. He penned several (unpublished) manuscripts. It was after Bob's completion of *Claus: The Untold Story of Kris Kringle*, that he decided to work with his younger sister (and editor), Taylor Brantner, on cleaning up the story until it was fit for publication. After some success with *Claus*, Bob dug out his previously edited (however, unpublished) manuscript of *Five Hundred Feet Above Alaska*. He teamed again with Taylor and re-edited the material. The reception of *Five Hundred Feet Above Alaska* was terrific and still is selling strong.

Bob's mother's first job was as a stewardess in 1965 working for United Airlines. Through her experiences, Bob's mom Deni, instilled in him a lifelong passion for aviation. His latest novel, *Skyheist* is more than just an exciting aviation adventure, but is an homage to aviation's golden age of the 1960's.

Bob is a certificated Airline Transport Pilot and is type rated in the Beech 1900, Boeing 737, 757, 767, Airbus A320 and A220, as well as the DC-9. He is also a rated Flight Engineer. Bob served in the Flight Engineer position working on the Boeing 727 during his time at TWA. He also holds a commercial sea plane rating that he obtained while in Alaska.

Skyheist is Bob's fourth published book. He wrote the afore mentioned *Five Hundred Feet Above Alaska* and *My Year as an Alaskan Bush Pilot*, drawing from his experiences flying in "The Last Frontier."

Bob is married to Kelly Kaczka Brantner and they have one daughter, Madison, and a dog, Fergus. They live just outside of Annapolis, Maryland.

Made in the USA
Columbia, SC
22 May 2023

17131950R00204